MY PARENTS' MARRIAGE

MY PARENTS' MARRIAGE

A Novel

NANA EKUA BREW-HAMMOND

AMISTAD

An Imprint of HarperCollinsPublishers

MY PARENTS' MARRIAGE. Copyright © 2024 by Nana Ekua Brew-Hammond. All rights reserved. Printed in the United States of America. No part of this book may be used or reproduced in any manner whatsoever without written permission except in the case of brief quotations embodied in critical articles and reviews. For information, address HarperCollins Publishers, 195 Broadway, New York, NY 10007.

HarperCollins books may be purchased for educational, business, or sales promotional use. For information, please email the Special Markets Department at SPsales@harpercollins.com.

FIRST EDITION

Library of Congress Cataloging-in-Publication Data has been applied for.

ISBN 978-0-06-297673-4

24 25 26 27 28 LBC 5 4 3 2 1

For my parents,
their parents,
and your parents, too.

Marriage is like a groundnut—you have to crack it to see what is inside.

—AKAN PROVERB

A RECORD OF NUGA MARRIAGES

1941

Mawuli Nuga and Abui Dei marry
(Customary and Ordinance) in the Gold Coast.
They have four children: Yao (1942), Antony (1943), Fafa (1947),
and Emefa (1949).

1945

Mawuli Nuga and Julia Weber have one son in Germany: Festus.

1947

Mawuli Nuga and Rebecca Laryea marry
(Customary) in the Gold Coast.
They have three children: Elikem (1947), Elinam (1948),
and Esime (1949).

Mawuli Nuga and Hannah Koomson have one daughter:
Comfort "Connie" (1947).

1948

Mawuli Nuga and Hannah Koomson marry
(Customary) in the Gold Coast.

1949

Mawuli Nuga and Micheline Miadogo marry
(Customary) in the Gold Coast.
They have two children: Kokui (1950)
and Enyonam "Nami" (1953).

A RECORD OF NUGA MARRIAGES
(*continued*)

1962

Mawuli Nuga and Hannah Koomson divorce in Ghana.

1963

Mawuli Nuga and Rebecca Laryea divorce in Ghana.

1964

Mawuli Nuga and Hemaa Prempeh marry
(*Customary and Ordinance*) in Ghana.

Mawuli Nuga and Abui Dei divorce in Ghana.

1972

Mawuli Nuga and customs officer's wife have one son: Kofi.

1974

Kokui Nuga and Boris Van der Puye marry
(*Customary and Ordinance*) in Ghana.

1

It was the last Friday night before Christmas, and Accra's Ambassador Hotel ballroom was thick with the funk of celebration. Soldiers twirled their partners around the parquet floors, a few in the higher ranks guarded by officers at attention. Lines of sweat outlined the men's rifle holsters, while perspiration separated the tight curls ladies had scraped back to join fake flowing ponytails. At tables skirting the dance floor, beautiful young women held court surrounded by mostly older, married men in decorated uniforms. Colonels, majors, and captains kept the two- and four-top tables heavy with highballs, goblets, flutes, and snifters, while the Ambassador staff stood by to take fresh orders and empty ashtrays.

Many had taken the party to the ballroom veranda for air or a smoke—Kokui Nuga had gone out for both. Leaving her sister, and the officers sponsoring their drinks for the evening, Kokui wedged her way into a dark corner and exhaled. She leaned against the enclosure, the railing indenting her arms, and looked past the blinking lights of the Christmas tree, trying to discern her future. She lit up another Tusker, the smoke curling around her heart-shaped, night-colored face, her mind dancing with scenarios.

She could go back to London, try to find a university that would accept her. Her father would not immediately agree, but he would let her stay in the apartment until she found her footing if she made a strong enough case, which she could. She was almost twenty-three, the same age he had been when he left Ghana to work in Jan Weber's paper mill in Germany. A year later, he returned with the beginnings of the fortune he now used to control her and everyone else in his life. Maybe she would stumble on a fortune of her own.

Or, she could stay with her mother in Togo for a while. Kokui was not looking forward to asking her mother when they saw her this Christmas, but she had to. The clock was tick-tick-ticking to '73 and all the demands the new year would make. She needed time, and space away from her father's house and her life in Accra, to sort out what she was meant to do with herself.

Her second cigarette down to a glowing nub, she inhaled, squaring her shoulders for her return to the party inside.

"Ei!" Kokui hopped back from the attendant who had crouched wordlessly in her path. Her heart beating from the surprise, she bent to detangle her left heel from the hem of her white dress as she watched him sweep the smoking butt of her cigarette into his dustpan. "Today, dear, they go promote you to head sweeper."

He cut dead eyes at her comment, and her performance of it in pidgin, but she wasn't mocking him or his station. She envied his focus on this menial task. She wondered sometimes if her ability to discipline herself had been scattered between the revelation of her father's lie and her mother's resulting retreat to Togo—but her sister, Nami, didn't have this problem, and she had had this

2

problem before everything crumpled. It was her problem that had uncovered it all.

She winked at the attendant to communicate her admiration and smiled to lift her own mood. It was about to be Christmas, she reminded herself, and whatever uncertainties the new year held it also offered the hope of a fresh page. She smoothed the edges of her hair and, with her ponytail swinging behind her, made her return to Nami and the soldiers splashing their cash on them for the night. She didn't have to figure out her life this minute, she decided. She couldn't. In the meantime, she would allow herself to celebrate.

2

Kokui's eyes fluttered open at the sudden flare of the car's interior light. Wiping the dribble of her post-Ambassador doze from her chin, she sat up in the soft leather seat. Their driver, Nelson, was lowering the radio volume as he inched toward the rifle-toting officer leaning into the vehicle in front of them. Another policeman stood beside him making sure incoming traffic didn't drive past.

"Do you have any small bills?" Nami asked her.

Kokui lowered her purse between her knees to check. "Nothing smaller than five cedis."

Nelson's gaze darted to the rearview mirror. "Sister, I have pesewas. They should take coins and be satisfied."

They watched the policeman dismiss the vehicle ahead with a clap on the cab, and narrow his gaze with shrewd calculation at the three-pointed Mercedes star on their car.

"Here we go," Nami said.

The officer pointed a flashlight through the glass. Kokui breathed in to prepare for the interaction and rolled down her window.

"Afyehyiapa o!" She sang the season's greeting as she found the man's eyes above the beam. "Ɛyɛ sɛ this Christmas, dear, you chop like never before. All you do for our country—it's not easy, koraa."

The policeman raised an eyebrow at Kokui's act, but kept silent, enjoying it.

Kokui tapped Nelson's shoulder. "Let's find the officer something to appreciate him, eh? Something to make his Bronya sweet. Something so his wife won't turn her back to him tonight."

The officer chuckled, closing his fist over the coins in Kokui's hand and keeping it there. His crudely cut nails both tickled and scratched the hollow of her palm. "Who says I have a wife?"

"Barima fine like you?" She withdrew her hand. "I know you have a wife. And girlfriends. Plenty. Nelson, let us go before he does his juju on me and Nami."

"You ladies are the ones doing juju in this Ghana here." He stepped back, grinning widely, and clapped the top of their car.

Nelson sneered. "These people have no shame."

The show over, Kokui settled back into the leather cocoon of her seat as they continued along the Achimota School road. Past their old secondary school campus, the streets were black, ambient with distant forest croaks, until they turned onto their street.

Nami sprang forward as their two-story house came into view. "Yei! Has Daddy returned? Why is the gate open at this hour?" It was close to three a.m.

Nelson stopped the car on the side of the road. "What do we do?" he asked. Their father would punish Nami for sneaking out, and he would castigate Kokui for taking her, but he could sack Nelson for driving them.

Headlights abruptly presented a new problem, slashing the

night through the parted iron. An old Opel screeched out of their compound, a woman screaming out of the passenger side window.

"Mawuli Nuga," she hissed, jabbing a long, skinny arm above the lowered glass. "I curse your daughters. Each and every one will know the shame you've caused me."

The words scratched out of the woman's throat in the pitch of a strangled animal.

"Heh!" Nelson gaped, his head twisting to follow the car, but she was gone, around the corner, absorbed into the darkness.

Kokui turned to Nami, her chest empty of breath, the scene too familiar to speak on.

"Well, it's not an armed robber," Nami said. "But Daddy is back."

Nelson eased the car to a stop between their father's Range Rover and their stepmother's Benz. Gingerly opening her door, Nami paused, then flinched at the night sounds creeping into the car.

"Is that a baby crying?"

The sisters scrambled outside, Nami into the house, Kokui over to the gateman and the other driver.

"Evans, who was that woman?"

"Hmmm." Their security guard said much through pursed lips.

"What happened?"

"She says she has given birth for your father."

Kokui recoiled, her grip tightening around her handbag as she tried to control her short, ragged breaths.

This kind of thing happened all the time, she told herself, brusquely turning away. Mawuli Nuga was rich, handsome, and magnetic. Men with that trinity of power could do whatever they wanted to whomever. It was up to the women to leave. But still. As a daughter whose mother had left without fully leaving, Kokui felt the betrayal of, and in, her sex. Her father had shared himself with yet another woman who had not known about the others, and he had devastated another mother. He had created yet another child who would have to negotiate the throbbing pain and disrespect of the woman who had labored to deliver them with the indifference of a father who afforded every security except the emotional stability of a peaceful home.

Passing Nelson and the cars, she went inside and shut the front door.

Every light in the house was on, but every door was closed. She walked past the room that had belonged to her father's first wife, upstairs past the pair of rooms that had belonged to his second and third. They were all gone now, his current wife sharing the master bedroom suite with their dad. The house was empty of all the kids, too, except for Kokui and Nami—and this baby who had displaced Nami as the youngest, wailing down the hall.

Kokui looked for Nami in their bedroom. Her sister was leaning out the window that looked onto their father's bedroom balcony. Mawuli Nuga stood gently swaying a swaddled bundle in his folded arms. His white singlet, pale-blue pajama pants, and even his brown skin looked yellow in the bedroom light. Behind him hovered their cousin and maid—Sister Eyram, they called her.

A knock yanked Kokui and Nami's attention to the doorway. Their stepmother—Auntie Hemaa, they called her—stood in their room now. Even in this witching hour, their stepmother was ever the chic and composed royal. The cornrows she usually covered with a sleek, face-framing wig were exposed in neat lines against her shining scalp. Her gauzy periwinkle morning gown, knotted at her waist, was incandescent against her smooth, obsidian skin.

"I told him I allowed you to meet your friends," Auntie Hemaa said, addressing their now-forgotten fear of their father's reprisal. "In any event, he's focused on other things. Come and meet your father's Christmas miracle."

Nami sniffed at Auntie Hemaa's parched joke while Kokui searched their stepmother's unlined face. No wild-eyed rage or red-eyed pain. No twisted lips of bitterness. No shame. At least none that she could see. Auntie Hemaa was nothing like the others, Kokui thought, at least not yet. How long, Kokui wondered, could she withstand the cheating, the disrespect?

"Yes, Auntie."

She and Nami followed the swaying fabric of Auntie Hemaa's robe into her and their dad's commodious bedroom. Past the framed black-and-white of Mawuli's mother, the four-poster bed, swooning couch, and vanity table and chair, Kokui walked tentatively onto the balcony behind her stepmother and younger sister.

"Daddy," Nami said.

Mawuli turned to bestow his winking smile on each woman, the dimple at the corner of his mouth and the center of his chin conspiring as they always did to allow him to charm even as he offended. The moon shone on his pate, the silver roots of his thinning, black-dyed curls showing through, pronouncing his widow's peak.

"We saw that woman as we drove in," Nami went on. "Screaming her head off for the whole of Achimota to hear."

The ribbing of their father's singlet formed parentheses around his soft paunch as he tilted the baby so they could see the little face. "Girls, this is your brother. Kofi Eledzinye Nuga."

As he crooned the name, the baby turned up the treble in his howl. Mawuli turned to his cousin. "Eyram, take him, eh? We need our sleep for the drive to Togo."

"We're still going?" Again, Kokui's eyes leapt for Auntie Hemaa's reaction.

"Why wouldn't we?" Mawuli said. "Your mother is expecting us."

Auntie Hemaa had moved to Sister Eyram's side. "Keep him

with you in your room for now. We'll sort out a place for him when I'm back."

Sister Eyram nodded and took her exit with the baby.

"Let's go to bed," Auntie Hemaa said. "You all have a long ride in just a few hours, and so do I."

Kokui and Nami returned to their bedroom.

"Are we telling Ma about our nouveau nɔvi?"

Nami turned for her sister to unzip her dress. "Let him tell her. It's his to tell."

Kokui nodded slowly. It was his to tell, she knew, but would he?

She unpinned her ponytail, casting the hairpiece onto her bedside table. Nami followed her into their bathroom.

"After he tells her, we can add the things he won't say," Nami continued. "Like how emaciated that woman was—like a kwashiorkor case. Didn't she just have a baby? This Kofi is no more than six months." She bent over the sink to scrub the pancake from her face. "And Ma can pretend not to care that she is still his 'grande Madame Nugaga.'"

A wry smile touched Kokui's lips at their father's pet name for their mother, Micheline. "Still his 'mansion woman,'" she added. "Still 'ma Micheline.'"

The sisters regressed to the kissing sounds of their youth, tittering through the grimaces they made. At the bottom of their laughter, Kokui heard the disgust, the weary disappointment.

Nami switched off the lights. As was usual, Kokui left her bed empty and joined her sister under the oversize cloth, one of many they had taken from their mother's glorious pile of castoff designs.

"She was very slim, wasn't she?" Kokui said, fear rising with the comparison they had just giggled at. "That Daddy's woman. Her arm poking out of the car—it was like a snake. Did you hear her curse us?"

"Ho," Nami scoffed. "They all think their juju is stronger than the others', until they find out it isn't stronger than his. Only Ma knows better."

"How do you think she does it?" Kokui asked after a long, thought-filled silence.

"Ma? I think this was always the better arrangement for her. She was never meant to be someone's madame."

Kokui started to ask Nami to elaborate. What did that even mean: "meant to be someone's madame"? They were both Mawuli Nuga's daughters—stepdaughters to four different "madames." She could bet Nami didn't know what she meant either.

"I was talking about Auntie Hemaa. Why do you think she's lasted this long?"

"It's only been ten years. Auntie Abui stayed twenty-one years before we got here, and through two additional wives, three, if you count Ma."

Kokui shuddered. "I could never."

"I couldn't do it either," Nami said.

"Hmmm."

Kokui folded herself around her sister's back, her belly cushioning Nami's firm, full thickness. Curled together, their breaths found a rhythm that tempered the night's adrenaline, lulling them with the medicine of a sleep that was needed, even if it wasn't sound.

3

The cock had crowed more than three hours ago, but the Nugas were only now about to leave. The day had started late because they had. The revelation, and cries, of the newest member of their household had made rest impossible. But bleary as they were, they were in their cars now, Auntie Hemaa in the back seat of hers, and Mawuli in the driver's seat of his, Kokui beside him, Nami behind him. Each ignition hummed in readiness for their respective drives.

"Give this to your mum." Mawuli handed Kokui an envelope fat with one-cedi notes to pass to Auntie Hemaa.

It chafed Kokui that her father insisted on referring to Auntie Hemaa as their "mum." She liked the woman—admired her grace, her composure, her beauty—loved her, even. It felt like betrayal to her mother to look up to Auntie Hemaa, but she did. She had lived with Auntie Hemaa almost as long as she had lived with Micheline. Together with Sister Eyram, Auntie Hemaa had raised her. Yet only one woman had birthed her. Only one woman was her mum. But that wasn't why she couldn't look her stepmother in the eye as she stretched from her passenger side to push the money over to Auntie Hemaa's lowered window.

She felt deep pity for her stepmother—and perplexed by why she endured this arrangement with her father. Auntie Hemaa was a Prempeh, from the royal line. If she had wanted to share a husband, she could have chosen to. Polygamy was legal for royals and Muslims in Ghana—and informally enjoyed by anyone who had no claim to a title other than "man." But she had entered her marriage unaware Mawuli was married to Kokui and Nami's mother.

It boggled Kokui's mind that her father opted to lie to his women. Mawuli had grown up in the Evangelical Presbyterian Church, under an uncle who, he always told them, preached fidelity, charity, and integrity to him. Yet, Mawuli was unwilling, or unable, to remain faithful to his wives. Why not confess up front, and at least let the women agree or understand what they were getting into?

She wondered, too, about the women. Auntie Hemaa was a University of Science and Technology graduate, and she was far wealthier than their dad. She had inherited, and now ran, her uncle's transport business. She commanded a fleet of twenty-six trucks moving goods all over Ghana and across the neighboring borders. She did not need Mawuli's money. None of his wives had. But still, many had stayed far too long, as far as Kokui was concerned, and there Auntie Hemaa was, holding on—while Kokui and Nami's real mum held her own thorny ground in Togo.

"That should be enough for your petrol and the checkpoints." Mawuli spoke to his wife over Kokui and the hum of the engine, his foot on the brake, his hands resting lightly on the steering wheel. He turned to Auntie Hemaa's driver. "Nelson, carry Madame safely to and from her people, eh?"

"My greetings to your cousins," Auntie Hemaa said. "And no arguments with any of the boys at the border."

He released the handbrake. "I'll be on my best behavior."

Auntie Hemaa leaned back into her seat, the bangs of her wig swaying in a soft part as Nelson pulled out of the gate Evans held open.

Braking in their wake, Mawuli handed Evans his own thick envelope.

"Sir, Afyehyiapa." The gate man gripped the envelope in one hand and raised his other hand to his temple in salute. He stayed in position until they drove out of sight.

"Daddy, are you okay to drive?" Nami asked a yawning Mawuli. "I know Ma prefers just us, but"—Kokui could see Nami choosing her next words carefully—"you are tired. We should have told Victor to drive us this time."

Mawuli raised a love-crinkled face to the rearview mirror. "My Nami, I know if everyone leaves me, you will remain by my side."

Kokui arched an eyebrow at the smirk her dad and sister shared. "Eyei. *MyNami* and *MyDaddy*."

"Am I lying? Your brothers and sisters have all left me to run this business I built for all of you, and between the two of you it's only Nami who is interested."

Kokui turned to the window to roll her eyes. "Daddy, I didn't mention the business."

"It's the business that pays for all of you and all of this." He swept his hand outward, the thick gold ring on his finger glinting.

"I'm trying," Kokui said.

"Not hard enough." Mawuli paused to direct Kokui to retrieve the envelope of police bribes from the glove compartment as he slowed at the checkpoint for a new officer on shift.

"Boys, Afyehyiapa o. M'on di Bronya, wai." He acted out the obligatory pleasantries with a smile—the skin around his mouth tightening again when the officers released them. "Kokui comes to meetings totally unprepared."

"Daddy, that was an impromptu meeting."

"And so? What do I always tell you? Prepare for every eventuality."

She sighed. "Daddy, I'm learning the business. It will take time."

"You grew up watching me and you're still learning? Kokui, you will be twenty-three years, and you don't know your left from your right. Your sister is three years your junior and she knows what she is about—now she's started university, overtaking you. You should be setting the example."

He turned into the filling station and switched off the engine, absently stretching a tip out to the masqueraders performing at his window. A newsboy approached, pushing the day's paper at the window. FUEL PRICES REACH RECORD HIGH, AS MORE SUFFERING PROMISED IN THE NEW YEAR. Mawuli gave him money, too.

"If not for money"—Mawuli twisted in his seat to face Kokui again—"with those your second-try exam results, I don't know which university in Ghana you expect to accept you. 'C.' 'C.' 'C,'" he listed. "You want to be like your brother Antony?"

Kokui bowed her head as the station attendant came to fill their tank.

"If you like," Mawuli said, "continue delaying your future."

"Daddy, was the coup my fault? You said I should go to London and work while we waited for things to settle for me to re-sit the exams."

"And you saw what your options are over there in Abrokye. If you want to go back to the UK and nanny, or do some other odd job, by all means. All I can do is leave you what I have. If you let the business die, then see what you will pass on to your own children when the time comes."

Kokui leaned her head against the window, the smell of the petrol thickening in her throat. "I've heard you, Daddy."

"Daddy," Nami said, "I've told you not to have Kokui reviewing the ledgers, or sitting in revenue meetings. She can't choose between weights and grains of paper."

"Nami—"

Nami spoke over her sister. "You know your daughter, already. She needs to be with the workers, whether in the grove or at the machines, keeping them motivated, and sweet-talking the clients."

Mawuli barked. "Enyonam, I don't need you to tell me what my daughter can and cannot do. That's my mother's namesake."

Kokui met the chastened droop of her sister's gaze from her side mirror. *"My mother named Kokui after herself,"* she mimicked her dad. *"That was a woman with a vision! She changed her surname from Nuvi to Nuga because she saw bigger things in her future. She wanted a ga-ga life and I got it for her!"*

Mawuli snorted at Kokui's dramatic gesticulating and baritone. "It's true." He peeled ten ten-cedi notes from the envelope in his rock-gray blazer and paid the attendant. "Now we are ready to set off."

"Togo, we are coming o!" Nami made the pronouncement with her arms thrown wide, but Mawuli met his youngest daughter's performance with a yawn.

"Let's listen to some music, eh?"

Kokui stretched to switch on the radio, happy to change the mood in the car. Horns and drums accompanied the soprano section of a Twi Christmas chorale, drowning out her father's upbraiding with rhythmic glee. She turned to the window, escaping into the sedans, lorries, and pickup trucks rumbling around them on the road that led to the motorway. She pointed out the goats, cows, and chickens tied to various vehicles, challenging Nami and their dad to guess the meals they would end up in.

"Fufu and light soup!" Mawuli said of a mottled white bull on the back of a flatbed truck, its bones jutting through its skin.

"Ah, Daddy, I know light soup is your favorite, but this muscular cow, too? It will take days to cook him down," Kokui said.

"You see your sister's problem, Nami? Too impatient. Tough meat is the sweetest if you can wait for it to break down in the pot."

Was that her problem? she wondered. What was his?

When the tarred road yielded to the red earth of the villages connecting the Eastern Region to the Volta, new meat appeared. Past a painted sign of Mami Wata, the goddess's tail the color of the sea, a boy held a fresh and fat grasscutter by the ears, its slit throat dripping. Yards later, another child hawked a dried grasscutter carcass stretched across a latticework of sticks.

Mawuli stopped to buy the cured delicacy. "Your mother's favorite."

Kokui smiled at her dad, in spite of the truth, indulging the fantasy of this trip, as she allowed herself to do just a little every year. For one whole week, it would be just her parents, Nami, and her—the four of them waking up to eat and be together, like it used to be.

They bumped on the rough road until they reached the smooth stretch that led to the Adomi Bridge. Hawkers engulfed the car, holding up to their windows skewers of dried clams, steamed corn patties, and sachets packed with thousand-strong schools of minuscule fried fish.

"Yesssss, fressssh abolo!"

Kokui called for the corn patties, each steam-wrapped in its own banana leaf. "How much should we buy Ma?"

"A sack, if you think she'll want as much."

She pulled the envelope of bills from the glove box while Mawuli motioned to the adɔdi seller.

"Ma doesn't eat adɔdi," Kokui reminded their dad.

The clam-snack trader pushed her way to Mawuli's window.

"You know Daddy likes to buy for the family," Nami said.

He didn't. Their father gave his cousins and their children money, and went on his way. But maybe, Kokui thought. Mawuli Nuga did what he wanted, when he wanted.

He paid for enough clam kebabs to tear part of the newspaper page the hawker had wrapped them in. He passed the redolent bulk to Nami to hold in the back seat.

Just after the bridge, he turned onto the long, rough road that led to the bungalow he had built for his cousins and their families in Juapong, and parked at the tap in front of the house. Stray cats and dogs watched as Mawuli's eldest cousin, Cletus Nuvi, led his siblings and children to swamp the Range Rover. They pulled Kokui, Nami, and Mawuli out of the car to serve them glasses of water and calabashes of palm wine on the veranda, then led them behind the house to the black marble headstone that marked Mawuli's mother's grave.

"You know we can't keep long here." Mawuli slipped Efo Cletus an envelope before they got back on the road.

"Oh, Daddy! We forgot to give them the adɔdi," Kokui said. "We're not too far to turn back."

"Focus on your front." Mawuli switched on the radio.

Kokui turned to Nami's face in the sideview mirror and shared her mother's anticipated sneer. "You know I don't eat those roadside clams," she would say when she saw the adɔdi.

* * *

When they reached the border, the sun glowed orange in the dusty sky. The cement customs building stood framed by an arch crowned with the black star of Ghana's flag. Customs officers in navy uniforms moved among the mix of vehicles and alighted passengers, inspecting bags. On the periphery, soldiers in up and down cocoa brown kept watch as hawkers presented snacks and money changers peddled cedis and CFAs.

An officer peered at Mawuli's window, and shook his head. "Nuga, come out from your car. Quickly!"

Kokui turned from the uniform to her father. "Does he know you, Daddy?"

"All of you. Out of the vehicle. I said quickly!"

Mawuli sucked the color from his teeth. "Out of my vehicle for what?"

A second agent came up behind the officer.

"Do you know who you're talking to?" Nami snorted at their uniforms.

A third came around to Kokui's side and opened her door. Kokui's stomach seized. She gripped the door handle, trying to restore the barrier of steel between her and the officers as she searched each face for eyes to make soft contact with.

Nami jerked forward in her seat. "What's happening? Daddy!"

"Tell your supervising officer not to try this nonsense with me. If you touch my daughters . . ." Mawuli punched the steering wheel, letting the horn's roaring beep finish his threat.

"Officers." Summoning the vigor of a morning bird, Kokui chirped over the horn. "Meɖeku, ƒe yeye na mi lo. What is the problem?"

"Ask him."

"If you want to play games," Mawuli said, "just know that I own the team and the club."

Kokui cupped her hands to beg. "Officer, please. Tell me what we can do."

"It's not me who can answer," the agent said. "We've been ordered not to let him pass."

Kokui's head whipped to face her father. "Why, Daddy?"

Mawuli started the car. "Tell your commander to come out and face me. I will tell him what his wife tastes like."

Kokui drew back in her seat. They all knew her father was libidinous, but he had never been so crude. Not in front of her and Nami.

"Heh!" The agent at Mawuli's window waved over a soldier while another put a hand on the hood of the car, the engine purring beneath his flattened palm.

"Nami, give me the adɔdi."

"Daddy, no," Kokui said.

"Nami, I said pass me the clams."

The rustle of the newspaper wrapping filled the car.

The soldier strode toward them, his hand resting tentatively on his rifle, his darting gaze trying to assess the level of the threat. "What's the issue?"

"We've asked this man to alight from his vehicle."

"And I said I won't. Is it my crime that their commander cannot satisfy his own wife? She said the baby is for me, and I've taken the boy off their hands. What next?" Mawuli sucked his teeth again. "Let me give you your Christmas to share, and release me to mine."

The soldier appraised the pearl-colored Range Rover Nelson had washed that morning, before taking in the stone-colored blazer and crisp white buttoned shirt Mawuli had given Kokui money to buy for him in London. He noted the gold that dangled from the sisters' earlobes and wrists. He pulled the customs officers aside.

Kokui watched her father retrieve one of the kebabs and sink his teeth into the top clam. They waited without words until the soldier returned to the car.

"Sir," he said. "I've tried for you, and they have agreed to let you pass."

"And I have agreed to forget this matter when I meet with your colonel in the new year." Mawuli peeled several bills from the envelope in his jacket and passed them to the officer, along with the clams.

He released the clutch. As they passed under the arch that welcomed them to Togo, he nodded in the direction of a roadside chicken coop. "These fowls will be sweet in some groundnut soup, eh, girls?"

"Yes, Daddy," Nami said.

Kokui looked past the coop, silent. Staring at the palm trees that dotted the Togo shoreline as they bent to the salt breeze, she wondered where the clams would end up—and how their dad would explain to their mother why they had been delayed.

4

Nami sniffed as Mawuli parked the car.

"She's repainted."

"I like it," Kokui said of the noon-yellow walls bleeding into the morning-blue shutters and door.

"You like paint on the ground?" Nami thrust an accusing finger at the splatter on the red clay. There were also paint droplets weighing down blades of the scraggly grass tufts in their mother's front yard.

"You know your mother, already. She loves wild things." Holding the cured grasscutter like he had killed it himself, Mawuli preceded his daughters to the door.

But not all wild things love her, Kokui thought as her knuckles hit the moist blue wood. The door yielded, stopped softly by a red and purple sheet dripping with dried color. One of their mother's designs. The cloth flapped in their faces. Kokui pushed it aside.

"Ma?"

Surprise softened Nami's face and tone. "It's tidy."

In the wide front room, cushions zipped in khaki covers stenciled with milk bush flowers sat in neat rectangles atop the bamboo-backed armchairs and two-seater. One of their mother's massive old woodblocks sat between the single chairs, holding up a black leather-bound Bible topped with a dish holding four cowrie shells. Behind the seating, the carpenter's table that did double duty for dining stood battle-scarred with the grooves of innumerable knife lines and stained with infinite dyestuffs, but it was clear of clutter.

Beyond the table, just off the double doors that hid their mother's bedroom, a thin secondary school student's mattress lay on the terrazzo floor—where their mother would make their father sleep. Topped with a white pillow, the mattress was encased in blue and green cloth printed with the massive perched profile of a cock.

Mawuli smirked at the bedding, setting the grasscutter on the table.

Kokui moved past the mattress, through the painted cotton sheet that covered the door to the outdoor kitchen and yard.

The ordered disarray behind the house was more like their mother. The pestle and mortar were wet with recent use, but the pots on the stove were tepid. The sinks were gray with the rinsed-off blue and yellow house paint. Below them, dye-stained stacks of calabash stamps, different ones carved into leaves, flowers, birds, and abstractions, lay in scattered witness of the cloth that bore their images. The dyed panels of fabric covered the compound, stretched out to dry under the setting sun, a gallery of the beauty that winged through their mother's mind, held down at the edges with rocks.

"Where is she?" Nami asked, peering behind Mawuli who now stood behind Kokui.

"I'm here."

In unison, they turned to find her.

Micheline Miadogo Nuga.

Standing in the back doorway, Micheline made a castle of her cottage, the cloth that covered the door gently waving behind and around her. The boubou she wore quivered against her stout frame, the dark-gold silk and its matching headscarf almost indistinguishable from her skin. Mawuli appraised all seventy-two inches of his wife, like the soldier at the border had done the Range Rover. Kokui and Nami watched their mother pretend not to notice him. In solidarity, Kokui held her mother's determinedly averted gaze.

"Ma." She exhaled, rushing to latch on to the firm, fleshy folds of her mother's side, stretching to tuck her head under her mother's armpit.

"Atuu." Micheline cooed in her eldest daughter's ear, chasing the tender murmur with a succession of pecks on her daughter's temple.

Kokui lapped up this tenderness, like a newborn latching on to a nipple. It wasn't often she got to smell her mother's breath, hear it in her ears, feel her mother's love on her skin. Micheline lifted her other arm to make space for Nami. "You didn't open my bedroom doors," Micheline said.

Mawuli folded his arms. "Hide-and-seek."

"Your favorite game." Micheline looked past Mawuli, addressing the ether. "Have you seen your bed?"

Mawuli's lips curled with amusement, his dimples winking even as his eyes narrowed to twinkling slits. *This* was his favorite game, Kokui thought.

"Have you seen your grasscutter, ma Micheline?"

Micheline released her daughters. "I only just sent Afi to her house. She was here to cook and serve you. What kept you people?"

"The Nuvis wouldn't let us leave," Kokui said. She did not want to spend this week managing her mother's reaction to her father's latest indiscretion.

"Of course not," Micheline said. "It was the annual visitation of their god. Mawu li nam nu ga lo."

Mawuli covered a yawn.

"Tired? You used to be able to do this drive twice in one day," Micheline said.

"Who says I can't?"

"Girls, go and bring the fufu Afi pounded and heat the light soup for your father to eat and rest his bones."

"How can bones rest when there is still fat inside to suck, ma Micheline?"

The sisters arched their eyebrows at the suggestive shift in their father's octave and the shudder that rippled through their mother.

"Kokui, follow your sister and help her bring the fufu. If it's gone hard, it's your fault for coming so late."

Kokui and Nami transferred the food to the table, and the four of them sat to eat like this was their norm. They dipped their fingers into their respective earthenware bowls, pulling out slippery, savory mouthfuls of the breast-shaped mounds of fufu, swallowing with slurps the gingery pepper soup studded with fish, goat meat, and beef. Kokui felt her shame of her father, and for her mother, again yielding to the fantasy of an uncomplicated family. All four of them seemed to be under the spell of this delusion. Micheline cracked jokes at the cacophonous production Mawuli made of breaking and sucking the marrow from each bone in his koli. Kokui performed her dad's guttural gobbles. Nami tried to copy Kokui.

Every year, this pilgrimage made Kokui wonder what might have been if her parents had chosen a different way. If Micheline had not left her and Nami at the house in Achimota, when she found out it existed along with, then, three other wives and eight other children. If she had opted to take Kokui and Nami to Togo with her,

24

or kept them in the house at Ridge, the only house they had then known. If Mawuli Nuga was a different kind of man.

"You can take the boy out of the village," Micheline said of her husband's beastly bone cracking, "but you can't take the ko*fetɔ* out of the boy."

When the time came for bed, Micheline raised bashful eyes at the husband she had left eleven years ago but never divorced. "Sleep well, Old Man," she said as he lowered himself onto the thin mattress.

Behind the closed double doors of Micheline's bedroom, Kokui and Nami began to shed the long day. Micheline, too, peeled off her scarf and boubou and settled into the bed.

"No one else makes Mawuli Nuga sleep on a floor mat," Micheline said as her daughters quickly arranged themselves around her.

Kokui ached at the pride masking hope in her mother's voice. The truth was no one knew who or what made Mawuli Nuga do anything he did—and no one made Mawuli Nuga do anything he didn't want to do.

"Ma, why do you always make him sleep out there the first night?"

"Only to boot us onto the floor the rest of the week, and let him in," Nami added.

"The first night is to punish him," Micheline said, "but a whole week would punish me."

Kokui inched deeper into her mother's armpit. "Ma, why don't you leave Daddy and remarry?"

"Remarry?" She sliced the word into two, seemingly considering the question for the first time in her life. "Marry who again?" She shook her head. "No."

"Why?" Kokui emptied her chest of breath, overcome with sadness for her mother. "Because you love Daddy?"

"Should I let him give another woman what I've earned?"

"What have you earned, Ma?"

"As long as I am around, what he has is yours. The others have divorced him. Their kids have left the country."

"They're still his children, Ma. And he is married to Auntie Hemaa, too."

"Hemaa has no children."

"Have you spoken with Daddy about this?" Who knew how Mawuli would decide to divide his estate in his will, Kokui thought, or if there wasn't some other wife somewhere with children who could also stake a claim? "He can leave his things to whoever he wants."

"Don't worry about what my husband and I speak about." Micheline began stroking her daughters' heads. "How are things at your father's house? With your stepm—Hemaa?"

Kokui winced at the studied nonchalance in her mother's query. She asked this question every year. "She's still there."

"She's there, Ma," Nami repeated, "but Daddy has gone to—"

Their mother's stroking stopped. "Has gone to do what, Nami?"

Kokui inhaled. Nami wouldn't tell their mother about their new baby brother. Not after she had insisted the news was their father's to tell. Not on their first night of the only week they spent together as a family every year. "Ma—"

"Daddy has gone to bring another baby to the house."

Kokui gasped at the sudden crack in Nami's voice. Gone was the judgmental seal of set lips her little sister often wore when they discussed their mother, and absent was the sycophantic defense she often made for their father. Nami's mask of sarcasm had broken, her face agape with dry sobs.

"A baby boy," Nami rasped. "He cried all through the night. That's why Daddy was yawning—"

"Did he keep the baby in his room with him?" Micheline asked.

"On the way here, we learned that the woman, the baby's mother, is the wife of one border agent. The agents tried to pull us out of the car, opened Sister Kokui's door, called a soldier in." Every few words, the crack in her voice deepened. "They almost arrested us at Aflao."

Kokui swiped the tear sliding across the bridge of her nose. "No, Ma, he didn't let the baby sleep with him like you say he used to do with us."

Micheline wheezed now, silent tears shaking her body and the bed. "I chose wrongly," she said. "I chose wrongly. I chose wrongly."

Nami croaked, "If you say he is wrong, Ma, then we are wrong."

Kokui reached across her mother's belly to clasp her sister's hand.

"Be wiser than I was."

"How, Ma?" Kokui asked. It wasn't Micheline's fault Mawuli had deceived her. How could she have chosen differently when she hadn't known who or how he really was?

"I don't know," Micheline admitted.

They lay in their respective lakes of sadness, their throats taut not only from the weeping but the whispering. God forbid, Kokui thought bitterly, Mawuli hear and accept that the knife he had plunged in the hearts of his wives had cut his children, too. It was so confusing to her, this impulse they all shared to protect Mawuli from the pain he had caused them.

"She cursed us, Ma." Kokui brought it up because she had not been able to keep the woman's words down since she heard them. Lying next to her mother and sister, she could see the serpentine arm of her baby brother's mother stabbing at the darkness.

"Who cursed you?"

"The boy's mother."

"Ho!" Nami scoffed. "You think she's the only one that's cursed Daddy? Even Ma cursed Daddy."

"But she didn't curse Daddy," Kokui said. "She cursed us."

"What did she say?" their mother asked.

Kokui conjured the woman's desperate, acrid rage. *"Because of the shame you've caused me, not one of your daughters will marry happily."*

"Is that a curse?" Nami asked, wiping her mask back into place. "Who do we know who is happily married?"

Micheline let out a sad breath. "You can hope for something better, Enyonam." She caressed Kokui's arm. "You can be happier than I wa—" She stopped herself. "Than I am."

The quiet hum of their grief hung in the air for many minutes before Micheline spoke again. "I'll go to marché and see what they tell me to do."

"I will come with you, Ma." Kokui wanted to ask the priest what to do about the shame of rootlessness she had felt long before her father's latest woman had uttered her pronouncement.

"And have your father chop my head and say I am turning you all into witches? No," Micheline said. "Now, Kokui, what are you doing about university?"

Kokui rolled away from her mother and sister and stared into the darkness. "Daddy says he is getting me a place at Legon. I don't want to go to university in Ghana, Ma."

"Where do you want to be?"

Happy, she thought. Was there such a place? "London. Or here. With you, Ma."

"Here?" Micheline tutted. "And do what?"

Kokui felt her eyes go hot with fresh salt, her mother's rejection stinging. "I could help you with your designing, Ma."

"Kokui, you were never interested in sitting still with me. Discipline is not in you."

"Ma, I can't stay," she said, her voice breaking like Nami's had. "Like you couldn't."

"You leaving is different than me leaving," Micheline said. "You have to know your father's business. He will give it to the one who knows the business best. The two of you will inherit Nuga & Heirs Paper Mill. I have seen to it myself."

Kokui released a deep, low growl. "I don't want it, Ma. I don't care how paper is made. I can't sell paper. I don't want to work for Daddy."

"I know the business, Ma," Nami said.

"I don't care about the business."

"You don't care about the money? Kokui, everything I have is for the two of you. This house. The house my father left me. The money in my accounts. But I also want you to have everything your father has to give. For what he did, he owes us that," she said. "You have to be wise."

Kokui bucked against the bind of her birthright as Mawuli Nuga's daughter. She had not chosen to marry this man and yet she was trapped in the transaction between him and the wife he saw once a year. "I have to leave," Kokui said. "Help me talk to him, Ma."

Micheline answered her after another thick silence. "He's your father. He will listen to you before he listens to me."

Kokui breathed through the congestion and heat of her tears. They all knew Mawuli Nuga did not listen to anyone.

"I'll back you up," Nami said. "Whatever you want to do."

Kokui closed her eyes, clarity slowly forming. She had no idea what she wanted to do with her future, but she knew she had to choose a much different path than her mother's and her father's.

5

"He's leaving."

Kokui didn't follow Nami's furtive gaze over the veranda railing, or echo her sister's relief at their father's exit from the Ambassador's poolside area with an entourage of young women and old men. She pushed back in her chair, letting the metal scrape the stone that tiled the ballroom's veranda floor. She almost wanted him to see her there. "Colonel, let's go and claim our place by the pool, eh?"

Their father's friend rose to his shoes and planted a guiding hand on the small of Kokui's back. His colleague, Lawyer Denu, did the same with Nami.

"It's good I saw him first," the Colonel said. "If your father had seen us . . ." He gave his head a firm shake and his voice trailed away at the thought.

This man had helped plot the coup, and yet he feared her father. What was it about Mawuli Nuga that had so many in his thrall, Kokui wondered.

"He was here with his girlfriend."

"And so? You are his daughter."

And so? What did it mean to be a daughter when fathers betrayed mothers, and other men's daughters? Wasn't the woman her father was with also someone's daughter? Kokui didn't bother asking the Colonel. She knew he didn't care; after all, he was there with her, only afraid of her father seeing him with his daughter. Instead, she quickened her stride—a feat in her taut column dress and heels—eluding the Colonel's arm as it started to slip to the lower curve of her buttocks.

She knew she shouldn't marvel at this old man's presumption that anything sexual was going to happen between them, given how her father was, not to mention the makeup of the guests milling between the hotel's restaurant and poolside and her and Nami's own exploitation of the Colonel's and Lawyer Denu's egos. This kind of thing had been going on forever.

The Colonel was almost sixty years old, with children her and Nami's age. The Colonel, Lawyer Denu, and every bloated-belly "big man" in Ghana disgusted Kokui. They had the money, so they saw everything and everyone as a transaction. The last time she and Nami had been at the Ambassador, they had run into the Colonel and he had pulled rank on the lieutenants they were sitting with and bought their drinks for the rest of the night. It being the eve of the new year, Kokui simply wanted him to do it again. She would take as much as he would give, drain him as dry as she could, but she would give him nothing because she owed him nothing—and because she didn't have to. In moments like this, she thanked God she wasn't poor. Being Mawuli Nuga's daughter was a dizzying circle of irony.

It was a hypocritical game she was playing with the Colonel. She knew this. The Colonel was a married man. But she was not his wife, she rationalized. She had not entered into any binding arrangement with this man. She would take his drink and dinner money—likely pilfered from Ghana's coffers, anyway—but she would do nothing to make his kids siblings to other children they would struggle to love for fear of hurting their own mothers.

Tailed by the Colonel's rifle-toting guard, they took their seats right by the band at the table her father had just vacated.

"Nice girl like you shouldn't smoke," Lawyer Denu said.

"Who says she's a nice girl?" Nami's face brightened with a mischievous smirk.

Her unlit cigarette suspended between her lips, Kokui smiled with her sister. It made her happy to see Nami back in sarcastic form after her breakdown at their mother's. "I'll be back."

She took her cigarette to the edge of the poolside patio and leaned against the column by the door marked STAFF. She watched as the uniformed servers trooped out of the kitchen, laughter and banter abruptly yielding to the silent docility of professionalism when their feet touched the patio floor.

Kokui noted one server spying her from a distance, waiting, she knew, to collect the butt of her cigarette when she dropped it. She blew out the last cloud and walked the nub to the rubbish bin, only to find another server with his hand out.

"Ei, Head Sweeper." Kokui saw the annoyance flicker across the man's face, but she had no other name for him. "I'm Kokui."

"We're about to clear the bin, madame."

"If I were a madame, I wouldn't be here," she said. "I'd be waiting at home for my husband to leave his girlfriend at the Ambassador to open the new year with me."

"No," he said, "you would be waiting at the Continental."

Indeed, Auntie Hemaa was at the hotel across town, the plan for Mawuli to meet her there before the crossover into the new year. "Working here, I'm sure you see a lot of things."

"I only see what needs to be cleared, and whatever small thing a guest is kind enough to dash me."

Kokui raised an eyebrow at his unsubtle ask for a tip.

He shrugged, nodding toward the band. The singer was crowing a cover of Barrett Strong's "Money (That's What I Want)." "You have to verbalize what you desire."

"Something my father would say."

"The way you made your face when you said 'my father.'" He tilted his head toward the moon and dropped his lower lip in an expression of adoration-cum-admiration.

"I didn't say it that way."

"I can't compete with Cinyras o."

Kokui had no idea what he was talking about, but she was clear that this server was flirting with her. She respected his ambition. "Cinyras?"

"The hero in Greek mythology. He slept with his daughter."

"I don't want to sleep with my father—I prefer a one-woman man, if such a man even exists," she said. "And trust me, you can't compete with him. Neither of us can. At my age, he was on his way to becoming a millionaire."

"Who says I'm not on my way?"

She appraised him in his uniform, the burgundy jacket and ruffled white shirt. "Well, you're not even a manager."

Irritation tightened his smooth brown face, his eyes growing hooded, his full lips drawing a straight line. He was a good-looking man.

"Like every Ghanaian whose father isn't a millionaire," he said,

"I have to start where I can. I was working at the Ministry of Finance, but when they sacked the administration, I had to find another way."

"The Ministry of Finance?" She lowered the corners of her mouth, impressed. Jobs at the ministries were impossible to get unless you knew someone. "Couldn't the one who got you that job get you something else?"

"The person my professor knew was in the last administration." His lips bunched in a small smile, like he was chewing on a good secret. "My time here is temporary, though. I'm going to America."

She gave him a patronizing smile. Everyone had a right to dream, she thought. "Why America?"

"I've been accepted into university there."

She squinted at him, appraising him again. "You mean it. You're actually going to America?"

"I am."

Kokui felt her throat constricting, jealousy surprising her. "How did you manage that?"

He chuckled. "I applied."

"You must be very brilliant."

"I guess God gives us each something to work with."

She dropped her cigarette butt in the rubbish bin.

"Some of us have beauty and riches," he continued, "and some of us have a cousin in New York who helped them apply to university there."

He had a cousin in New York? Kokui knew Ghanaians were everywhere, but America was not the first place their people went. They were children of the British Empire. Yes, Ghana was independent now, but close to four hundred years of praying "God save the King," then "Queen," had tied the countries' souls together. "When do you leave?"

"It will have to be next year. I'm raising the funds for my ticket."

"But you've been accepted. Will they keep your place for a year?" She wanted to know every detail—and how she might follow suit and make her way to some place that was totally unfamiliar.

"They allow one year deferral."

"But—"

"How long does it take to smoke a cigarette?" Nami was behind them now, glancing between her sister and the server in confusion. "The countdown is about to start."

"I was just chatting with my friend . . ." She turned to him to finish her sentence.

"Boris. Boris Van der Puye." He tipped an invisible hat toward her sister.

Nami eyed the small bag of rubbish he had pulled from the bin.

"Happy New Year, Boris, and good luck in America."

He nodded. "Thank you, madame."

"I told you I am Kokui."

"Madame K," he said, a smirk touching his lips.

"Why were you speaking with him?" Nami asked as they walked back to their table.

"He's going to university in New York, Nami. He applied. I've been thinking London, but maybe—"

Nami sighed with the patience of a schoolteacher addressing her dullest pupil. "Even if you were to get a school there, we don't have anyone in America."

"Daddy didn't have anyone in Germany."

Again, Nami exhaled, impatient. "Why do you want to suffer, Sis?"

Kokui clasped her little sister's hand and squeezed, like she had in their mother's bed. "I don't," she said. "I don't want any of us to."

The Colonel put a flute in her hand. She tried to shake off the envy and awe that tingled on her skin at the thought of Head Swee— Boris's—acceptance at a school in New York, and reprised her role as the Colonel's chirpy drinking companion. She clinked his glass enthusiastically, but she couldn't stop thinking about her exchange with Boris as the band began to count down. He had opened a new door in her mind. A future of her own choosing seemed attainable as the old slipped into the new. Ten! Nine! Eight . . . 1973!

6

The sales office of Nuga & Heirs Paper Mill and Press sat two stories above the high street it perched on in the commercial Tudu neighborhood, but from Kokui's back-seat window the dusty-blue building was dwarfed by the kinetic rush that coursed outside of it. The eight a.m. crowds danced around one another on the thoroughfare, dodging beeping vehicles and stepping over goods displayed in distinct piles and rows on the ground. Passengers lugged suitcases and overnight bags to and from the bus station as drivers' mates shouted their destinations. "Ta'di!" "Ho!" "Lagos!" "Lomé!" Hawkers beckoned prospects with deep, low kissing sounds while money changers whispered black market rates.

"Daddy, I get pound sterling, dollar, CFA," one informed Mawuli breathlessly as her father shut the car's back door. "Sister, tell him I go give him good price on new naira."

Kokui turned to her dad as they made their way onto the

stone-paved compound of Nuga & Heirs. "He go give you gooooood price, Daddy."

"That is not the offer he needs to make." Mawuli waved his hand at the line of money changers behind them. "All of his colleagues are offering a good rate. In business, you have to distinguish yourself."

Kokui braced herself for one of her father's sermons.

"When I started out passing tracts for my uncle, I quickly learned you have to offer more than the thing everyone says they want. What they say they want is cheap. You have to offer what they need. And I'm not talking about material need. I'm talking about respect. Love. Those are the things a soul eats," he said. "For those things people will pay—or give—anything you ask."

Kokui looked up at her dad. What had happened to him that he was advising her to manipulate the human need for respect and love to make a sale?

"The secret to succeeding in business is the same secret to making it in this life, Kokui: You have to find out what a person's soul is hungry for. You have to know the need beneath the want. Once you know that, you have them in your hand."

Kokui endured the lecture until she watched her father's taut evangelistic expression loosen with lust at the sight of the office receptionist. She noted her father's lingering gaze, and the knowing that slanted the woman's stare. What was under her father's want with women? What did he need that five wives and myriad girlfriends had not been able to satisfy?

They walked past the employees finishing up their boiled eggs and porridge in the staff room, down the corridor to the row of offices. Opposite the three sales managers' offices, the bookkeeper's office sat empty between Mawuli's and the one Kokui had been working out of.

"Kokui, bring me the ledgers you entered the transactions in yesterday."

"I wasn't able to finish, Daddy. I'll do it now."

Mawuli followed her into her office. "Kokui, I've told you never to leave the ledgers out and open for anyone passing to see." He sank onto the vinyl chair behind Kokui's desk and pulled the A-4 notebook close. "Where are the receiving slips?"

"Locked in my desk."

"With the key in the lock." He opened the wooden drawer and pulled out a fistful of limp carbon papers.

"When are we getting a new bookkeeper, Daddy?"

"Kokui, this business is for you. If you don't know how to keep the books, you will be cheated—bankrupt before you can say 'fi-afitɔ.'" He studied the page in front of him, then furiously started turning to the ones before it. "No. No. Kokui, what shambolic work have you done here? You haven't entered the figures correctly."

Kokui swallowed the frustration thickening in her throat as she moved around the desk to stand over her father's shoulder.

"You see this column?" He traced his finger from the top of the page. "You enter the amount spent here—what we have on the receiving slip—then you subtract it from this column here. You have to ensure the amounts leaving the credit side are equal to the amounts on the debit side or we have a problem. You understand?"

Kokui crinkled her brow and nodded, performing the closest approximation of interest she could conjure.

"Kokui, I'm serious."

"I know, Daddy."

He abruptly pushed the ledgers away and rose from her chair. "Kokui, you have two options. Forget school and continue working with me here so I can teach you the business myself, or take the place I can get you at Legon and commit to being a serious student."

Kokui groaned. Always this pressure from him. Nami would fulfill his dream of carrying on the family business—why was he obsessed with conscripting her into something she did not want to do?

"With your results, even a two-by-four school won't take you in London. You want to go and work for peanuts over there when I have worked tooth and nail to give you everything you need here in Ghana?"

"If I can get a school in London, will you help me, Daddy?"

"You won't get a school with a proper accreditation, Kokui," he huffed. "But if you can, we'll talk. Now use patience and finish these correctly."

Kokui slumped in the vinyl chair and opened the notebook. All she had to do was enter the amount on each slip in its own line on the debit column and subtract accordingly from the credit column. She could do it, but reading the product descriptions on the pale-yellow slips, she didn't want to.

JUAPONG TEACHING HOSPITAL
    MARITAL EDUCATION BOOKLET (15,000 COPIES,
        4-COLOR)—¢35,000

EVANGELICAL PRESBYTERIAN CHURCH (HEAD OFFICE)
    FAMILY STABILITY MANUAL (15,000 COPIES,
        4-COLOR)—¢35,000

CAPE COAST CATHOLIC MISSION SEMINARY
    GOSPEL TRACTS (5,000 COPIES, B/W)—¢625
    FAMILY EDUCATION WORKBOOK (15,000 COPIES,
        4-COLOR)—¢35,000

EGLISE EVANGÉLIQUE PRESBYTERIENNE DU TOGO
    TRACT ÉVANGÉLIQUE POUR LES FAMILLES
    (2,000 COPIES, B/W, EWE)—¢500
    (2,000 COPIES, B/W, KABIYE)—¢500
    (2,000 COPIES, B/W, FRENCH)—¢500

They were more than halfway through the year's first quarter, and her father had earned more than most Ghanaians would see in a lifetime, printing materials preaching marital and family strength. Perhaps even more absurd to her was that her father studied each pamphlet before it went to press, correcting misquoted Bible verses and offering colloquial translations where he found them necessary. He had grown up under his uncle, a businessman and part-time clerk at the Evangelical Presbyterian Church, and he had made sure all his kids had attended Sunday school. She couldn't understand how her father reconciled his behavior. The irony of life, she supposed, as she, Mawuli Nuga's daughter, sat stuck in this office entering these paradoxical figures into the record, while Head Sweeper planned his future in America.

Kokui felt a fresh surge of envy thinking about the hotel attendant's achievement of escape, remembering their conversation at the Ambassador in the last minutes of the old year. Admiration welled up in her, too. No matter how smart he was, she couldn't imagine the process had been easy for him. Only top athletes and musicians seemed able to make their way to America from Ghana. He said he had a family member in New York who had helped him apply to school. Kokui wanted to know more about Boris—and she wanted his help in applying to school in America, too.

Her task completed, she delivered the ledger to her father. Mawuli turned from the pile of slips on his desk to study her entries. "That's more like it," he said. "I know no child of mine can be daft."

She watched him clap the notebook shut. "Remember what you promised me, Daddy."

"What did I promise?"

"You said if I can get a school abroad, I can go."

Her father laid the ledger on the desk and folded his hands over it. "Kokui, close my door and sit down."

"Daddy, you said I entered the figures correctly."

"I said close the door and come and sit down."

She did as she was told.

"What do you see on my desk?"

Kokui eyed her father suspiciously. "Receiving slips."

"And what do you see behind me?" He waved in the direction of the black two-inch, three-ring binders standing in a line on the filing cabinet against the wall.

"Binders."

"And what is in the binders and in the cabinet under the binders?"

"Files?"

"And what are the files and receiving slips made of?"

She exhaled. "Paper."

"And what do we make?"

"Paper, Daddy."

"Eh-heh. And what does paper do?" He didn't wait for her to answer. "We communicate with it. We pass information with it. It's how we teach. How we've recorded life for thousands of years, from Egypt to China to Rome. Birth. Death. Business. Marriage. Paper outlives it—and us—all, Kokui. It tells the generations we will never meet how we lived, and that we lived. It's not just paper. It's proof of life!"

"Isn't life itself proof of life, Daddy?" What was the point, Kokui wondered, of passing information to the next generation, on paper or in speech, if it kept them locked in the bondage of the past?

"Paper is what your ticket to Abrokye will be printed on," he said. "If you can make it there."

Kokui met her father's shrewd gaze, his dimples smirking at her. He'd mentioned the ticket to get her attention, and he had it. She looked at the flaccid receiving slips again, which looked crisper, firmer.

"I wasn't more than your age in 1944 when Jan Weber bought

my ticket to his office in Germany because I was selling their prod-uct so well. I had accounts for them all over the place."

She continued for him, mimicking his delivery. *"The Catholic and Methodist mission schools from Winneba to Sekondi. The Governor General's office here in Accra."* Kokui had heard the story so many times.

"I made soooo much money for Jan Weber, his sons, and his daugh-ter, they took me to their mill in Steinau an der Straße to study the operation. I was there less than two years, he was so impressed he gave me the money to start my own mill. I left Ghana a paper salesman," she said, raising her pointer finger for emphasis as her dad did when he told this part, *"and when I returned, I had the money to start my own paper mill. Today, in the whole of Ghana, there is only one Harris offset press machine and only one Fourdrinier paper machine in the whole of West Africa. I own them both. And it all started with me as a small boy helping my uncle Theophilus in his printing shop."*

Mawuli watched her performance with the squinting alertness of a critic. "You can recite the story, but you haven't let it teach you anything."

"Daddy, you are a successful man," she intoned in her own voice now. "You've been successful from the start."

He barked. "I don't need your flattery, Kokui."

What did he need, then? Kokui was desperate to know.

"From your youth, I took you and your sister 'round with me. We were at the mill in Bolga, and at the press in Industrial. The older children were under their mothers, but you and Nami, I took with me. Do you remember?"

How could she forget? Her father's workers had practically folded themselves in two, bowing to greet Micheline. "Madame Nuga," they chorused, and each time, Mawuli corrected them: "Madame Nuga*ga*."

43

This was before they knew his insistence on the superlative was not more evidence of his decadent love for their mother—the kind of *ga* amour she and Nami mooned about wanting when they married, before they began to question what this type of eros, or any kind of love, demanded. Weeks later, when they learned of Mawuli's whopping infidelity—that he had three other wives and multiple children in a house in Achimota—Kokui would wonder if Mawuli meant it literally. Micheline, his "mansion woman," was the most *ga* in size of his succession of wives.

"I remember, Daddy."

He shook his head. "I don't know why you are squandering this opportunity. I just don't understand."

How ironic, she thought, that he was perplexed by her. "I have to find the need under my want, Daddy."

"Then be serious about yourself, Kokui," he said. "Seek. Knock. Pursue. Go after everything that's for you in this one life, prepared for every eventuality."

Go after everything? There had to be an alternative to insatiability, Kokui thought, as she walked out of her father's office.

She admired that her father had built something that enabled eighty-eight employees across three offices to feed themselves, put children through school, and care for poor relations. Some of the staff had even been able to leave the company housing and buy land to build homes for themselves. She respected that Mawuli had managed to accomplish this with little more than smarts and will. Not everyone knew how to convert the benevolence of family and strangers into a business. She didn't. Maybe because her father had been born with nothing but the love of his mother, amassing "everything"—including women and children—gave him a sense of gratification. But that was not her story. She wanted, and needed, fidelity more.

7

Kokui parted the curtain of bottle caps that opened into Tokyo Joe's Chop Bar and Drinking Spot. She looked for Boris among the Saturday afternoon customers chatting over their heaping bowls and frosty bottles on the low wood tables.

"Madame K."

She smiled at his silhouette in the back doorway, surprised by how nice it was to see him in his element. Instead of the hotel uniform, he wore a white buttoned shirt, khaki trousers, and polished black shoes. She could see, based on the smocks, shorts, and chalewotes most of the other patrons had on, that Boris had dressed up for her. She felt less silly now, in her Akosombo Textiles jumpsuit and high heels. It still astounded her that Boris had agreed to help her apply to his school in the States without accepting her offer to pay him. They both knew five hundred cedis would get him close to the money he needed for his ticket to New York.

"We'll have more privacy than in here," he said.

She followed him outside to a courtyard bordered by the bar, a small house, and the wall that enclosed the outdoor kitchen. They sat at the small card table that leaned against the kitchen partition.

"Can I get you a drink?"

"You already know the answer."

"I'll bring you a Star."

Kokui looked around the compound as she pulled out a chair to sit. On the other side of the wall that the table was leaning against, a pair of women pounded fufu while another watched two barrel-size pots of bubbling soups. She observed the compound cat pacing near the women, hoping for a scrap of the fish one had dropped in, and she noted the pregnant goat that lay on the shaded veranda of the house behind the bar. Both the bar and the house were sturdy box-shaped buildings with corrugated iron roofs, each painted a bright aqua green.

She sensed eyes on her and followed the feeling to the little girl straddling the top of the wall. "Heh! Get down from there," one of the aunties in the kitchen shouted at the girl. Kokui exchanged a wave with the girl as Boris returned, balancing a tray holding two bottles, two glasses, and a small dish of groundnuts.

"You said this is your uncle's place? Your mother's brother?"

She was trying to figure Boris out. He told her he had been working at the Ministry of Finance before the coup. He had played coy when she asked him about it, but those kinds of jobs only came through serious connections. Tokyo Joe's was a small place, but it was full of customers. She knew from her father that it took envelopes to the area chief and relevant ministers and ministry clerks to open any kind of establishment in Accra. The bar, the house, and the land they stood on were valuable real estate. Perhaps he had a benefactor of his own.

"He's not a blood relation," Boris said, "but Uncle Joe and my mother grew up in the same house."

"Here in Mamprobi?"

Unconsciously, he tipped his head in the direction of the old colonial quarter of the city. "No. British Accra side."

"But you grew up in Mamprobi? Do you live nearby?"

"Not too far."

"You said you live with your brothers and—"

"Focus on the questions you have to answer."

Kokui arched an eyebrow at the sudden bite in his voice. What serpent had she uncovered with her questions, she wondered.

"Were you able to get the form from the embassy?" he asked.

She pulled the Erie Community College application from her handbag and smoothed the folds of the three pages on the table.

"You see the form is simple? Just add your name, your secondary school, and detail your academic plans."

Kokui gulped her beer to mask her insecurity. Leaving her father's haunted house of disrespected women was the only plan she was clear on. "Do you think the school is expecting a certain answer?"

"To what?"

She took another deep swallow. "What did you write for your academic plans?"

"I'm here to help you."

The passion-cum-stern condescension in his voice faintly reminded her of her father. She smothered the irritation, the feelings of inadequacy, and the eagerness to prove herself that rose in her chest as she looked down at the listed fields of study. She had no interest in Data Processing. She skipped past the Education field—she liked children all right, but not enough to sit in a classroom with them for a whole day. Health Sciences intrigued her, but she had never been good at anything science related.

"Remember, it's a community college," Boris said. "It's not your end. Choose something that can prepare you for the course you will do when you transfer—and for your life. Something that will have stability and longevity, like Business Administration or Office Management."

She chafed at Boris's course suggestions. She had grown up steeped in both curricula, taught by Mawuli Nuga himself. She wanted to do something totally new, but faced with choices that left her uninspired and wary of entrapping herself in something that wasn't right, she succumbed to insecurity and impatience. Maybe it was wiser to start with what she was familiar with. Kokui wavered and glanced at the list again. She didn't care. She just wanted to leave her father's house. When she got to America, she would figure the rest out.

"Number Six!"

Kokui looked up from the form she had begun to fill out. Happily postponing concentration on the weighty question of what path she was meant to pursue, she focused on the muscular older man who now stood over them, eager to learn Boris's connection to him.

"You didn't offer your guest anything more to eat than groundnuts?"

"Number Six?" she asked Boris.

"He's his mother's Baby Last."

She watched Boris's jaw twitch at his uncle's explanation.

"Uncle Joe, we won't be keeping long."

"Oh, your uncle Tokyo Joe!" Kokui shot to her feet and half-curtsied. "Hello, sir. Thank you for hosting us in your establishment."

"Hello, beauty." He appraised her. "Why won't you be keeping long?"

48

"Uncle Joe, I'm helping her with an application to university in the US."

The old man looked down at the papers on the table. "Erie Community College, eh?"

"I told her to try my strategy," he said. "It might be easier for her to gain entry into a two-year program before transferring for a four-year degree."

Boris's uncle gave him a smirk. "Your friend here is too poshly dressed to be eating peanuts. You think she'll tell her colleagues to come here from—where do you stay, my dear?"

"Achimota, Uncle."

"Ei! Rich-imota!" He threw his hands up. "Up, up, up, up. Boris, kill the goat for this Achimota girl."

Kokui laughed. "Oh, Uncle, I'm okay. Thank you."

"Watching your figure? Remember, we need big handles to grab on to."

She forced more laughter, quickly lowering to her seat to elude the hand he had reached out to demonstrate with. "No," she said. "Uncle, we are almost finished."

"Take your time." He rested the hand she had ducked on the cap of her shoulder, caressing her joint with his thumb. "Young lady, I hope I will see you again. You are welcome anytime."

When he left, Kokui scratched at the memory of his finger on her shoulder and resumed filling out the form.

"I'll add more to the academic plans later," she said. She passed Boris the pages to read.

"Then it's left with your school report and A-level results."

She swallowed her saliva, the beer finished. Once the school saw her triple Cs, she feared this exercise would end in denied admittance, and embarrassment. "Are you sure you don't want money for helping me? If I don't get in, at least you will have something for your trouble."

He tutted at her. "You haven't submitted the application and you're planning for rejection? Forget about the list," he said. "If you could be paid to do any work, what would it be?"

"Determine what makes men how they are." She chased the words with a dry chuckle, but she was serious. "Unable to pass a woman without touching or reaching or brushing. Unable to commit to one woman at a time. Why they would mess up a home to satisfy themselves." She searched Boris's face for agreement, or an excuse, but his set lips were unreadable. Was he a shoulder grazer, a handle grabber, a profligate philanderer? In their three interactions, he had been an absolute gentleman with her, but still she wondered.

He had to be attracted to her, if he was turning down airfare and sacrificing his personal time to help her—but who knew if Boris didn't bring other women to Tokyo Joe's? He was ambitious and driven and handsome, and he was on his way to America. He was a catch.

"To study why human beings are the way we are, Philosophy or Anthropology are there," he said.

She snorted at his clinical answer.

"Whatever the case," he went on, "I don't want any payment from you. I don't want you to confuse my interest in you for money."

"Interest in me?" Kokui repeated it because she wanted him to say it again, and elaborate, but he didn't. Instead, his admission ballooned between them. The air that had formerly been feathery with the awkward tickle of flirtation was now weighted with the fear of rejection and the uncertainty of what would come next if she reciprocated.

Kokui felt the suspicion of a desire too quickly fulfilled. She was

Mawuli Nuga's daughter. She could offer him a lot more than five hundred cedis. Perhaps he had a longer-term strategy in mind, to use and humiliate her. "You are interested in me, and you have me at your uncle's place? How do I know you don't have a wife at your house?"

"How do I know you only exchange drinks with that soldierman you were counting down to the new year with?"

She flinched with embarrassment.

"We'll just have to trust each other," he said.

"Hmmph. Trust." She returned her application to her bag and pushed back from the table. "I should be going. Two hours on just these peanuts." She winked at him.

"You haven't told me if you are interested in me," he said.

Kokui searched his face for mockery and deceit. All she found was the earnestness she had noted the night Boris had almost made her fall collecting the cigarette she discarded—but what if she was wrong?

She exhaled and emptied her mind of her vacillating reservations, allowing her admiration for him to win. She was fascinated by him, as interested in him as the little girl who had been watching them the whole time, ignoring the calls to come down from the wall. She wanted to study this man. She wanted to ask him every question about himself she could think of. She wanted to do more than wave at him.

"I'm interested."

They both looked away, each releasing a half laugh. She chewed the left curve of her upper lip, relief joining the thrill and fear of declared, and shared, attraction heating up her face. He took her hand, folding his palm over hers, lifting her to her feet, leading her out to her car. Kokui blinked at their mutual grip, marveling at the sight and feel of his hand sweating into hers. *Head Sweeper!*

She had not envisioned any of this that December night at the Ambassador.

Nelson sat up in the driver's seat when they came out, wiping the dribble of sleep from his chin.

"I'm at the Ambassador every night this week."

"I'll be there," she said, too quickly, but caught herself as Nelson started the car. "If I can make it."

She had to be careful, she thought, as she stared at the hand Boris had just held. She was in awe of Boris. He had a big vision for himself, and he had the determination and discipline to see it through. But, like her father, he was a man.

8

Kokui bent for her sister to pin her ponytail in place. "How I've missed you!" she cooed. "I suffer to do my hair when you are in school."

"All I'm good for," Nami said wryly. "Take advantage. Lectures resume in two weeks." Nami gently pulled the ponytail. "Is it secure?"

Kokui gave her head a firm shake in front of the head-to-toe mirror, the waxen curls brushing the back of her silver jumpsuit from shoulder to shoulder.

Nami sniffed. "All dressed up for the chop bar."

"Nami, if you want to join us, just say so."

"Join and do what?"

Kokui met her sister's reflection in the mirror and turned to fold her into the tightest embrace. "Don't worry. You will always be my sweetheart. My first love, I never go leave you."

Nami squealed and squirmed out of her big sister's squeeze, the cynical screw of her face softening with the placidity of assurance.

"Get ready and let's go, eh? Maybe you will meet your own tonight."

"My own Guy Friday?" Nami scoffed as she slowly walked over to their bureau.

"Nami, do you know something?" Kokui sat on the edge of her bed to strap on her sandals. "I like that Boris doesn't have money. I like that he doesn't have an envelope to make anyone kneel at the altar of his bad behavior."

Nami pulled out a dress. "That means he has something else, Sis. We all have something."

Kokui feared the same thing. Since their mutual admission of interest, she had spent almost every evening with Boris, sitting at the Ambassador's poolside bar while he worked, or meeting him for a drink at Tokyo Joe's, watching him. It had been almost two full months, but she still knew few basics about him. She believed he meant it when he said he liked only her, because he shared the time he stretched to work as many hours as he could with her—but he never let his hands complete what his gaze appraised. He never reached for her. Never let his palm slip to her bum. She didn't want a man who grabbed every woman's handles, but she did want him to grab hers! They had yet to kiss.

He still hadn't shown her his home or introduced her to any of his friends or family except Uncle Joe. She suspected he was ashamed of his house, and she hadn't pressed the issue because she was also ashamed of her home—she wasn't racing to explain the multiple vacant rooms emptied of heartbroken, embittered wives, or the baby that wasn't her stepmother's, or her feelings about either. But she worried, too, that Boris's reasons for limiting her access might be more sinister. That, like her father had, he was hiding something.

Kokui sprang up from the bed. Strapped into her heels, she was as tall as their mother. "I like that I'm the one with the envelope."

"So you can make him eat your adɔdi," Nami said.

Kokui grimaced as Nami turned for her sister to zip her into the bright orange cotton.

"Am I lying?"

"My clam isn't dried, Nami." Kokui's ponytail swished with another shake of her head. *"Yessss, fressssssh!"*

They giggled at the memory as they could only do with each other.

"What are you girls hee-hee-ing about?"

They turned to find Auntie Hemaa in their now-opened bedroom doorway, the picture of regal polish in her wig and kente.

"Nothing, Auntie Hemaa."

"I'm off to the Continental for dinner with a client," she said. "And you?"

"We're going for some Homowo festivities," Kokui told her.

Auntie Hemaa arched a plucked eyebrow. "Homowo, or homo sapiens?"

"Eish, Auntie Hemaa!" Kokui giggled. "Just a small Homowo planting season opener."

"Whatever planting has you going to Mamprobi, you are of age," she said. "Just drink your tea. We don't need any more babies in this house."

They waited for her car to leave before trooping down the stairs. On the veranda in front of the house, Sister Eyram paced back and forth, balancing baby Kofi on her back with a tightly wrapped cloth. *"Ameka fa dzedze vi, lo?"* She sang the lullaby's question and crooned the answer. *"Isn't it my Kofi who is perfect? Isn't it my Kofi who is worthy?"* The boy had stopped crying for his mother, but his eyes darted in disappointment when he saw Nami and Kokui.

"Is he asleep?" Sister Eyram asked them.

"His eyes are wide open."

"Still looking for your mother," Sister Eyram said over her shoulder, her tone as tender as it was sharp, as if the boy, not yet one year old, could understand. "We are also your family. You can sleep."

Kokui turned away from her brother's sad eyes, not sure if it was better that he had been separated from his mother before he could grow to remember things differently.

In the car, behind Nelson, they settled into the leather seats for the ride. Kokui felt her smile returning, covering the cloud of empathy for her little brother, as they exited the house gate. The quiet of their street gave way to the evening hustle: the kelewele sellers frying wide pans of the spiced plantain chunks and the chichinga sellers turning speared cubes of meat over on their grill grates, flames on wicks swaying beside them. The kenkey sellers wove through them, calling attention to the fermented balls of sustenance. "Kalayeyɔlei!"

There were neon cones blocking the stretch of road immediately in front of Tokyo Joe's. Revelers spilled beyond them, filling the street, as passing cars and trɔtrɔs maneuvered around them, some honking their horns in agitation, some in solidarity with the celebration.

"Nelson, we'll get down here so you can park."

The sisters stepped out into the symphony of drums, strings, and voices blanketing them from the speakers and the merrymakers.

"Boris might be in the back." Kokui led her little sister past the red bulb that glowed above the bottle-cap curtain.

"That's him in the corner there."

His head was tilted in low conversation with a lady, their foreheads practically touching. He wouldn't have told her to come if he had invited another woman, Kokui told herself, but still, jealousy at his intimacy with this woman she had never met taunted her. He was playing games with her, her distrust said. What could a smart, focused man like him see in a daft woman like her? "Boris."

He lifted his head, his face taut from whatever he and the woman had been discussing. "Madame K."

The woman turned to sweep her gaze from the peak of Kokui's ponytail to her shining toenail polish.

"This is my brother's wife—"

"The eldest brother's wife," she said. "Tsotsoo Quartey."

Kokui's heart softened, the tightness of envy yielding to relief. She moved her bag from her right hand to her left to greet Boris's sister-in-law with a soft shake and a half curtsy. "Hello, Sister Tsotsoo."

Tsotsoo looked at her hand, her bag, and then at her face again. "You have caused many problems in my house, 'Madame K.'"

"Me?" Kokui turned to see if her sister had heard the same thing.

"Our Baby Last has broken a good heart and left a scorned woman in its place because of you."

She turned to Boris, the coals of insecurity heating her up again. "What's going on?"

"I'll explain later."

Her shoulders wilted with disappointment. She felt Nami's palm on her back. "Explain now, Boris."

His sister-in-law laughed. "Madame K, I said he broke her heart for you."

Kokui watched Boris look away.

She dropped her head with disillusionment and pulled a cigarette from her bag. It wasn't three wives and eight children. She supposed it was unrealistic to expect he had had zero attachments when they met, but still, it hurt to know there had been another heart in the background. How important had this connection been that his sister-in-law knew her, that his ending things had brought trouble to his house? She knew he was a man, but she had hoped he could be a different sort than she was used to.

An older man came up behind Tsotsoo. "Is this the one?"

"Madame K," Tsotsoo confirmed through lips pursed to drink tea. "This is my husband. Boris's eldest brother, Kwate Quartey."

Kokui saw Boris shrink into himself, like a child caught sneaking meat from the soup pot. She could understand why. Though slimmer and shorter than Boris, Kwate Quartey had an imposing carriage. His hands hung at his sides loosely curled, ready to clench into fists—or shake hands on an agreement shrewder than anyone who dared accept the grip could propose. His lancing stare seemed permanently narrowed into a squint of suspicion.

"Bro Kwate, my name is Kokui Nuga," she said, half-genuflecting.

He nodded, his gaze shifting from her to Boris. "But can you afford this girl?"

Kokui reached out to gather Boris's hand into her own. "I've been wondering whether I can afford him," she said. "Yankee-bound man like this."

"If they sew your patch and his patch together, the both of you will rip," Kwate said.

She felt the hairs on her arms rise. If not for the fact that he was Boris's brother, she would have returned his curse on his own head. "Ah, but Bro Kwate," she said, performing a playfully placative tone. "You don't know sasa fabric is the most beautiful kind? The best matches are unexpected."

"It's true o," Tsotsoo said. "Sometimes the patchwork is more beautiful than the individual pieces."

Kwate's face glazed with lost interest as another man approached. "Is she the one?"

"She is the one," Tsotsoo said.

"Ei, Number Six's girl."

Kokui's head began to bobble, turning at new voices, new men, and a circle of women gathering around her. Uncle Joe cut through the cluster, snaking his arm out to hug her.

"My Rich-imota Girl is here!" he said. "And her friend."

"Her sister," Nami said sharply.

"Bring the sisters some food to eat! My daughter," he called Kokui as he gripped the flesh between her waist and hip. "You are welcome. Both of you."

He dropped his hand and grabbed Nami's, leading them away from Boris out to the back where more of Boris's family congregated. They pulled her, hugged her, handed her and Nami beers.

"I like your dress," one of the wives said.

"It's a jumpsuit," another said.

"You are beautiful."

"But you are a smoker," one said with a frown.

Another tapped her temple. "I hope you are correct. The girl our Baby Last was moving with went completely off. I mean, how do you steal eight thousand cedis and make it appear as if the one you say you love stole it, all because he has seen another woman?"

"She wasn't smart to take the money for herself! Foolish girl!"

Eight thousand cedis? Kokui's eyes bulged at the easy revelations, and the boisterousness of their welcome. Boris had simply told her to come for a drink.

"You haven't answered. Are you correct?" The woman tapped her temple again. "You can have all the money and still be a madwoman."

"Don't mind her." Tsotsoo was next to her again, wedging between her and Nami. "She's been drinking from morning,"

"Sister Tsotsoo, you, too, you were drinking with me."

"But am I slurring?" Tsotsoo took Kokui's hand and pulled her toward the outdoor kitchen. "It's quiet here. We can talk."

Kokui nodded, tentative and curious, hopeful for more disclosures about Boris. "Okay?"

"What are your intentions toward our brother? I don't know what he has told you, but he is our Baby Last. We don't play with him at all, at all, at all," she said.

"He hasn't told me anything."

"He and his brothers have had a hard life. Not too hard," she conceded, "but not easy."

Kokui leaned in.

"Their mother had properties all over Accra. Ei, Auntie Christie! They used to call her 'Auntie Shika' because of her wealth and generosity. She gave loans to plenty people, and she gave plenty time for them to repay, but there were some jealous ones.

"They saw her with the big house here in Mamprobi, and her half-caste husband, and they reported them that they were in cahoots with the British—even though the man was of Dutch heritage. Nkrumah's people seized everything! If not for a misspelling of her name on the registry documents of the house in Mamprobi, the Lands Commission would have taken it, too!" She shook her head. "She died in custody when Boris was twelve years old."

Kokui inhaled this revelation about Boris. She had known it wasn't just her admiration for him that had drawn her in. Boris, too, understood the devastation of abrupt, cataclysmic upheaval in childhood.

"It was his brother Kwate and me who took over raising him. Kwate had to become their father," she went on. "They think he is

60

strict because they have different fathers, but that's not the case. I've never heard him call them his half brothers.

"Anyway, Boris is a good boy. Very smart. A little 'nose in the air,' like you." Tsotsoo tilted her head to demonstrate.

Kokui gasped at the woman's assessment, her free hand flying to her nose.

"But it's okay," Tsotsoo said. "You have found yourselves."

She felt Boris next to her now.

"Boris, this one is a nice girl. Not simple, but very, very nice. Except for the smoking."

Tsotsoo yanked her into a fleshy hug. Kokui could smell the pomade in her hair, the beer on her breath, and the lavender on her skin. It made for a surprisingly pleasant bouquet. "Thank you," she said.

"So now you've met the family you've been so curious about," Boris said when Tsotsoo left them.

"But not the girl your sister-in-law mentioned."

"I don't want to talk about that."

Kokui flinched at the bark in his voice. "Boris, I need to know what's going on. You say you are interested in me—"

"You." He stopped himself, and sucked his teeth. Even in the dark, Kokui could see his face creasing and tightening with all sorts of thoughts. "Come."

"Where?"

"To my house. So you can see for yourself where I stay."

"Sis!" Nami hissed as they moved past. "Where are you going?" She gave her sister her beer. "We'll be back just now!"

She followed him silently up the dirt road, keeping impressive pace in her heels.

"It's here." He stopped at the dented iron gate of a sturdy two-story building that dominated half the street.

The corners of Kokui's mouth slid down. She was impressed. A few shutters were missing from the windows and a few of the exterior lights were blown out, but even under the cover of night, she could see the house had been built to be a home for generations.

"Christiana Naa Dede 'Auntie Shika' Quartey House," she read the name under the center lintel light.

"Number Six," the old man across the street waved at Boris as he twisted the padlock open. "Now you have your key, eh?"

"You didn't have a key?" Kokui asked.

"Don't mind him." Boris folded her palm into his and pulled her over the threshold.

On the other side of the gate, she scanned the property while Boris locked them in. It was neat, the dust clear of rubbish, only a football under an old mango tree. A parked car was under a protective cloth cover. Warm squares of light glowed in a checkered grid.

"My brother hires out the extra rooms. That's how we keep this place."

"You must fetch a lot of money," she said, thinking of the eight thousand cedis Tsotsoo mentioned. "It's a big house."

"He must fetch a lot of money. He gives us nothing but the rooms we sleep in."

"He's the eldest. Isn't that how it works?"

Bitterness squeezed Boris's face. "He can share so we, too, can do something for ourselves. This is our mother's house—the money should be there for all of us when we need it."

She nodded, the picture widening. He wouldn't need to defer a year at school to work for airfare if his brother helped him.

"If we were lions, Kwate would have eaten me and my brothers long ago and enjoyed licking the blood from his teeth."

Kokui grimaced. "What?"

"My cousin Sammy in New York," he said. "That's how an elder brother behaves."

Boris walked her into the dimly lit stairway and up to a spacious room. Two beds sat on wooden frames under the single bulb dangling from a ceiling of decorative wood squares. "This is my bed. My nephew—Tsotsoo's son, whom you met—sleeps on that one," he said. "So now you see there is no secret wife or girlfriend."

"Who is the girl they were all talking about?"

"Kokui, she's not around anymore."

"But she was." She folded her arms at her waist. "Boris, I have three ex-stepmothers, and my father's current wife isn't the mother of the baby a woman dropped at our house just before Christmas. I have eight siblings—that I know of—whom I barely know. And my mother." She stopped herself. "I like you, but I will not be with anyone who cannot be faithful to me. I don't want my parents' marriage."

He sighed. "Madame K, she was a nice girl. I liked her." He shrugged. "Until I met you."

"How do I know you won't like someone else?"

"Ah! But how can you know that, any more than I can know that you won't want someone with more to offer you?" he said. "All I can say is I'm not your father. Even if I could afford five wives, I only want one."

"Your sister-in-law was asking about my intentions toward you. What about yours for me, Boris? You're leaving for America soon. We have to decide whether we want to continue if I don't get accepted. I want to continue."

"Madame K, who says you won't be accepted?"

She closed her eyes, his belief in her a prayer.

"We've only just started," he continued. "Let's cross that bridge when we reach it. I want to have something for myself before I bring someone into my life."

"Someone, or me?"

He pulled her hand to his, threading his fingers through hers. "Madame K, you are used to a certain lifestyle. How can I come to your father and ask for you at this stage of my life?"

She wondered how he would feel if she told him that she liked that he was a working man. He had all the qualities she admired in her father, without the money to corrupt him. "Money isn't the most important thing, Boris. Trust me."

"Hmmph," Boris said.

She pulled their entwined hands to the bodice of her jumpsuit and kissed him. On his nose, his eyelids, his lips, his ears.

"Kiss me," she said. "Touch me."

He disentangled their palms to cup her face. "You," he said, his voice winded with exasperation.

"What have I done?"

He shook his head and traced her lips. Kokui tried to control the quiver of her mouth as he brushed the plump folds, lingering at their partition. Slowly, he lowered both thumbs over the darts of her breasts, rubbing her hardened nipples through the shining fabric. His mouth followed, and Kokui arched to give him way, exhaling as his tongue slipped under the material. She felt his hands emboldening, searching for the zip of her outfit, and she guided him to it, before freeing the buttons on his shirt and trousers from their loops. She lay back on his bed, the strands of her ponytail sticking to her moistening back as she widened for him.

"I love you, Boris," she said, her certainty as strong as her desperate hope he felt the same, that he saw her as worthy of loving her truly, faithfully.

He stopped. She could see him thinking. She held her breath, embarrassed by how much she needed him to reciprocate.

"I love you, too."

She exhaled into him, curled around him tightly, her whole body tingling. *Homo sapien, indeed!* She wished she hadn't invited Nami along. She wanted to lie with him forever.

"Promise me you will always be faithful to me," she said when they leaned on their sides facing each other, their bodies rising and falling with the stakes of this new intimacy.

"Madame K, I've told you, I can't compete with Cinyras."

"He can't compete with you," she said.

"I promise." He gathered himself and sat up. "I'm sure they are looking for us by now."

"Nami must be fuming at how long I've left her alone. And who knows what Sister Tsotsoo is saying." She pulled her jumpsuit from the edge of the bed, relieved and ecstatic. "You have a nice family, Boris."

"Do I?"

"You're all together. Very different from my family. You'll see."

9

When the receptionist delivered the envelope to her office, Kokui sat it on the table unopened. So much rested on the decision folded inside. She would either have the freedom to explore a path of her own choosing in America with her father's financial support, or she would have to submit to her father's choice to go to Legon or commit to working for him. If Erie Community College denied her admission, she could plot another way out of her father's house or Ghana. Save the allowance her father gave her, pay her own way abroad, make her way without any support. If they didn't accept her, her family's prophesies, and her own, would be true. She swallowed the fear collecting in her throat as she imagined the scenarios attached to rejection, and the work required to dig her way out of all the things that seemed to be keeping her stuck in place. But if Erie accepted her, she and Boris would escape to America together. She closed her eyes, conjuring the day Boris had told her he was leaving for university in New York. How different would her life look attached to his drive and discipline, and his belief in her?

Kokui tore the envelope open. Wondering was more agony than declined admittance would be, she thought. She inhaled before permitting herself to look down at the unfolded page.

Dear Ms. Nuga:
It is with pleasure we write to offer you—

She shot up from her desk and went out to her car to shout. *Heyyyyyyy!* She clapped her palm over her mouth in disbelief as she reread the letter. She had done it. With no word from Mawuli Nuga and no exchange of closed palms or fat envelopes, she had gotten herself into school in the US, surpassing her mother's, father's, and Nami's low expectations, and her own. And now her father would pay. Breathing fast and hard, she couldn't wait to tell Boris. *Oh, Boris.* He had been the only one who believed.

She drove into the gathering traffic, fidgeting like the bubbles in a bottle of Fanta as the congestion slowed her reveal.

The sky was the color of tea by the time she bounced past the Christmas tree at the Ambassador's entrance, to the bar beside the pool. She tried to catch Boris's eye from her entry, to teleport her news, but he was focused on the two customers he was serving.

"Ah!" one of the men was shouting at Boris. "'Tis the season of enjoyment."

"What are we enjoying?" she asked.

Boris exhaled at the sight of Kokui. He really did want her around, she marveled. "I didn't know you were coming tonight."

"I have news."

"Ei, what kind of news is this?" the bombastic one asked.

Kokui raised an eyebrow at the man's prying audacity. "Not that kind of news," she said, leaning her midsection into the bar and thrusting her hand forward. "I'm Kokui Nuga. And you?"

She watched the men's backs straighten from *C*s to *I*s. "That is not a common name. Are you connected to Nuga & Heirs Paper Mill and Press?"

She nodded with the practice of her twenty-three years on the job. "That's my dad." She didn't like to drop her father's name, but she could see this man needed a push back in place.

"Okay, hello. I'm Solomon Kusi."

"Solo and I were at the Ministry of Finance together, and he was here with me for a bit at the Ambassador before he left for the Ministry of Lands."

Kokui heard the tightness in Boris's introduction.

"I'm the Chief Lands Clerk," Solo said.

"You've both done well," she said. "Boris on his way to university in America. You, at Lands."

Solo nodded. "We've been reviewing the land grants under Nkrumah and noticed your father's very sizable tract in Bolgatanga. You know the administration is carefully examining every grantee, but my colleague and I have been trying to contact grantees directly to allow them to clear up any discrepancies we encounter in the paperwork, and any deals that were egregiously disadvantageous to the country."

Kokui felt her smile fade. Her eyes shot to Boris to make sure she had heard right. Boris, too, looked surprised. Was this man really angling for a bribe not to put her father's land grant under investigation? She laughed inwardly. This man did not understand his place in the pecking order. The Chief Lands Clerk was not the

Minister for Lands. Her father ensured the minister pecked his fill so he wouldn't have to do business with low-level civil servants like this.

"I'm sure you and your colleagues know how much land is needed to grow enough trees for the paper your files are made of," she said.

Solo's face tightened with embarrassment or offense, Kokui couldn't tell which. She forced a fresh smile. "What were you all enjoying before I came?"

"We were offering Boris a tot to enjoy for the holidays," Solo's colleague said, "but he's refused, even though no one is watching him."

"He has integrity." She turned to beam her pride at Boris. His character was one of the things she loved about him. She took one of the glasses Boris had just filled. "But I will raise a tot with you. To Lands and to country."

"Kokui Nuga's boyfriend," Solo said. "Now I know why Boris is turning down offers of better work."

Kokui searched Boris's tightening face. "Which offer?"

"You know the salary here is peanuts."

She watched Boris's countenance fall.

"I was telling Boris there is opportunity at Lands," Solo continued.

"Boris is doing just fine on these 'peanuts,'" she said.

Solo raised mocking eyes at Boris. "This man doesn't need a thing!"

Boris wiped the bar clean when the men left. "I know you were trying to defend me, Madame K, but I don't need you to talk for me."

"I was talking for myself. Telling me about my father's 'sizable' land grant. What was that for?" She sucked her teeth. "He doesn't know what my dad can do to him."

"Don't go and tell your father anything," Boris barked. "He didn't say anything bad."

She recoiled, surprised by his anger. "He just tried to humiliate you in front of me and his colleague."

"Now that he has a small post at Lands he thinks he can talk anyhow, but he shouldn't forget that just as we lost our jobs at the Ministry of Finance without warning, he can lose this one, too."

"All the more reason for us to evacuate this country." She dug in her bag to slap her opened envelope onto the bar.

Boris's face loosened with joy. "You got into Erie."

She nodded, her ponytail slapping the back of her neck, pride swelling her chest. "I don't know how or why, but I did."

"You did it!"

"I can't wait to tell my family. Especially my father." She paused to retrieve and light a cigarette. "They had no confidence I could do anything like this on my own."

She opened the envelope to reread the acceptance letter aloud.

"They didn't offer you a tuition waiver?"

She frowned at the typed-up sheet. "Tuition waiver? Did they do that for you?"

"How else—"

She could hear his jealousy. She folded the letter and returned it and the envelope to her handbag. "Well, I got in," she said, her shoulders slightly slumping. "Now my father has to make good on his promise."

"What promise?"

"He swore to me he would pay, if I could get into school in Abrokye."

"Great," Boris said.

Kokui arched an eyebrow at him.

"What?" he asked.

"The way you said it."

"Said what?"

"That's great," she repeated through clenched teeth.

"I didn't say it that way."

"Boris." She took her time to gather her next words. She didn't want to offend him. "I've told you my dad needs a bookkeeper. I don't know how much he can pay you, but I'm sure—"

"Madame K, you don't like working for your father, and you think I would? I have six months. I can come up with the money for the airfare to New York."

How could he come up with the airfare making thirty cedis a month? Unless someone dashed the money to him, it would take him years. Nevertheless, to encourage him as he had encouraged her, she nodded. "I know you will." She inhaled, summoning courage to add another item for him to consider. "I've told you we go to my mother's in Togo the week before Christmas every year," she began. "I know it's high season for tips, but if you can make it for one or two days, it would be nice for you to meet my mother when we are all together."

Boris gulped.

"My parents—they have a strange relationship. I've told you," she repeated. "But I know your family, and it's time you knew mine."

Kokui's eyes bore into his, waiting for an answer. If he declined this invitation, she wouldn't interpret it as him not being able to afford to pass up the money he stood to make in the most lucrative week of the year. She would understand it as him declining a future with her.

"I'll go," he said.

Her face softened, her chin lifted, her ponytail swung. She watched the apple in his throat move up and down with uneasiness.

"Don't be scared, Boris. My father and mother won't eat you."

"Madame K, I never want to use you for a ladder—or confuse you that that's what I'm doing."

He didn't need to tell her this again. She had also been careful to keep the financial pressure on their time together low, content to sit with him while he worked at the Ambassador or join him at his uncle Joe's place for free drinks and food. "I know, Boris."

"I worry sometimes about our compatibility," he said.

She swallowed, fear sobering her glee at his agreement to meet her family.

"You don't understand the life I'm living," he went on. "You just sit in your father's car behind your driver and go—you don't know about the fuel prices."

"Yes, I do," she said. "I know they are rising. I've seen the operation costs in my father's ledgers."

"But have you ever sat in a trɔtrɔ? Do you know what it is to take transport and pay twenty-five pesewas on your way to work, and pay thirty pesewas for the very same ride on the way home from work because of fuel prices?"

She rolled her eyes. "Just because I don't have that particular experience doesn't mean I cannot understand you, Boris. I could take the path my father is laying out for me, but I'm trying to find my way, just like you are."

"I know." He went silent for a moment. "I wish, as you said with such force, that I was doing fine." He looked away from her. "I don't want you to ask your father about the bookkeeper position on my behalf. I will ask him myself."

"Okay."

He poured her a half tot of the VSOP before quickly screwing on the cap and putting the bottle back in its place.

She squealed.

He whirled around, alarm seizing his face. "What is it?"

"Boris, we are going to America! New York! Alice Annum will greet us at the airport. Marvin Gaye will drive us to your cousin's place. We'll have lunch with Diana Ross."

Chuckling, he swatted her with the cloth napkin he had been using to mop the wet rings the tot glasses had left on the bar's polished wood.

"Don't worry, Boris. I'll let you sit in the front with Marvin."

10

Kokui watched from the front passenger window as Mawuli clapped the top of Auntie Hemaa's car.

"Sis, you're brave," Nami said. "Boris in the back seat, and Daddy at the wheel, for seven-plus hours?"

"It has to be done." She had carefully considered when to invite Boris to her home and introduce him to her parents. Now was the time. She needed Boris to understand her family in its full complexity—or at least see it for himself, as she herself didn't fully comprehend it. If he saw Nami preen for their father's affection, if he watched Kokui ricochet from banter with Mawuli to bent head, if he saw her parents' marriage, Mawuli teasing Micheline with innuendo, Micheline pretending she didn't need her husband's attention—if Boris saw it all and still wanted to be with her, then she would know they were ready to not just go to the same school in America, but to go with each other. She had been careful not to mention marriage after their first discussion about their future, but many months had passed. They were approaching the bridge, and she needed to know if Boris was ready to cross it.

Nonetheless, as Mawuli advanced in their direction, Kokui felt her anxiety rise. "You're right, Nami. Let me get down for you to sit in the front."

The sisters switched places as Nelson drove Auntie Hemaa out of their open gate.

"What's this musical chairs all about?" Mawuli slid into the driver's seat.

"Daddy, you remember we are picking up my friend in Mamprobi, before we set off to Ma's."

Mawuli eyed her from the rearview mirror. "Your friend or your boyfriend?"

Kokui swallowed nervously. Their father had not raised them to play demure, but she had never felt comfortable discussing or introducing her partners to anyone in her family, except Nami— not that she had ever dated anyone seriously enough to do so, until now. As far as she was concerned, her parents' marriage, and her father's marriages, had disqualified her parents from having any moral authority to approve or disapprove of a mate she had chosen. But still, this was her family—to know them was to know who she was and why.

"He's my boyfriend," she said.

"Boyfriend or intended?" he asked. "I want to know what you expect us to talk about trapped in this car on the long journey to your mother's, which I don't even invite a driver to join."

From her side-view mirror, Nami smirked. A silent "I told you" as their father started the car. Past Evans at the gate, Mawuli maneuvered them across town toward Mamprobi.

From the junction, past Tokyo Joe's, she directed him to Boris's place.

"This is the house, Daddy."

Kokui could see her father mentally appraising the property as he squinted at the name on the lintel.

"Didn't you say he's called Van der Puye?"

"It was his mother's house. She's passed on. That's him." Kokui got out of the car. "He admires your house," she told Boris.

Boris's eyes darted like a chased housefly, from her to the Range Rover and back again. "But the house is not for me alone."

"Well, he knows that, Boris. Otherwise, you would be a rich man," she said.

He looked stung by her words. She wasn't sure why.

"I haven't told him about my acceptance at Erie. I want to tell him and my mother together. But he knows you are going." She led him to the car as Nami stepped out.

"Daddy says I should sit in the back with you, Sis."

"Boris, is it? Come and sit beside me."

Boris's facial expression suggested a bowel movement as he marched stiffly around the car.

"He won't swallow you," Kokui whispered. She took Boris's bag and set it between her and Nami in the back, before sliding in behind him.

"Young man, how do you see your future?" Mawuli asked as Boris gingerly shut his door.

"Sir, I'm going to study Accounting in the US."

"I didn't ask about your studies," Mawuli said. "I asked about your vision."

"My vision, sir?"

Kokui knew her father would interview Boris, but he had just sat down. "Daddy—"

"Kokui, let the man answer, if he can."

"I can, sir. I'm—I see my future in America with a good job, a nice house. Settled," he said.

She heard the timbre in Boris's voice getting stronger.

"Do you mean to stay there indefinitely?"

"Yes, sir. Ghana is not the place for a man like me."

Mawuli frowned, his eyes finding Kokui's in the rearview mirror. "What kind of man are you?"

Kokui's face stretched with pride before he answered. A man she could trust.

"I'm not a man of means, sir, and I don't have strong connections to keep a good-paying job. My cousin Sammy is in New York. He's finished school. He's working. He is doing well for himself and his family over there."

"What kind of work is he doing?"

"He is working at a hospital, as a clerk supervisor."

Kokui searched her father's reflection in the side and rearview mirrors. She didn't expect him to be impressed, but not everyone could boast a Jan Weber in their life.

"If your cousin were in Ghana," Mawuli told Boris now, "he could be doing more."

"Sir, he didn't have money for university fees. Neither do I. I took a certificate course, but without a degree, it's only connections that can help me, and I didn't have the kind strong enough to sustain a change of government. And even then, there aren't many jobs here."

"You young people have to stop looking for work. You have to create work for yourself."

Kokui rolled her eyes. "Daddy, if you'd never left Ghana, you wouldn't have gotten Mr. Weber's investment to start the company."

He barked. "I always tell you, I was on my trajectory. Jan Weber simply recognized it and was in a position to support it. I would have soared with or without him," Mawuli said.

Her father made it all sound so easy: *The old man saw success in me. I had a plan, and he wanted to attach himself. That's why he gave me the money to open the mill. Not a loan, a gift.* As a child, Kokui had taken the story at face value, but now that she was older, she knew there had to have been more to Jan Weber's decision to give her father enough money to open his own mill in Ghana, no strings attached.

Kokui performed what Mawuli would say next. *"It's okay to get your education and save some money there, but settling in Abrokye is not the dream it seems."*

"Exactly!" Mawuli said. "I'm sure you know about their race problems. They will make it difficult for you."

"Sir, I don't intend to involve myself in any of those racial things. I just want to work and make money in my corner. Whatever they have over there is better than my prospects over here."

"Is your status so low? I saw the advertisement on your wall for a room for rent."

"I'm the last-born, sir. My eldest brother is in control of the property."

Mawuli met Kokui's eyes in the mirror. "Kokui, you cannot go to America without a degree, and you will not get a proper school there. Over my dead body will you go the way of your elder brothers and sisters. I hire people to do the jobs they are chasing in London. I didn't build this company for it to die when I do."

"Daddy, I'm here," Nami said.

"You can't do it all by yourself, Enyonam."

"I can, Daddy!"

"You cannot. Yes, you are in university. Yes, you have the smarts, but your sister has the flair, the charm, the beauty."

Nami lowered her head.

Kokui sighed. "Daddy—"

"Young man, you said you're going to do accounting. I'm in need of an accountant here."

"Yes, sir."

Kokui heard the squeak of relief in Boris's voice. She, too, was grateful her dad had brought it up unsolicited.

"It's settled. You can start in the new year."

"Sir, you know I will have to leave by June, for school."

"Young man, let's see if you will even work out in my employ."

"Sir, I will work out," he said.

"A confident man." Mawuli smiled. "You have to be."

Kokui saw Boris's jaw soften for the first time since they got on the road. She felt herself loosening, too. It felt good to help Boris. She often wondered if her father would have been faithful to his first wife if the investment in Nuga & Heirs had come from her.

"He's keeping up with Daddy," Nami said, when they stopped to urinate. "Can you really see yourself with this man, Sis?"

Kokui squatted in the bush. Boris hadn't given her reason to doubt him in the almost one year they had been together, she reflected— aside from the girl who had come before her that he hadn't mentioned. "He's honest. Trustworthy. He works at the Ambassador Hotel. He could be chasing air hostesses or sugar mommies, but all the man does is work so hard. I've seen it for myself." She wiped herself dry and stood up.

"Well, he's passing Daddy's interrogation. Let's see how he handles Ma."

They returned to the car, the vehicle smelling of cured grass-cutter and four bodies, and rode on, stopping to drink palm wine with the Nuvis before continuing to the border.

"Maison Micheline," Mawuli announced when they reached their final stop.

Last year's marigold cottage was now white with crimson shutters. An emerald cloth hung in the front doorway.

"Ma?"

Micheline sat enthroned on the armchair in her sitting room, a green-and-gold tie-dyed boubou spilling over the sides. "This time, no trouble at the border?"

"It was a smooth ride, Ma," Nami said.

The sisters hugged their mother, bending into her seated hold and her temple kisses. "Kokui, you won't introduce your guest?"

Kokui straightened, proud. "Ma, this is Boris Van der Puye."

Boris looked more comfortable now, tenderized by Mawuli's pummel of questions.

"Let's sit down to eat, and get to know ourselves." She pushed off the chair with a grunt. "Afi!"

Her mother's assistant emerged from the back of the house, glancing quickly to and away from Mawuli's poker face. Kokui swallowed her disappointment. She decided the pain it would cause wasn't worth alerting her mother to what might have passed—or would pass—between Afi and Mawuli.

"We are ready to eat," Micheline said. "Go and help her, Nami." She stopped Kokui from following. "You stay with your husband here. Dear, what is your name?"

"Boris, madame."

"I told you, Ma."

Micheline looked past her daughter, smiling like she had smelled a latrine. "Kokui says you are a server at a hotel."

"As of the new year, he works for me."

Micheline blinked from Boris to her husband. "Doing what?"

"Accounting, madame. I was—I used to be at the Ministry of Finance."

"Doing what?"

"An assistant to the deputy minister's assistant."

"And what happened?"

"The coup."

"Lucky you to get this job from my husband. The right somebody can really take you places. But where can you go with the wrong somebody?" she asked Kokui.

Kokui exhaled as Nami and Afi filed in, carrying the fufu, soup, and bowls. Her mother was being excessively harsh.

"Ma, Boris is off to uni in the States."

"Well, that is promising. Which university?"

"Erie Community College, madame, in Buffalo, New York."

"Community college?" Micheline frowned. "You couldn't get a better school?"

Boris's smile drooped as they set the food before him.

"Ma, I wanted to tell you and Daddy together," Kokui said. "I've also been accepted to Erie Community College."

Mawuli's face stretched with surprise. "Is that so?"

Kokui tilted her nose toward the ceiling fan. "It is so."

"So, you'll be leaving Ghana for a community college, when your father can get you a place at University of Ghana? And what will you be studying?"

"I put down Business Administration."

"A clerk." Micheline turned to Mawuli. "You're going to let your daughter become a clerk, like your other children."

Micheline liked to underplay her stepchildren's professional accomplishments. Aside from Antony, most had respectable jobs in government services. Elikem had a very successful business training child theater performers in singing, and Connie was reading law.

"We'll discuss this later."

Kokui turned to her father. "Daddy, you promised you would let me go if I could gain admission."

"I said we will resume this conversation when I am ready."

Micheline pointed to the mattress on the floor after they ate. "Make a mat for your husband, next to your father's." She looked at Boris. "A man must earn his way into the bed from the floor."

Kokui could see the thin vellum of patience falling from Boris's face. "I'm not her husband," he said.

"Then why are you here, dear?"

"Definitely not to earn your daughter."

Kokui felt every muscle in her body contract, the bite in his voice breaking her skin. She had watched her father humiliate her mother and stepmothers too many times, and vowed each time to never sit still for such disrespect from any man—but now she bowed her head.

Her mother had used the spousal term as a test of Boris's intent, and he had submitted his answer, daring them to fail him. Kokui narrowed her eyes at her mother, an easier cushion on which to pin her blame and shame. From the moment they had walked in, Micheline had been picking at Boris. But why wouldn't she, Kokui asked herself. How could her mother be happy for her when she wasn't happy herself?

"You think you can be happy with a man like that, Kokui?" Micheline asked when she and her daughters were behind her bedroom door, leaving Boris and Mawuli on the floor outside.

"A man I don't have to share?" It hurt to cut her mother, but her own wounds ran so deep.

"Kokui, don't speak to Ma like that."

Micheline jutted her chin. "A man who doesn't want to earn you."

"Ma, I don't want him to earn me. I want him to love me."

"Kokui, you are too expensive to make yourself cheap. If he can't withstand your mother holding him to the fire, then he is not the lasting sort. I've made my choice, but you can choose differently."

Kokui lay taut in the bed between her mother and sister, embarrassment and confusion competing for control of her mind. How much differently could she have chosen, she asked herself. She had climbed over the wall that separated her and Boris's stations because she believed it could make the difference—that together they could defy the dysfunction she came from, and that she could find her focus with him. But he had made himself clear. *Definitely not to earn your daughter.*

Even if he had said it to salvage his pride, he had still said it. Why hadn't he just borne her mother's roasting, for her? She replayed the vision he had shared with her dad—he had not mentioned her in his plans. Maybe he had agreed to come on this trip only to ask Mawuli for the job.

It had been some time since her brow had furrowed over baby Kofi's mother's curse, but now the pronouncement rose from the dust of her mind. *Each and every one of your daughters will know the shame of marrying unhappily—if they marry at all.* She hadn't asked her mother if she had gone to the marché priest to cancel this dark oath spoken over her and Nami's future.

Nami didn't believe the woman's curse had any power, but Kokui didn't see how the anguish in her proclamation could be impotent. How could it mean nothing when it meant so much to her? Kokui heard it like a refrain, an echo of the strangled grief she had felt when she learned her father could not be trusted with a heart, when she watched Micheline spit her own curses at him. That kind of pain had to land somewhere.

She woke up the next morning with the determination to ensure the pain wouldn't stay with her, or fester in the tender space she had allowed Boris to enter. The shame and grief of Boris's rejection taunted her as she sat up, and she reminded herself Boris had been clear about his intent toward her. He had come to Togo for the job, she decided, and that only—that was why he gave up his shifts at the Ambassador during the most lucrative week of the year. He had said he didn't want to use her as a ladder, but now she believed he had lied. Their relationship had always been about pulling himself up, she concluded. What had he lost with her but time? If she wasn't sitting with him at the Ambassador pool bar, she was at his uncle Joe's place where they ate and drank free. Her mother was right, she told herself. She had given herself away cheaply—and still, he didn't want her.

It was early, the morning's first light a soft announcement of Micheline's vacancy in the bed. Her mother was probably working outside, Kokui mused, exorcising their argument on a piece of fabric or a block of wood. Nami was still sleeping. Kokui resolved to go to the marché herself. She slid on the dress she had worn the day before and pushed through Micheline's double doors.

"You are up?"

Kokui started at Boris's voice, her eyes jumping past him to her father's empty mattress. Where were her parents this early morning?

"You're awake." She answered the question on his face. "I'm going to the market."

"The market? At this hour? Since I've known you, you've never mentioned going to the market."

"That's in Ghana. We are in Togo." She felt a cold relief now that she knew they were done. The curse had been fulfilled, and, she would ensure, fully satisfied.

"Madame K," he spoke to her back. "What if we left for the States earlier than planned?"

She stopped, the door's handle in her hand. "What do you mean?"

"Now that you've been accepted at Erie, you can go for your visa. I have mine. We can stay at my cousin's place in New York, and work until school starts."

Kokui squinted at him, baffled by the incongruence of his words to her now and her understanding of his rejection the night before. "Boris, we don't need to go to America together. I thank you for helping me apply."

His brow furrowed. "What are you talking about?"

"You made yourself clear yesterday. You didn't come here to earn me."

"Madame K, I've told you before that I don't want any confusion about my interest in you. I won't transact with you, or for you."

"You don't want to be with me."

She watched annoyance seize his features. "I could be earning one hundred cedis in tips, but I'm here because I want to be with you."

The proof she needed was commitment to a lifetime of fidelity. "If you want to be with me, marry me."

"Kokui," he huffed. "You won't wait and let me put myself together?"

She felt she had been too placating with him. He needed to face the facts for what they were. He had everything to gain being with her, she told herself now. "When will that be, Boris? Think about it. My father would pay both our airfares and give us an allowance, if we marry."

"Kokui, have you heard anything I've just said? I don't want to be indebted to your father, or to you."

She sighed. "Boris, I admire your integrity so much. You know I do. But pride is a rich man's prerogative," she said. She could see him recoiling, but in that moment, she saw his need tangled with her want, and her own desperate need to be someone's nu ga ga, so she pushed. "It wouldn't be a debt. Once we are married, it will be our money. You work hard, Boris. Everyone who knows you knows that. But you still needed help to get the ministry job. Taking help doesn't make you less. I didn't know you, but I asked you for help applying to Erie, and look at us now. You helped me. Let me help you."

She let the silence hang between them, allowing him to think.

"I have almost four hundred cedis saved," he said finally. "If I work for your father, keep my evening shift at the Ambassador, and support Tsotsoo at her stall in the market, we won't need to borrow anything from him and still leave Ghana by June."

She rolled her eyes inwardly. "Or we can leave Ghana earlier, go to New York with the money Daddy gives us, and work to make our own money."

Again, he was silent.

"Don't punish me, Boris, or yourself, to prove you aren't with me for money. I know that's not why you are here."

"Morning whispers are the loudest."

Kokui turned toward Nami. She hadn't heard her sister exit their mother's bedroom.

"What are you all in tilted-heads conversation about at this hour?"

Boris opened his mouth to speak, but closed it when Kokui grasped his hand.

"You were going to say something, Boris?" Nami said.

He took a deep breath in. "Madame K and I are going to put our lives together. We've decided to marry."

Kokui exhaled.

Nami's eyes darted from Boris to Kokui. "Congratulations," she said, her tone tentative.

"Thank you, Sis."

"Have you told Ma and Daddy? Where is everyone?" Nami asked.

"Your father went out early, and your mother went out to find him. She asked about Afi," Boris said.

Kokui tightened her clasp around Boris's hand. Morning had barely broken and her mother was out searching for her father. She didn't need to go to the marché. At least not now. Boris was right here with her.

11

The last time Kokui had seen her mother at her father's house was the day Micheline dropped a twelve-year-old Kokui and a nine-year-old Nami outside Mawuli's gate. Watching only to ensure that they went inside, she refused to enter the compound of the home her husband had been keeping with other women. Twelve years later, Micheline stepped out of the taxi that had brought her from the Ambassador Hotel and crossed the threshold of the gate, but she would not go much farther. Shining in an embroidered kente boubou and matching head-tie, she stopped just before the veranda and averted her gaze from Auntie Hemaa, also in a gold kente, and the husband they grudgingly shared.

Kokui could see her mother summoning every power within her to avoid peeking into the sliver the opened door revealed.

"I will not step foot inside that house," Micheline said.

"Please, Ma."

She had begged her mother to come to Accra for her and Boris's

Knocking ceremony. She wanted her parents to be together when Boris came with his family to ask for her hand. She hoped and believed the presence of both Mawuli and Micheline, united in this purpose of receiving a proposal of marriage on behalf of their daughter, would challenge the spirits that lingered in this house, and seal the success of her marriage. If she could, she would have asked Auntie Hemaa not to attend. It surprised Kokui that her stepmother had not made herself scarce as usual.

"Please."

"We will do it on the veranda," Mawuli said.

Kokui huffed the familiar tortured vapor of exasperation and pity for her parents, Auntie Hemaa, and herself. Love and pride had ensnared them all in this humiliating web.

"It's okay," Auntie Hemaa told Kokui. "Let all of Achimota see we are marrying our daughter."

Micheline spoke over her rival. "Mr. Nuga, tell your people to bring us chairs to sit on. And some groundnuts to crack."

Kokui left her parents to their marriage as she prepared to make the first step toward her own. Inside, her father's cousin Efo Cletus was regaling his siblings and their children with a story, his grip firm on a Star beer bottle. They were all giddy with drink, the adults with beer, the children with Coke and Fanta.

"Was that your intended at the gate?" Efo Cletus asked her.

"It was Ma."

"Hmmmm." He stretched his sneer like okra.

"Ei, Efo Cletus, meɖekuku, hide your dislike for my mother, small." She slapped the back of her hand into her palm theatrically, making them laugh, though she resented their open display of contempt. They supported her father's philandering, with no sympathy for the pain it had caused his wives and children, because Mawuli financed their lives. It was his house they lived in.

His money that had paid for the bus and driver that had brought them to Accra and the one that would take them back home.

"Please, bring your chairs," she told them. "We are doing the Knocking on the veranda."

Kokui took the stairs two at a time to resume getting ready.

"Ma is here," she told Nami.

Her sister was zipping herself into her kente. "And Auntie Hemaa still hasn't left?"

Kokui shook her head. "She was putting her mouth inside the arrangements."

"Staking her claim to her plot of Mawuli Nuga," Nami said. "Ready to be a wife?"

"That won't be my story."

"We know o," Nami said. "Your own will be different."

Kokui winced at her sister's reminder of her confrontation with their mother. She had not meant to slice so deep, but she stood by her avowal. "When your time comes, do you want their marriage?"

She raised her arms for Nami to yank her kaba down in place over its matching skirt.

"My big sister, you concern yourself with unnecessary things. If you make it bigger than it has to be, it will crush you."

Nami put on a good show of nonchalance, Kokui thought, remembering the sobs that had racked her sister on their mother's bed. "Even when you pretend it's not there, it crushes you."

"Yo-oh." She cooed the dismissive acquiescence. "Bend."

Kokui ducked for her sister to pin her ponytail, then separate, lift, and coil the long waves into a weighty bun. She gave her head a test shake.

A car horn beeped outside the gate.

"They're here." Kokui felt her stomach turn to water. What if her own wasn't different, she wondered. What if it was worse? It wasn't as if Boris had initiated the proposal—she had sold it to him, dangling the need that throbbed under his want. She closed her eyes to her accusations. "How do I look?"

"Worth every item Ma and Daddy have listed on your dowry," Nami said. "You and your Kofi Brokeman will live happily ever after."

The sisters leaned on each other to step into their heels, and continued leaning into each other, their hands clasped tightly as they descended the stairs together.

Under the overhang of the veranda, Micheline and Mawuli sat enthroned on the rose-printed armchairs from the sitting room. In front of them, Efo Cletus perched on the edge of his chair ready to perform. Kokui settled next to Auntie Hemaa in the row behind Mawuli and Micheline, looking past her parents to Boris. Uncle Joe fronted the Van der Puyes, leading Boris and his family in a procession to shake each hand. Kokui held Boris's palm and his gaze, her stomach strengthening with his smile. She had pushed him to decide about her, but she hadn't forced his decision to be "yes."

"Agoo," Uncle Joe intoned the customary greeting, raising the bottle of palm wine Boris's brother handed him.

"Amɛ," they all chorused.

Efo Cletus cleared his throat. "What brings you to our family home on this melodious Saturday afternoon?"

Melodious? Kokui and Nami shared a laugh with their eyes.

"Our son has seen someone in this house. A delicate flower that he is hoping to pluck."

She was delicate, Kokui agreed, but she felt more like an egg. She knew she had the potential to produce something good if handled correctly.

But Nami was giggling. "So delicate."

Efo Cletus eyed the palm wine now. "You've stated your intentions. I hope you have brought something to refresh us."

"We have." Uncle Joe dug in the pocket of his batakari and produced an envelope. "Palm wine tapped fresh for the occasion, a bottle of Schnapps, and something small for those in your household to treat themselves as they wish."

Micheline rose to take the money before Efo Cletus could close his fingers around it. Mawuli tipped his head and Nelson collected the palm wine.

"We have duly received your gifts." Efo Cletus leaned forward. "You say your son has seen a flower in this house. We have many flowers here." He moved his pointing finger over all his assembled nieces, stopping at Nami. "Is she the one?"

"No," Uncle Joe said.

"I'm not delicate o," Nami said, eliciting much laughter.

"Is she the one?" Efo Cletus continued, pointing to Kokui.

"She is."

"Please, for our clarification, let your son describe the flower he has come to pluck."

Kokui held her breath as Boris rose, his kente slipping from his shoulders. He was not a man of melodious words. He was not a performer like she was.

Boris inhaled, settling his eyes on her. "I came for the one and only Kokui Nuga." He raised his arm to point her out. "The only flower whose petals I smell."

Kokui turned to her family. Had they heard what he had said? Could they see how different her marriage would be?

"Eish." Efo Cletus sniffed the air. "Our daughter Kokui, you have heard the proposal and you have seen the drink they have brought. If we drink this drink, we cannot take it from our stomachs and put it back in the bottle. Should we accept and swallow?"

She nodded through her uncertainty, not of Boris, but of marriage itself. "Yes."

Mawuli tipped his head and Nelson began to pour the tots to serve.

"Our flower has accepted your proposal, so we can begin the background check. If all on your side is clear, we will present the dates of the engagement and wedding." Efo Cletus reached for the thick fold of papers Mawuli passed him. "For now, you are free to start assembling the dowry to present for our daughter."

Uncle Joe leaned forward to collect the dowry list. Kokui could see Boris's smile tighten as the men leaned to survey the sheet. It was the same look he had had at the Ambassador the night his friend had called his bartender's salary peanuts. She would help him buy the items, she decided, as Nelson handed her a small glass of the palm wine.

12

Marriage was a strange, strange thing. Their ceremonies had followed the usual rituals: A month after the Knocking, Boris had engaged her according to the custom, with Efo Cletus returning to the house to officiate as Boris's family presented Kokui and her family with the suitcase of gifts the dowry had listed. There were wax prints, kente, shoes, jewelry, underwear, and lump sums to her and the family—all the things a woman needed to leave her family home, set herself up in a new one, and start a business, with remuneration to her family of their loss of her earning potential. The following day, they exchanged vows at Mawuli's home congregation, the E.P. Church in Juapong, she in a white tulle dress and he in a black tuxedo, and signed the marriage register. But the shift that came with her vocalized assent to the nuptial presents as well as the reverend's pronouncement did not feel at all rote to Kokui. She and Boris were now bound ancestrally and legally—she felt the transfer in her soul.

This was what Kokui had wanted, a commitment that promised to transcend the dysfunction she had grown up in, but she was still adjusting to the weight of the newness. It surprised her how resistant she was to changes she had said she desired. Boris's brother Kwate had offered them a room in Auntie Shika House to begin their lives, but she declined the escape she desperately craved, to retain the control she had in the familiar. She felt a primal need to be on known ground as she plotted how to cultivate a good marriage—and yet, through Boris's eyes, she felt the cold emptiness of her father's house all the more.

With Nami on campus, all but two of the nine rooms were vacant, and she and Boris had moved into the suite of her father's first wife. It chilled Kokui to begin her marriage on that bed, but the discomfort she bore in her father's house was more comforting than the unknown.

Boris chafed at the dizzying onslaught of novelties their marriage brought. He had gone from counting coins to pay a trɔtrɔ driver to joining her and Mawuli on the morning drive to the office, sitting behind Nelson in the Benz. He now called Mawuli Nuga, one of the wealthiest men in Ghana, his father and his boss. He didn't like it. His pride flared at the power his father-in-law and wife now wielded over him, but he, too, did not want to live in the house his brother had co-opted.

In Mawuli's house, he was not "Baby Last" or "Number Six"; he was the sole son present, and Mawuli treated him as such. Her father saw in Boris the heir he had always wanted Kokui to be when it came to the business, and he sought to lure Boris to keep Kokui in Ghana by giving him carte blanche to direct cost-cutting efforts. She could see her husband walking taller, the power of the responsibility and the opportunity to apply his acumen rebuilding the dignity he had lost collecting cigarette butts from the floor of the

Ambassador Hotel. Boris took seriously his charge to plug the holes where he found them, but he did so with their escape to America in sight. She and Boris had agreed on a new, accelerated timeline: they would be gone next month, not coincidentally on the sixth of March, Independence Day. In three weeks, they would be gone.

"Nelson, you know the AC burns fuel?" Boris asked the driver that morning when he dropped them off at her father's paper processing plant.

Kokui saw Nelson's nostrils flare as he switched off the engine, silencing the air conditioner and the radio. "You want him to sit in the heat," she said. Nelson had grown cold on her since the marriage, the echo that had remained of their childhood flirtation-turned-friendship now silenced.

"We have to stop burning money," Boris said, closing the car door behind Kokui.

Mawuli clapped Boris on the shoulder as they passed workers unloading one of Auntie Hemaa's trucks, the men bowing and tipping their hard hats as the three of them crossed the threshold under the sign that read NUGA & HEIRS—EST. 1946.

"Are you sure you want to leave for America?" her father asked. "You can join Nami at university—the education is the same as you'll get in the US, and more relevant to our needs."

Kokui smirked as Boris said what he always did. "Yes, sir, I am sure."

His answer was absorbed by the rushing river sound that whooshed in the hangar. The Fourdrinier paper machine was a mammoth contraption, the length of two football fields with multiple mechanized parts conspiring to transform the grayish-brown slurry of wet wood pulp into rolls of flattened white sheets ready to be cut, packaged, or printed on. Its motors, and the pair of industrial strength generators that powered it, were a brick bath that bludgeoned every sense. Kokui did not come to the facility often, but when she did, she remembered her first time, she and Nami wearing the hard hats the workers had latched on to their heads, her father effusively insisting above the roar that Micheline be addressed as Madame Nugaga.

"We are the only ones in West Africa with this capacity," Mawuli roared now. "With you here—even if you stayed till June, like we first talked about—we could triple revenue. Kokui can go around with you helping to secure new accounts."

Boris nodded respectfully, not telling her father what he had told her.

"There's a reason there is only one Fourdrinier in West Africa, Madame K. It's cheaper to order the paper from Europe."

She knew the machine required fountains of water from the boreholes they had drilled to pump, and fuel to motor the process.

"Your father is so enamored with this twenty-nine-year-old machine, he is ignoring how impractical it is to maintain it. You know how much he spent flying those mechanics in? Then, he is paying Auntie Hemaa to use her trucks to transport the wood from Bolga, not to mention the kickbacks he pays to keep the government ministry accounts." He shook his head. "I've told your dad if things continue as they are, the company has five more years of solvency, if that."

Kokui had reviewed the ledgers, too. Yes, the company's expenditures had bloated as fuel costs continued to rise. Yes, a few of the churches and mission schools they printed materials for had reduced their business, choosing to take their religious texts from the mother churches in the UK, Germany, and Switzerland to cut the cost of printing original literature in Ghana. But they were still earning more than they were losing, and her father had more than the business. He had properties all over Accra and Juapong, and the apartment in London. And if he lost everything today, Kokui told herself, she had no doubt her father could rebuild something better tomorrow.

They followed Mawuli to the waiting foreman.

"We have to figure out how to reduce the amount of fuel we are using," Mawuli told them.

"Sir, we are already—"

Mawuli cut him off. "Boris, you have some ideas for savings."

The foreman turned to Boris, his face quivering with resentment. Kokui didn't blame him. The man had been working at the company when she and Nami came as kids to visit with their mother. Meanwhile, Boris had been keeping the company books for less than a month. But she also knew the foreman would be happy to do the same if she had married him instead.

"I'm wondering if there is a way to perform any of the functions manually," Boris said, "like the way we chip the wood ourselves?"

The man's face contorted. "We are not paper masons here."

Mawuli barked. "Then what are you?"

"Sir, if you want the same quality and uniformity, it's not possible to do the processing manually."

"No. I want to know what you are, since you are not paper masons. Tell me," Mawuli said.

The man stared at him.

"I said tell me. Are you or are you not willing to get the job done by any means necessary? Before this machine existed, people were producing paper by hand."

"Sir—"

"Do you know what I was doing before I built this company? I was walking from office to office, school to church looking for people to sell paper to. I would leave Accra with kene in my pocket and beg for a ride to Cape Coast and Ta'di, all the way to the north and back again!"

The foreman struggled to maintain a mask of deference.

"When I got the chance to go to Germany and work in the mill, I did everything they asked of me. At a point, my sole responsibility was carrying water from one end of the unit to the other."

"Sir, I—"

"How do you think I came home with an investment to start this place? Humble yourself, or you will be humbled," he said. "I didn't build this business to watch it collapse. We must bring our costs down. And if you can't do it, I will look for someone who can. Are you hearing me?"

"Yes, sir."

"Now, Boris, you were saying what?"

"Another consideration is doing what you can on one generator instead of the two."

"It barely runs on the two we have. We need—" The foreman closed his mouth under Mawuli's glare. "We will do our best, sir."

"Don't do your best," Mawuli said. "Your best is the reason we are in this crisis. Do better than your best."

"Yes, sir."

Kokui and Boris followed Mawuli out, the heat beading on their skin in the sizzling cab of the truck.

"They've been pampered," Mawuli said as Nelson turned on the engine and the AC. "Business is not a game. It's survival. Every blessed day. Hunting. Catching. Killing. Eating." His voice trailed at the sight of a shapely alasa seller outside his window.

Kokui's eyes flew to Boris, fearful her father's behavior might catch.

When it came to women, her father lacked the discipline that had enabled him to build this business. She would never cease to wonder how he could be so strong in one way, and so weak in another. It sickened her, thinking about it, even as her mouth pooled with the nausea of the earliest weeks of pregnancy.

Boris looked past the seller. "Sir," he said, pointing to the newsboy. "That's why I am sure about leaving Ghana. Nami should leave, too."

ACHEAMPONG CLOSES ALL UNIVERSITIES—AFTER PROTEST, STUDENTS NEED "COOLING OFF PERIOD"

Mawuli turned from the window. "Please leave my last daughter in Ghana with me," he said. "Nelson, raise the volume, eh?"

The lunch hour news filled the car as they rode back to the office, Kokui swallowing her nausea.

13

aby Kofi was on his feet. More than a year into his arrival at the Nuga house, he had taken his first steps, and in the months since he had perfected a running trot. Like a coach, Sister Eyram chased him up and down the veranda's length, and each time he was about to reach the edge, she overtook him and opened wide for him to crash into her arms. "Atuu," she sang, sweeping him up by his chubby legs.

"Ma," he squealed.

Kokui alighted from the car and moved around them toward the house. The boy's presence made her uncomfortable, and his relationship with Sister Eyram more so. She could see his mother's jabbing arm, and hear her strangled cry. Kokui could feel her skin beading at the memory of the border agents circling the car. She could smell the adɔdi. She wondered if his mother regretted dumping him at this house. Did she miss her son? Was she uttering new curses against his sisters to draft new recruits into her pain?

Sister Eyram, who had devoted her life to raising Mawuli's kids, shone with pride. She called Kokui out of her averted gaze. "Look who is happy now."

Kokui left them on the veranda, making her way to her bedroom. Her door closed behind her; she stepped out of her shoes and entered the bed. She was becoming used to calling her former stepmother's room her own for the moment, but lying on the mattress sometimes transported her to the abyss of terror she had lived in during her first days in this house, when her mother had left her and Nami there.

Curled under the sheets, she clutched her belly under her blouse. Pinching and poking, her hands found the familiar folds soft and yielding, but in her spirit, she could feel the new being inside her protesting what she intended to do. Kokui had spent all her energies on marrying better than her mother, and now that she believed she had done so, she also felt she had to ensure her and Boris's stability before she could begin to think about bringing a baby into her marriage.

"You are not supposed to be here," Kokui told this spirit waiting for bones, sinews, and flesh, attaching its destiny to hers. She had drunk her tea diligently, just like Auntie Hemaa had taught her.

As she lay shivering under the covers, she thought back to when Auntie Hemaa first came to the house. She had trembled with dread then, too.

Their father had a diverse appetite in women, and the four wives he had had before Auntie Hemaa had each imposed their own flavor on the house, and on the children.

The first wife, Auntie Abui, had been sour and heavy, like kenkey, and just as lasting. She had stayed in the house through three wives and the introduction of six children she had not birthed, divorcing her husband only after he had gone to knock for Auntie Hemaa's hand in marriage. For months after she left, Sister Eyram found her sewing needles hidden in Mawuli's clothes, his shoes, and his mattress.

"Adze!" Sister Eyram deemed her, but Mawuli defended the wife of his youth.

"It's not witchcraft," he said. "It's love."

The second wife, Auntie Rebecca, had been rock salt, prickly with an acerbic tang. Like their father, she was keen on dispensing lectures. Also like their father, she was a masochistic romantic. She negotiated a schedule with Auntie Abui for nights with Mawuli, and marshaled all the girls to help her serve him the elaborate meals she prepared. She serenaded him for all in the house to hear as he ate, crowing louder and growing more desperate as new women and children made it evident there was nothing she could do to make him only hers.

A year after her youngest daughter joined her sisters in London, her three girls pooled the allowance Mawuli sent them every month to buy a one-way ticket for their mother to leave Ghana and their father behind. Auntie Rebecca had the means to return—just as she had always had the means to leave Mawuli—but as far as Kokui knew, she remained in London and had remarried a man twelve years her junior.

The third wife, Auntie Hannah, had been almost childlike in her sweetness, and proudly refined. A sugar cube. She was made for the luxury that came with Mawuli's transition from paper salesman to paper mill mogul, but she dissolved when confronted with hot water, which is what happened when Kokui and Nami's mother, Micheline Miadogo, entered the picture. Auntie Hannah had fancied herself the love of Mawuli Nuga's new life: the true love of his maturity. She believed her husband when he told her his first two wives—successful working women—had nowhere else to go. When she discovered that Micheline had also become her husband's wife, she lost her mental bearings. Not long after Kokui and Nami moved into their home, Mawuli took Auntie Hannah to the hospital in Asylum Down for observation. She spent almost one year at Accra Psychiatric Hospital before her brothers came and took her to their hometown, where she remained until she died.

Kokui had watched her mother evaporate, too.

Moments before they found out Mawuli had three other families, Micheline sat Kokui outside the assistant headmaster's office at Achimota School while she pled her daughter's case. The school secretary had left her desk to go to the washroom, leaving the louvers of her boss's office open. Kokui could see and hear everything through the upturned glass leaves and mesh netting.

"Your daughter just didn't score well enough to gain admission here, madame, but she may have a chance at Accra Girls'."

Kokui bowed her head, a shame that was becoming familiar settling over her. She had studied for the exam, yet here she was.

"If she goes to boarding school, her sister will miss her."

"Madame," he said, irritation joining bemusement to dehydrate his tone.

Micheline spoke over him. "My children cannot be separated."

"Madame Nuga, she has to earn her place just like her brother and sisters did. If Achimota School was in the business of letting every child in solely based on means, we would not have the reputation we do, and you would not be here seeking a way around."

"Which brother and sisters do you mean?" she asked him. "She has only one sibling."

The man's eyelids fluttered. "Excuse me?"

"You said 'brother,' singular, and 'sisters,' plural. Did you mean, 'My sister, thank you for your generous contribution to this fair institution of academic excellence—it will support so many of our younger brothers and sisters'?" She played out the scene, adding her answer. "'My brother, aren't I your sister? Don't mention it.'"

He resumed the rapid blink of bafflement. "I meant your other children in Achimota School, madame. Antony, Connie, and Esime Nuga. Mawuli Nuga's children. Or?" His last question was an ellipsis.

Kokui had squinted at the eavesdropped information, like it was food that had been left out just a touch too long, unable to tell whether it was good or bad.

Replaying the moment in her mind ad nauseam since, Kokui realized, in his position, the assistant headmaster must have seen all sorts of family configurations. It was common for the man children called "father" to be an uncle, just as a brother could be a cousin by blood or friendship. With most of the students dropped off by drivers, it was enough to match the children's names with their paying guardians. Moreover, the primary school where Kokui and Nami were enrolled, and the secondary school Micheline was trying to get Kokui into, ran independently of each other. The assistant headmaster only knew Mawuli Nuga as the father of these children because he paid their school fees in person, and brazenly flirted with the secretary in the bursar's office when he did. The man had probably never stopped to consider that the Nuga children in his school, whether or not they had different mothers, which wasn't uncommon, didn't know the others existed.

Micheline began to emit short, heavy, wheezing breaths. Kokui chewed her fingers, still trying to connect what she was hearing to what she thought she knew. Her father lived with them. He ate every meal with them, except on weekends, which he said he spent visiting his ailing mother in Juapong, or when he traveled for work. Aside from his mother, there was only one Madame Nuga—the workers at their father's mill had treated Micheline as such. *Madame Nugaga.*

"Madame Nuga, clearly I didn't know your situation. Knowledge is an awesome terror, isn't it? A Pandora's box. An Eve's apple." Embarrassment, and possibly fear of reprisal from Mawuli, inflected and propelled the assistant headmaster's jumbled stream. "Difficult as our lesson has been today, I hope we can—"

Micheline slammed his office door behind her. She yanked Kokui from her chair, charged over to Achimota Primary, and pulled Nami out of her class. The whole way she incanted curses over their father.

"What's happening?" Nami kept asking from the classroom block to the car, and on the ride to their house.

Kokui slipped her sister's hand into hers. "I'll tell you when we get home."

Micheline dropped her daughters off and left.

What happened while she was gone those seven-plus hours, they heard later, from their brother and sisters.

Micheline returned to the school secretary to call her "other children" from their classes. When they came out, she told Antony, Connie, and Esime she was their father's colleague, and that he had asked her to pick them up.

These were not small children. Antony was close to nineteen, Connie fifteen, Esime thirteen. They knew their father did not work with a corpulent woman who spoke with a Togolese accent—and they knew their father. They went along for the ride out of feline curiosity, ready to commit every detail of the unfolding drama to memory so they could entertain their siblings with a fresh story of "yet another one of Daddy's women" when they got back home.

But what began for the children as an all-too-familiar comic spectacle twisted when they crossed the Accra city limits.

"Where are you taking us?" Antony asked.

"Bolgatanga," Micheline said through sudden tears.

"Ei, what are we going to do in Bolgatanga?"

Micheline wiped her face. "Burn your father's land. Let him use a different kind of paper to rebuild."

Watching her weep, they empathized. In humiliating their mothers time and again, Mawuli had broken his children's hearts, too.

"Madame, let us rather go to the machine," Connie said. "It's the Fourdrinier we have to burn."

"The only one in the whole of West Africa," Connie, Antony, and Esime mimicked their dad.

Micheline turned the car around, and at the factory that housed the machine the length of two football fields, she tried, but her heart, rent like paper, wasn't in it. The sheet she lit did not catch to its spool, the jets of washing water immediately dousing it. One worker inhaled too much of the smoke that rose. Two others suffered torn skin trying to contain Micheline. The foreman sent for the police, but once the officers realized it was a "husband-and-wife matter," they left them, after a bribe, to sort out the mess.

Micheline drove her heretofore unknown stepchildren to the rented bungalow she shared with Mawuli, Kokui, and Nami, and directed her daughters to pack what they could. The older children led them to their father's house.

When they reached the two-story home minutes from the Achimota School campus, Auntie Abui, Auntie Rebecca, and Auntie Hannah were wringing their hands in separate chairs in the courtyard behind the house while their husband, still in his suit, looked down from his bedroom terrace. They clung to their children, checking the kids' clothes for chicken feathers and their skin for ritual cuts. Mawuli came down and took his youngest daughters' palms in his, leading them to the congregation of offspring that now filled the courtyard, formally introducing them to their siblings and cousin-caretaker, Sister Eyram, without mention of their mother.

The next time Kokui and Nami saw Micheline was the week before Christmas, in Togo.

Their father drove them himself, almost eight hours from the house in Achimota across the border, past the city center in Lomé to the town of Aného. Together, they stayed in the orange cottage with tomato-red shutters their mother had purchased for herself. Micheline cradled her daughters and cursed their father.

The first night, the girls shared their mother's bed. The second night, Micheline invited their father in, the four of them huddling together. The third night, Kokui and Nami were relegated to sleeping mats in the sitting room, listening outside the bedroom's closed double doors, giggling as they playacted the kissing they imagined was going on.

The holiday drive to Togo with their father became their annual ritual. The week before Christmas belonged to Micheline Nugaga, even after Auntie Hemaa arrived.

The fifth wife, Auntie Hemaa, was gari. Reliably sustaining, brilliant in her simplicity, she got on so well with everyone that people forgot how gritty she actually was. She was the one who prepared the tea for Kokui when she caught her lingering with the driver's son, Nelson. Pawpaw leaves and hibiscus petals boiled to a bitter infusion the color of blood. "Drink," she said. "You are your father's daughter, but you are a woman. You have to be smart."

Kokui woke up to a black room now, the bed wet with her sweat, the house still, Boris's warmth rising and falling beside her.

"You're awake?"

"I am, Boris."

"How are you feeling?"

She could barely form words, exhaustion, fear, and panic mingling with her memories, stinging her eyes, gripping her throat. "I'm pregnant."

"You're sure?"

She swiped the tear sliding past her nose. "Why would I tell you if I wasn't certain? I am."

"I thought you said you've been taking tea."

"I said that because that's what I've been doing." They had been together for over one year, married almost seven weeks, but it was the first time she had snapped at him. She exhaled her regret. She wanted to be a wife who spoke softly to her husband. "I don't want a baby now either, Boris. I, too, am ready to leave for New York."

"So, what do we do?"

"I'll ask Auntie Hemaa."

"Auntie Hemaa? Won't she advise you to stay in Ghana and deliver?"

She felt her patience thinning again. She didn't have the energy to calm his anxious thoughts when she was managing her own. "Do you see any children from Auntie Hemaa in this house?"

"I thought she couldn't have children."

"Maybe she can't, maybe she can. I don't know. But I know she has an herbalist."

"I'll take you," he said.

Kokui rolled closer to Boris and lay her cheek on his chest. That was all she had needed him to say from the beginning. "I'm sorry for speaking roughly," she said. "I wasn't expecting this."

"We can't control everything."

She frowned, gently pulling at the hairs on his chest. That was the problem, she thought, wasn't it?

14

Auntie Hemaa's herbalist, Comfort Koranteng, lived in a small bungalow near the Dansoman Junction behind a black gate and clay-colored perimeter wall that advertised her two businesses: COMFORT MEDICINE and COMFORT WASHING.

"She's gone to do some deliveries," her husband told Kokui and Boris, his arms bulging with the weight of the laundry bundle and the pair of buckets he carried.

Kokui felt laughter and rage tossing her between their paws. She had left her house at cock's crow to separate a part of herself from herself, but she would have to wait.

Boris sputtered his discontent. "But she told us to come at this time!"

Mr. Koranteng blinked at them, the muscles under the bristles on his cheeks and chin arranging to say, "And so?"

"So, what do we do?" Boris asked.

"Come inside, or go and come. She'll be here just now."

Mr. Koranteng stepped aside for them to enter the pedestrian gate.

They had been foolish to think this would be an in-and-out affair, Kokui chastised herself, as Mr. Koranteng pointed them to the plastic chairs under the overhang of the veranda. It was a Saturday morning in Accra, when all the business of home and life had to be handled before Sunday services.

"We should have brought our laundry," she said, trying to lighten her mood. So soon after talk of fragrant flowers, she and Boris were on another veranda, absently sipping the water the Korantengs' daughter served, about to terminate their first pregnancy.

She watched Boris swat the air aggressively, taking his impatience out on the flies that swirled. The side gate kept creaking open with clients dropping off their clothes for washing, but the time dripped by with no sign of Comfort Koranteng.

"Should we release Nelson and find our way back?"

Kokui raised an eyebrow at Boris. "It's his job to wait."

"Do you think he will tell your father where we are?"

"It's his job to be discreet."

"What should we—"

Kokui shouted over Boris. "Sir, please, how long before Mrs. Koranteng is due back?"

Mr. Koranteng looked up from the tub between his legs. "Your husband is worrying you, eh? Let him go," he said. "This is woman's matter."

"An immaculate conception," Kokui muttered, dropping her head to her lap.

"No, I want to be here." Boris checked his watch and looked toward the gate.

"Go find us something to eat." She was glad he had come, but she didn't need this extra burden of soothing him as she braced herself for the impending intrusion, and for the pain.

"Get food for yourself," Mr. Koranteng said. "It's better if her stomach is empty."

"I'll stay and wait," he said.

"Yo-oh, Young Love." The man snickered and resumed scraping the brick of soap in his hand against a submerged cloth.

The clothes that had gone on the lines wet and limp were flapping like flags when Mrs. Koranteng beeped her car horn outside the gate. The daughter opened the gate for her mother, and Comfort Koranteng rolled onto the red clay in a red Mitsubishi with a door decal bearing her laundry company brand.

"Oh, Mrs. Koranteng. We've been waiting-ahhh." Kokui attempted a dulcet tone, trying to manage her anger. It didn't work. Her words came out as hot as the day.

"Sorry-sorry o, Mrs. Van der Puye." She cupped her palms to beg. "Our boy has gone to his village for a funeral so the deliveries have fallen on me. Let me wash my hands and change my clothes so I can see to you." She disappeared into the house, Mr. Koranteng at her heels.

"Are you okay?" Boris asked her.

"Are you?"

Mr. Koranteng stood over them before either of them answered.

"Madame is ready for you." He turned to Boris. "She won't allow your husband."

Kokui threaded her fingers through Boris's. "Let her make an exception."

They followed the man around to the annex house behind the main building. The one-room annex was bigger than it seemed from the outside. The mineral scent of clay and green plants was almost edible in the damp air. A row of cupboards hung above a deep sink and a small fridge. There were two long wooden tables, one in the center topped with a student mattress neatly encased in a white sheet.

Comfort Koranteng—now changed from her curly wig, Japan Motors T-shirt, and floral skirt into a head-tie, sleeveless top, and wrapper—stood behind the center table.

"She says she wants her husband inside."

Mrs. Koranteng shrugged. "Let him see how we women suffer."

"Will she suffer?" Boris asked.

"You are sending the spirit back when the body has accepted it," she said. "Help her onto the bed."

Yes, she was sending it back, Kokui thought. It was too soon for it to come.

She lay back on the mattress, grateful for the cool white sheet and the ceiling fan that whirred.

"Raise your dress above your hips," the woman directed. She helped Kokui, tugging the hem of her dress up before slipping two fingers inside of Kokui.

Kokui gasped at Comfort Koranteng's painful digging, tears slipping past her temples as she joined the fan to watch from above.

For all his talk of "woman's matter," Mr. Koranteng faithfully assisted his wife, giving her a calabash of steaming water to clean her hands before pulling dried seeds and rocks of saltpeter from the shelves. He opened the small fridge to retrieve a crawling pouch.

"It's okay," Comfort Koranteng told their widened eyes of the black ants. "They have medicine inside."

Mr. Koranteng ground the ingredients into a thick paste, molding two balls, each the size of a young guava before his wife parted Kokui's knees and bent to slip one of the capsules inside.

Kokui bucked at the spreading sensation of liquid razor blades.

"Are you okay?" Boris kept asking.

"After the blood and tissue pass, so will the pain," Comfort Koranteng answered for her.

Mr. Koranteng was ready with a new calabash of soapy water.

"Lie for some time, and then you can go. My husband will prepare fresh tea for you to take." Mrs. Koranteng wiped her hands dry. "Now, for my payment."

Kokui twisted at the carving inside, tears pooling in her ears as Boris counted out thirty cedis before taking her hand again.

"Madame, try and be still for the medicine to work," Mr. Koranteng said.

When the tea was ready, Boris helped Kokui sit up. The slashing surged up and outward, burning her chest and scalp, numbing her fingers and toes. Her lips felt like rubber as she fought to pucker for the calabash Mr. Koranteng tipped to her mouth.

"How long will the pain last?" Boris asked.

Kokui almost laughed at the question. She had been wondering about its answer for the last dozen years.

"Everyone is different," Mr. Koranteng said. "It takes time, but she will be well. I've been supporting my wife in this work twenty-three years. The pain is normal." He tore a sheet of cotton wool and padded Kokui's underwear. "You can go now."

Every step to the car sliced through her. She wept like Baby Kofi as Boris lowered her gingerly onto the leather seat.

Nelson's head jerked from Kokui to Boris. "Is she okay?"

"Just take your time driving," Boris said, trotting to the other side of the car to sit and hold her. Between his feet, he rested the Coke bottle filled with the tea. "I'm sorry you're in such pain, Madame K."

She was, too, but what they had come to do was over. It wouldn't be long before they were in America, and this day, and this pain, far behind them.

15

Their last week in Ghana, Kokui went to see her mother.

"Let Nelson take you," Boris said, but she didn't want company on this trip.

She wanted to be alone with Micheline.

She boarded the State Transport Coach at the station near her father's office, switched at Lomé, and caught the trɔtrɔ from the capital to Aného. She was disappointed to find her mother's house the same shade of white as on their last visit. She had been looking forward to a fresh hue.

Kokui pushed through the fabric flap at the door, and dropped her bags to follow the sounds of chatter in the backyard. Bathed in the afternoon sunlight, her mother sat with Afi tying thick knots along a length of grey baft. Afi screamed her fright at Kokui's sudden, unexpected presence.

Micheline playfully swatted her assistant with the cloth. "Ho!" she scoffed at Afi. "As for you, everyone is a spirit."

The younger woman's closeness with her mother plucked at Kokui. Afi could be with Micheline any time she wanted. She did everything for Micheline, cooking, cleaning, doing her hair. Recently, she had graduated to helping Micheline execute samples of the designs she sold to different textile manufacturers in Ghana and Holland. If not for the pain it would cause, Kokui would share her suspicion about Afi and her dad with her mother.

Kokui rushed to make space between Afi and Micheline and bent into her mother's embrace.

"Afi, cook us that nice fish we got in the market."

Afi half-genuflected. "Yes, Ma."

Micheline turned to her daughter now, inspecting Kokui's face for trouble. "I thought it would be some time before the happily married woman graced me with a visit."

Ignoring her mother's sarcasm, Kokui lifted the fabric that slumped on Afi's chair and took her seat. "We leave for America one week from today."

Her mother frowned. "I thought you would wait small. Why are you rushing to the cold?"

"We want to go and work, Ma, make some money before we start school."

Micheline arched an eyebrow. "You want to go and work?"

"Ma, I'm not lazy as you all think. I was able to gain admission to school in New York."

"Yes. To a community college," she said. "If it were me, I would remain in Ghana, go to university, and secure what my father has built. But you are not me. You've made that clear."

Kokui bowed her head. Since the night she and her mother had argued about Boris, she often went over the words they exchanged, more so after she had seen Comfort Koranteng. So much of her confusion and resentment over her parents' marriage was bound up in her mother.

She was twelve years old when Micheline left her and Nami at their father's. She had always understood why Micheline left Ghana—when betrayal came, her mother had needed to tend to herself in the soil she had grown from. But it wasn't until she lay on Comfort Koranteng's table that Kokui began to consider that something other than abject callousness had propelled Micheline to leave her and Nami behind.

She picked up the gray baft to continue the knot.

Micheline snorted at her. "That's not how you do it."

"Show me, then."

"Will you sit for me to teach you anything?"

Kokui rolled her eyes, returning the cloth to a dormant lump on her lap.

"How is your husband? How are you?"

For a brief moment, she entertained telling her mother about Comfort Medicine, but she didn't want to satisfy Micheline's cynicism. "All is well, Ma."

"You must be excited to be going to America."

"I am, Ma, but I will miss you."

"Ho." Her mother dismissed her with a wave. "What is there to miss? You are in Ghana, just here, and I don't see you more than once a year."

She met her mother's eyes, surprised to hear the hurt in Micheline's voice. "I didn't know you wanted us to visit more."

Micheline looked away. "What mother doesn't want to see her children? Everything I do is for you and your sister."

"Ma." Kokui stretched across the space between their chairs to rest her hand on Micheline's thigh.

She was about to start fresh with Boris in America. Nami was at university. In spite of the temporary shutdown, she was on the path to settling her future. Their mother deserved to be free, too. Kokui inhaled the courage to tell her so.

"I know you are doing what you think is best, but you don't have to remain married to Daddy to secure our inheritance."

Micheline tore her thigh from Kokui's palm, lighting up like a flame. "You've been married these few weeks and you've come to tell me my life?"

Kokui sighed. "I didn't come to fight with you, Ma."

"Then what did you come to do?" Micheline resumed knotting the fabric, yanking the material in her fist, twisting it into itself. "You have no idea what you will encounter in this life, but know you will have pain upon pain upon pain. The suffering you are trying to outrun will overtake you, Kokui, and it will push you to your own," she said.

Kokui drew back from Micheline's words, watching them join her fears. "Ma, don't curse me."

"I'm not cursing you, my daughter. I'm telling you the facts of life. That America you are going to with your better husband than mine will show you. You will see. Then you will run home, back to your father for his help because you will need it, and then back to me, and you will tell me I was right, because I am."

"Ma." Afi stood in the doorway. "Don't say such things."

"Tell Kokui the same! Ask her if she could bring this nonsense to her father." Micheline whipped her head back to Kokui. "Can you open your mouth to tell Mawuli Nuga he doesn't have to remain married to me? Am I alone in this marriage?" She sucked her teeth. "Always remember that I am your mother, Kokui. It is I who born you, and not you who born me. I don't need your permission to live the life I've been given—the life I choose to accept for my own reasons."

Kokui rose from the chair, letting the gray baft fall to her sandals. She had tried to release her mother, but Micheline wanted to be bound to her father and to this marriage.

"Ma," Afi said. "Just wish her well."

"I wish my daughter a long life," Micheline said. "So she can stand in my place one day and tell her own children the same thing."

"Sister, I wish you well," Afi said. "Enjoy Yankee for me, with your handsome husband. And if you remember, write to us. I won't say 'no' if you add some dollars inside your letters. Hei!" She clapped Kokui's shoulder. Kokui did all she could not to roll her eyes.

"Foolish girl," Micheline called Afi tenderly, her steam distilling. "I thought you were coming to tell us the food is ready."

"Oh, Ma. I've only just put the rice on."

"Then come and help me finish this work instead of putting your mouth in my house."

Afi closed her hand around Kokui's wrist. "Sit down, Sister."

Kokui shook off her hold. "I want to walk a bit."

"The food will be ready soon. Don't keep long."

Back in the house, Kokui took her handbag from the chair and made her way out the front, her mother's words following. There were so many shadows behind her. Fears. Memories. Curses. She had to leave them behind when she boarded the plane to New York.

16

The first time Kokui had been to the marché, her mother had taken her and Nami for prayers of protection. After they told her Mawuli had married Auntie Hemaa, Micheline marched them through a stretch that cut through the market stalls and led them behind the booths and stands to a man holding court on a plastic chair on the back veranda of his house. "You have to be careful of that woman," Micheline had said of their new stepmother. "The Asantes have a powerful juju, but our own is stronger. We are Ewes." She slapped her chest.

It had been ten years, but Kokui was sure she would know the priest's thatched-roof house with the goatskin pouch of herbs dangling from the doorpost if she saw it.

Kokui took the path that curved off her mother's side street, through the village of people who had cleared and settled the land on the way to the main road. The network of mud and cement homes seemed to spread beyond her memory, even from her last visit, though she supposed she had not roamed the town much in the past few years. The faces had multiplied. More women and girls threshing palm nuts with babies on their backs. More men mending fishing nets with the boys old enough to help. They all greeted her as she passed them by. They had watched her and Nami grow on each annual trip.

At the marché's shuttered stalls, she tried to remember the way they had taken to the old man's house. It was not a market day, and the only activity was in the croaking, rustling bush. Kokui inhaled the courage of her purpose, and followed the trail of red soil that peeked through the green bush. She marched quickly, breaking into a sprint at the sound of a hiss she wasn't sure came from the bush or her mind, huffing to a stop where the path opened into a clearing, gathering her bearings.

The small village behind the marché had also expanded. A mix of thatched and corrugated iron roofs confused her memory. She wandered to the tap at the end of the stretch looking for some detail that would conjure more. A young woman filling a trio of jerry cans looked up at her in surprise. As a stranger, Kokui had ventured deep.

"Sister, who are you searching for?"

"The one who blesses," Kokui said.

The woman nodded. She tipped her head toward the flowing faucet. "Wait and I'll take you."

"You know the old man?"

"He has passed on. His sister has taken over."

Kokui liked that. A woman would understand.

She helped with one of the containers, trailing her guide through a narrow passage that ended on the back veranda she remembered.

"Sit. I'll go and call her."

Kokui noted the funeral poster of the old priest, next to a stack of boxes. The first anniversary of his death had just passed.

"Madame, you are welcome."

Kokui turned to find an old woman in a faded orange cloth stamped with blue leaves scratching an itch under the wig under her head-tie, a little girl behind her carrying a plastic chair for her to sit on.

Kokui got up to curtsy. "Good afternoon, madame."

The woman eyed her with suspicion. "What can I do for you?"

Kokui gulped, her heart racing with the hope of relief.

What she had always wanted was to feel still and settled, to close the gap between who she was and who she knew she could be, but that want had always been woven with her parents and their marriage. Even before her father was exposed, she had felt inexplicably unsteady, unable to focus on anything but fixing that feeling. Boris was the fix, she believed. Together, they were escaping. She was willing to do anything to protect their union.

"I am seeking protection for my marriage."

The priestess stared at her mouth, waiting for more.

"I've just married—almost three months now," she said. "But my father has disappointed many women, and one has said my marriage will be the source of my shame. My mother, too, in her unhappiness, has told me I will suffer in my marriage like she has. I am going to America with my husband one week from today. I don't want anything following us. I want something to ensure our happiness."

"Hmmm." The woman continued to study Kokui, taking in her ponytail, her red nails, the print of her blue-and-white dress, her black handbag, her brown sandals. "Why did you come to me for this?"

Kokui blinked at her. Hadn't she just said it all? "I know your prayers, and anything you can give me, will keep us protected."

"Give me your hands," the woman said after another long pause.

Kokui stretched her arms and linked palms with the priestess, bowing her head in readiness. The woman blew on her, a succession of huffs. Kokui shivered, the cool air tickling her hairline.

"Oh, Spirit of the Living God," she said, "in the name of Jesus . . ."

Kokui's head snapped up.

The woman's eyelids were crinkled with the tightness of her focus. ". . . release this woman from the spirit of fear. Oh, Lamb of God, I plunge her in the blood of your sacrifice. Every evil pronouncement spoken over her must come under the subjection of the better word you have spoken over your daughter. The curses are canceled. The snare is broken. Your daughter has been set free. Cover her and her husband as they journey to the US—let every foul spirit pass them by. I stand in the truth that she is a new creation in Christ Jesus if she accepts your salvation today."

Kokui sat dumbfounded as the woman resumed blowing on her.

She shouted a stream of syllables Kokui couldn't understand before rising to retrieve something from the box next to her brother's poster. She returned to press a small brochure into Kokui's palm. "My sister, read this, eh?"

She didn't have to. She had grown up seeing some version of the marital education booklet in her hand. Her father used to make her and Nami rubber-stamp them: PRINTED BY NUGA & HEIRS PAPER MILL AND PRESS.

Kokui rose quickly from her seat, her body tingling with disappointment. She could have gone to any roadside church for such a prayer, she thought. She had come for a power only specialists could wield.

"Madame," the priestess said, "it's a free gift, but anything you can give toward our ministry will be appreciated."

She restrained herself from flinging the CFA bills at the priestess, and scurried off the veranda, almost smacking into the woman who had led her there.

"You told me she has taken over for her brother!"

"Hmmm," the lady said. "She was her brother's apprentice, but now she says she is born again."

Kokui turned to retrace her path through the grass, but her guide stopped her.

"My sister, I showed you her house. Anything small you can give me?"

Kokui gave her the booklet and lit a cigarette before continuing her march back to her mother's home.

"Where did you go?" Micheline's face was taut with alarm. "I sent Afi looking for you. You don't know this place like you think."

"The place is changing," Kokui conceded.

"Nothing stays the same," her mother said. "Soon, you will be an American woman."

Kokui moved to the table to overturn the bowl Afi had used to cover her plate of food, and to put some distance between her and her mother. "I didn't mean to offend you, Ma."

Micheline folded her arms. "Your children will do the same, Kokui."

"Ma." She paused, the exhaustion of the day overwhelming her. "I just want you to be happy."

"Leave my happiness to me and focus on your own," her mother said. "Are you hearing me, my daughter?"

"I think that's what I came to say to you, Ma."

The women looked away from each other. Neither of them really knew what their own happiness looked like.

Abruptly, Micheline rose and went to her bedroom. Kokui began to clear away her plate when her mother returned with an envelope.

"It's one thousand dollars. Take it with you, but forget you have it. Hide it from yourself. Don't tell Boris about it either. Keep it down so if you ever need to leave, you don't have to ask anyone's help. My mother did it for me and now I'm doing it for you." Micheline pressed the envelope into her palm. "Travel safely, my daughter. I really do want it to be well with you."

17

Their descent was beginning. Kokui could feel it in her stomach. The dip in altitude, the scrambled eggs and second mimosa, the anticipation—it all bubbled inside of her.

"We're really here!"

She squealed through a closed mouth, but still the man in the seat in front of them jerked his head around in alarm. His face softened at her decorous attempt to contain her joy.

"First time in New York?"

"It is!"

Kokui giggled at the force of Boris's reply, in unison with hers. She felt lighter than the air they were cutting through, so grateful to be on the other side of this dream she had not even thought to have when she pondered her future on the Ambassador Hotel veranda that December night. She and Boris had each hurdled over so many low expectations to make it to this moment. Perhaps, she told herself, that was the only assurance she needed that no shadow that chased her could overtake them.

She pushed her head past his to peer outside the plane window. The oblong view presented an infinite and fastidiously organized grid of rooftops and treetops, parks and stadiums, each in their rectangles and squares. Roads bisected the network in straight and curving lines, animated by the cars and trucks that traced along them. Only the waters, shimmering gray under the morning sky, defied the deliberate hand of the city's architects with their indeterminate shapes. Kokui had lived in London for eight months, so the general look and feel of Abrokye was not new to her, but there was no end date to her stay in America. She was touching down into her new life. She was home.

"It looks like Monopoly," she said.

"The game?" Boris laughed through a puckered face. "Well, we are here to win."

The aircraft dipped lower, the buildings and cars getting bigger, their perspective narrowing to the white lines that mapped the airport runway, until they were on the ground, clapping with their fellow passengers for the pilot's safe landing, and for themselves. They had made it through the three-hour flight from Accra to Dakar, eleven hours in transit, plus a two-hour delay of their eight-and-a-half-hour plane ride to New York.

"Pan American Airways welcomes you to John F. Kennedy International Airport," the pilot announced over the speaker. "Local time is 8:03 a.m., and the temperature is forty-eight degrees Fahrenheit— just under ten degrees Celsius."

They unfolded themselves from the tight seats, stretching upward like plants in the sun. After waiting their turn to pull their bags from the overhead bin, Kokui stuffed her arms into her navy coat and buttoned her sunset-pink suit out of sight as Boris encased himself in the black wool coat and fur hat Uncle Joe had given him from his military days abroad. They both stood taller than their five foot nine inches, practically bouncing down the narrow aisle.

As if for an invisible camera, Kokui maneuvered the steep aircraft stairs in her pink pumps. She turned from the wind, her ponytail whipping, as she joined the mass of passengers marching toward the terminal.

"I don't see Diana." She pretended to crane her head in search of the Supreme, as they stood in the line to pass through immigration.

"Don't worry," Boris said, "she's waiting outside with our luggage."

"Next in line!"

Still giggling, Kokui strode to the immigration officer with Boris. As the man thumbed through their passports, she trained her eyes on his name tag: CZAPLA. His people, too, had come from somewhere else to find their way in America, she thought. She stood taller, sure he would understand the nervous excitement she felt.

"Coming from Ahcruh?"

"Ah-Crah," she corrected. "Yes."

"Eleanor Koh-kooey and Boris Van der Pooey?" He looked up at them, matching their passport photos to their faces.

She nodded past the first name she never used, her father's mother's name. "*Kaw-kwee* Van der *Poy*. Yes."

"And what brings you to America?"

Boris's chest puffed out. "We have been admitted to Erie Community College, in Buffalo, New York."

"School starts in August. What're you planning to do till then?"

"Find some work and make some mon—" Kokui shut her mouth as the man's left eyebrow crawled up to his hairline, her heart thumping in her throat as she realized her blunder. Their visa condition had been clear: employment was restricted to Erie's campus.

Her eyes skipped from Boris's frozen face back to the officer. She cleared her throat and thickened her accent so they could both blame misunderstanding. "We plan to find some time to work our way through all the sights to see in New York before we begin school, Mr. Czapla."

She held her breath as she watched him weigh whether to interrogate them further. If he opted to hold her to her first answer, she couldn't slip him a few cedis and walk away.

Slowly, his eyebrow lowered. "*Cha-plah*," he corrected her. "Make sure you get to Brooklyn for a pierogi." He stamped their passports. "Welcome to New York."

"Eyei." Kokui's heart was still flapping as she and Boris shuffled into the baggage hall. "He would have sent us right back."

"He would have sent you right back."

The bite in Boris's whisper further punctured her sobered levity. "Our bags are out."

They piled their luggage onto two trolleys and pushed past the customs officers into the arrivals hall, their eyes searching the small waiting crowd.

"Kwɛ! Is that Boris Van der Puye in America? Auntie Shika's special baby!"

They both turned to the slim, dark-brown man with the parted, low-cut Afro in the leather jacket, the bell-shaped bottoms of his tight trousers pluming around his platform shoes. Thick sideburns winged his high-cheeked smile, the jagged diamond-shaped birthmark by his left eye crinkling. His stare sparkled with mischief.

"Sammy!" Boris thrust himself into his cousin's arms, the wool and leather at their chests clapping.

Kokui ululated. "The famous Sammy of New York! Boris has been talking about you from the moment we met. *My cousin Sammy helped me get a school. My cousin Sammy is doing big things in New York.*" Kokui pantomimed as she spoke, overperforming to wave away the unease that had seized her in the encounter with Mr. Czapla.

Sammy pulled her into a hug. "You are welcome to New York, Madame K!"

She snorted. "Boris has everyone calling me that."

"It's okay. I call my wife, Frema, 'The Boss.' She can't wait to meet you. She wanted to come to the airport, but she had to see to the children."

"Oh, Boris said you have one child." Kokui had only had the seamstress sew a few dresses for a five-year-old girl.

"Yes, we have Jane, but Frema also babysits some of the neighbors' children," he said. "The way things are here, no one can stay home to look after their kids. She had the idea to charge so she could be home with our daughter."

"Very smart," Boris said. "Kokui was a nanny, too, in the UK."

Kokui started to clarify that it wasn't quite the same thing. She had been taking care of one child, the granddaughter of her father's business contact, a man who owned several mills in Germany. And she had been doing it in the mansion cottage he summered in, in Hampstead. But she stopped herself. She hadn't come to New York to continue performing the role of Mawuli Nuga's daughter. No one in America knew, or cared, who her father was. It didn't matter. That was the point. All that counted, moving forward, was who she was going to be.

"Let's go, eh. By now the rush hour traffic is in full force." Sammy loosened Kokui's hands from the trolley bar, and pushed ahead with Boris.

She followed the men back out into the chilling wind.

"Aren't you hot in that fur, Boris?" Sammy asked. "It's not so cold today."

"The way Boris has been looking forward to wearing Uncle Joe's hat, even if we had landed on a beach, he would keep it on." The laughter in her throat died at the hurt look Boris flung over his shoulder, and for the second time since they had landed she felt unnerved for blurting another truth.

"We are coming from Ghana, Sammy. If we aren't sweating, it's cold," Boris said.

"Then you will suffer at Erie. The winters in Buffalo are brutal."

They moved through the parking lot, passing row after row until they stopped at a yellow cab.

"You drive a taxi?" Kokui frowned as Sammy opened the trunk and began packing it with their luggage. "Boris said you work at a hospital."

"I do. Gyamfi—the one who drives this taxi—went to Ghana to bury his brother. He's gone the next three weeks so I've borrowed it to work. I'll pay the owner Gyamfi's share, and keep the rest of the money I make."

The three of them took their seats inside, Kokui at the back, Boris in the front, Sammy at the wheel.

"But how are you working both places at the same time?" she asked.

"Ah! Is it complicated?" Sammy quipped. "At night I drive the taxi, during the day I work at the hospital. I've taken the day off from the hospital to welcome you."

Kokui found it very complicated. She turned to the window in thought, lighting up a cigarette. Boris had said his cousin was doing well for himself in New York. She was realizing now she had never probed to understand what "doing well" meant to Boris.

"Madame K, you didn't ask Sammy if the smoke worries him."

"Don't bother your wife, man." Sammy stopped to pay the parking attendant, and they were off, joining the stream of traffic that coursed onto the four-lane highway. "Really, I got the taxi for you to drive, Boris. I'll share with you when I can, but it's yours to drive. The timing worked out beautifully. We were lucky to get it for you all to make some good money right from the start of your stay."

She watched Boris's head shoot to a profile, his eyes and mouth wide with gratitude. "But won't he need a US driver's license?" Kokui asked.

Sammy swatted her question away like it was a fly. "Half of these drivers don't have valid paperwork." He turned back to Boris. "You can make a hundred dollars a day, easily."

"A day!" Boris swiveled in his seat to share his excitement with her. "What about Kokui? What can we get for her to do?"

Kokui inhaled at the question that had taunted her growing up as Mawuli Nuga's daughter—and at some of the answers she had heard in these short minutes with Sammy. A nanny or a driver. She wanted to find work and make money to take to Erie when classes began. That was her and Boris's plan. She knew, too, as a newcomer, she would not have her pick of jobs. But still, she hoped to seek out a paid role that would spark her, and light her way forward.

"We'll talk to Frema. I know she can use help with the children she takes in. Besides, I'm sure we can help her find something."

"That's great," Boris said, turning to Kokui again.

Kokui studied the scenes panning outside her window. At eye level, the grid that had seemed so ordered from the airplane was a gritty maze. Peeking through the bare trees that stretched their gnarled branches like yawning bodies on both sides of the thoroughfare, the modest box-shaped homes near the airport gave way to towers of brick flats.

She took in the cars that cruised past, and the people and buildings that rose around them when Sammy exited the highway. Sammy slowed the car through a neighborhood of two-story apartment buildings. The solid brick structures, many with decorative stonework framing the windows, stood proud amid the odd edifice with knocked-out windows or a burnt facade. Each street seemed to have one of these condemned buildings, like a smile with one tooth missing.

He switched off the engine. "This is it. 'Do or Die' Bed-Stuy, Brooklyn. We're just up the block."

Boris chuckled at the neighborhood's morbid nickname, but Kokui frowned as they trooped down the pavement with their suitcases.

"That's life, isn't it?" Boris said. "Either you do, or you die."

Sammy led them up the front steps of a red-brick building. It stood next to an abandoned lot of stubborn weeds, broken bottles, and discarded diapers. The WET PAINT signs on the door indicated care, though, Kokui mused, consoling her growing disappointment as they walked into the first-floor apartment.

18

Kokui knew Boris's cousin didn't live in a mansion in Hampstead, but his boast that Sammy was doing well for himself had led her to envision a better place than this. The foyer, sitting room, and kitchen were one tight room. Two carved Asante masks hung on the dingy white wall directly above a fraying plaid couch. Crowded in front of the sofa was a playpen and a center table.

Sammy's wife, Frema, hunched over the toddler on the towel-swathed center table changing his diaper. A second baby was strapped to her back with cloth, asleep and mouth open, blissfully impervious to the grating volume of the singing advertisement on the television and the influx of noise they had brought in.

"Welcome!" Frema turned to shine a bright smile over her shoulder. She was very pretty, Kokui thought. As dark, smooth, and angular as the masks on the wall, though she looked exhausted. The faded nylon scarf that covered her hair showed off her unforced beauty, even as it made her appear to have just risen from bed.

"Sister Frema," Kokui called her out of respect for her role as their host and her older age—thirty-four to Kokui's twenty-four. "Thank you."

"Sammy, take their coats! I'm coming." Frema scooped the child up and dashed to dump the soiled diaper.

Kokui could hear Sammy's wife washing her hands in the bathroom. She saw one door in addition to the one Frema had just run out of, shaking her wet hands dry. Where would she and Boris sleep, Kokui wondered.

As Frema deposited the boy in the pen, the whole apartment seemed to shake with the child's shrill and droning whimper. Frema whipped around and raised a warning finger.

"Whining Willie! Try crying and see."

He slurped back his tears and the room went silent except for the television.

"Wow!" Kokui and Boris gaped at the boy now quietly gathering the rainbow of plastic rings scattered around him. Even more shockingly, the baby on Frema's back was still sleeping.

"Whining Willie no more." Sammy shrugged. "Didn't I tell you she's the boss?"

"Okay. Now!" Frema pulled them to the couch. "Come and sit. How was your flight? You must be tired. What will you drink? We have tea, water, Coke, beer—go and see. Whatever you want in the fridge is yours. This is your home. I've prepared some light soup for you. Will you take it with fufu?"

The questions swirled above Kokui. All she could focus on were the tiny quarters. "You pound fufu here?"

"Pound? You think I have energy to pound anything chasing these children all day?"

"I can attest she has no energy to pound anything," Sammy said dryly.

Kokui offered a polite chuckle, but she didn't like what she had just heard. She had not escaped the charged atmosphere of her father and Auntie Hemaa's fraught union to sit under another troubled marriage.

Frema rolled her eyes at her husband before turning back to Kokui. "We use mashed potato mix."

"Potato mix?"

"I'll show you," Frema said. "Boris, will you try some?"

"I'm here to try it all, and I won't say no if you add a beer!"

The corners of Kokui's mouth lowered with surprise. She supposed Boris was with his cousin, in his element, but she had never seen him look or sound so free.

"My dear wife," Sammy said, "make that two, please."

Frema wagged her finger again. "My dear husband, today you get served once in front of your family. That's it." She turned to Kokui. "If you don't make yourself clear, these men will take you for a slave. We are not in Ghana with help to send for this and that."

Boris was not a traditional man who demanded to be served, but now that Kokui thought of it, they had spent much of their dating days at the Ambassador or Tokyo Joe's. At her father's house, Sister Eyram, Nelson, Evans, and Victor had taken care of everything. Was he expecting her to wait on him now that they were in America? As she crossed the border of the living room carpet to the kitchen's scarred brown linoleum, she reminded herself she was in New York and on her way to Erie because Boris had served her. She took the men the bottles and opener Frema handed her.

"Cheers, brother," Sammy said.

Frema was pulling the carton of mashed potatoes from the cupboard when Kokui returned to the kitchen. "The pots are under the sink. Take one and put some water on to boil. I'll show you how to do it."

Kokui raised as polite an eyebrow at Sammy's wife as she could muster. She had just come off twenty-four hours of traveling.

"Sister Frema, I said yes to eating, not to cooking." She chortled as she said it, so her words could be mistaken for a joke if they were too candid for the moment. She quickly glanced toward the living room to make sure Boris hadn't heard her, though. He would not think anything funny about her saying more than "yes" and "thank you" to their hosts.

Frema pretended not to hear her, and Kokui decided it best not to repeat herself.

"How long have you all been living in New York?" Kokui asked as she filled the pot under the faucet.

"Almost eight years."

"And you like it?"

"Well, I like the money," Frema said.

"Sammy was telling us you have a babysitting business."

"I charge thirty-five dollars a week per head. Usually, I keep three children, sometimes more, but one stayed home sick today."

"Three children! In addition to your own?" Kokui thought of Sister Eyram. At one point, her father's cousin had been in charge of her, Nami, and their eight siblings.

"Hmmm. It's not easy. That's why we only have one child." She held Kokui's gaze as she handed her the box of powdered potato mix. "My sister, if you want to live in this country, take some time to get your birth control sorted. Otherwise, you will be running after babies, unable to work the way you need to, while the men are out, leaving you to manage on your own."

Kokui nodded, looking over at the sitting room where Boris

and Sammy had spread out on the couch. Boris had supported her through the abortion, but there was only so much he could do.

"I was taking herbs when I came, and still I became pregnant," Frema said. "I thought, 'Okay, this child's spirit must be strong,' but after Jane was born, I went straight to the clinic for the pill. I'll show you, if you like."

Kokui inhaled, disturbed by the similarity in their stories, and the prospect of what her and Boris's life could look like if they had a baby before they were ready. "Yes, please." She never wanted to be surprised by pregnancy again.

"So, you have almost six months before you start school," Frema continued. "I know Sammy has sorted Boris out with the taxi for now, and he will help him find something else when Boris has to return the taxi to Gyamfi. For you, I can take on some additional children so you can help me, and we split the money fifty-fifty."

Kokui tried to hide her grimace.

Frema arched her eyebrow. "You can also try one of the restaurants for a dishwasher position. The hospital is also there. Ask Sammy. They're always looking for cleaners."

"Are those the only jobs?"

Frema clapped her hands and shook them out as if she were drying them again. "The thing is, they won't let you find something better to do. You know the visa conditions. But, my sister, four years and you're free. You'll have your degree and you can pursue the kind of job you want."

"Didn't you and Sammy go to school?"

"Having the baby took me off course. I got a serious infection from the way they cut me." She half squatted to demonstrate. "I had to have surgery. I was in so much pain. The infection was so bad I almost died."

"What!"

"Hwɛ. I had to have a corrective surgery and stop everything, school, work, so I could properly heal. That's when Sammy started looking for taxis to drive on top of his work at the hospital." She gestured in the direction of the playpen. "I started the babysitting so he couldn't bluff me anymore when I asked for money. But now that Jane is in school, I can finish. Me, too, I'll be starting in August. When school resumes, the parents will have to find a new babysitter."

Kokui watched Frema's words pile up around her, alarm setting in. Her father had always told her to prepare for every eventuality, but she had not stopped to consider that some event or calamity out of her control could postpone or dash the fulfillment of her hopes in New York.

"Look at us," Frema said. "We didn't put the stove on." She turned a knob and felt the stovetop. "Good. It's working. It's been acting up of late, but the super came to fix it."

"Super?"

"The maintenance man for the building." She sprinkled salt into the water and shook out the potato powder. "Now you stir until it becomes thick like fufu. Let me get the soup from the fridge to heat for you."

Kokui stirred the pot thinking about the thousand dollars Mawuli had given her and Boris at the airport.

"How much does an apartment like this cost?"

"We pay ninety-five dollars a month, including heat, water, and electricity." Frema slammed her hand down on the counter. "These roaches." She scrubbed soap into her palms with a rough sponge. She peered over Kokui's shoulder at the bubbling starch. "When it gets thick like this, you have to chi it hard!"

Frema closed her palm over Kokui's fist and battled the swelling mass with her. The baby at her back woke up from the exertion. Frema sucked her teeth and loosened the crying child, transferring him to her front to cradle him just as the phone on the wall shrilled. "Keep at it," she ordered Kokui. "The bowls are in the cupboard above the sink and the spoons are in the drawer."

"Hello?"

"Mrs. Quartey, it's Diana from Jane's school. Jane just soiled herself again."

Kokui could hear everything the woman on the other end of the line was saying, as if it were her own ear on the receiver.

"Madame K, can we have another round of beers?"

Kokui burned with irritation as she turned to her husband. He was laughing on the couch with his cousin. Was he okay with everything they were seeing? One room. Babies crying everywhere. "Boris, don't you see us cooking?"

"Madame K," Frema said. "That was Jane's school. I have to go and pick her. Will you watch the children until I get back?"

Kokui frowned. "Shouldn't Sammy do it? Since the children don't know me?"

Frema was already grabbing her bag, putting on her coat. "He was driving that taxi all night. I don't want him to sleep at the wheel."

Kokui felt Boris behind her, his arms encircling her waist as he dropped his head into the curve of her neck.

"Thank you for doing this, Madame K." His whispered breath, though sour from the beer and their hours of travel, was warm in her ears. "I didn't know they had only one bedroom."

She exhaled. So he saw what she saw. This worn-down couple. This tight space. She wasn't being a princess. This wasn't what either of them had been expecting.

"What do you want to do?" With the thousand dollars her dad

had given them, they could rent their own place and begin their life in New York without the pressure of tiptoeing around Sammy and his wife, and she could take her time to find suitable work.

Boris looked toward the living room to see if Sammy could hear. "What do you mean?" he said. "Sammy and Frema have opened their home to us for free. Let's stick with the plan."

She hadn't expected Boris to say anything different. They had left Ghana to make a new life and living for themselves. It was what she wanted, too, even if the reality was already far from what she had dreamed. She sighed. They would only be with Sammy and Frema for five months. Soon, she and Boris would be on their own at Erie. He was studying Accounting and she would pursue Business Administration to start. They would get good campus jobs, save, find well-paid work when they graduated, earn enough to buy a nice home, and be in a better position to have children when the time came. Frema and Sammy's story did not have to be her and Boris's, and it wouldn't be. She would make sure of that.

Kokui forced a smile as she dropped a clump of "fufu" into a bowl, and hid its shapelessness with three generous ladles of soup. "Your first meal in America."

"Ours," he said, taking the bowl from her hands.

That night, she lay alone on the bed that pulled out from the living room couch. Sammy had taken Boris out in the taxi, to teach him how the taxi's meter worked and to give him a sense of the streets. The plan was for Boris to start on his own tomorrow.

Exhausted from the day, but unable to sleep, Kokui stared into the void of the ceiling trying to summon the excitement that had left her giddy and giggling just hours before. She lay like that, in a vortex of sleeplessness, until she woke up wondering whether she hadn't in fact been asleep the whole time, Boris sliding onto the bed beside her.

"You're back." She inched next to Boris, the wire springs under the mattress creaking with the movement. "How was it?"

"I made twenty-eight dollars after we split everything."

"So, not the hundred Sammy was talking about."

"More than Sammy is left with, I'm sure."

They both jerked up at Frema's voice. Sammy's wife stood steps away from them in the kitchen, glowering.

"Why wouldn't Sammy have—?"

"Madame K," Boris said, "don't worry about what Sammy has or doesn't have."

The kettle began to whistle as Sammy exited the shower.

"Good morning, all," he bellowed, the diamond mark near his left eye winking.

"I have to get Jane ready for school," Frema said. "Madame K, will you listen for the door? The Browns should be bringing Willie any minute now."

"Of course." What else could she say?

Frema took her cup of tea into her bedroom.

"I think they're having major problems," Kokui whispered to Boris.

"If they are, that's their problem." He rolled over and almost immediately began to snore.

19

Kokui looped her arm through Boris's as they made their way down the front steps of Sammy and Frema's apartment building. It felt good to be outside, even if the chill in the wind was stinging her eyes.

Boris wagged his finger, as Kokui wiped her weather-induced tears. "Whining Willie, try crying and see."

She snorted, leaning into her husband as they walked down the block to the taxi. "I don't know whether I'm happier to be free of the children or Frema. That woman . . ." Kokui chuckled. "For someone who makes clear she isn't here to slave, Frema is very good at giving orders."

She released his arm as they approached the cab.

"Sammy was saying she is willing to take on more children for you all to split the money," Boris said. "I think it's a good idea."

Kokui shook her head, her ponytail slapping the wind. "I can't be stuck in those tight quarters all day. While you and Sammy were out from afternoon into the night exploring, Frema had me changing diapers and cooking to feed the children. She was gone for close to three hours when she went to pick up Jane from school, and she told me to wash the dishes by the time she got back."

He snickered.

"I don't see what's funny."

"I'm sure she's been looking forward to the help."

"Well, she can look backward." Kokui ducked into the passenger seat. "I want to focus on looking for some office work. Maybe as a receptionist." Every visitor and correspondence passed through the woman who manned the front desk at her father's office. It was a good way to survey an industry and meet all sorts of people, she thought.

"Madame K, you didn't like working in your father's office, and you want office work here?"

She grimaced. "So, because I didn't want to work for my dad, I can't work in any office?"

"If office work were easy to get, don't you think Frema would be doing it?"

She narrowed her gaze at her husband. He had been so encouraging when she was applying to Erie. It wasn't like him to dissuade her from pursuing something hard.

"Frema told me she felt forced into the babysitting, Boris. Apparently, Sammy was bluffing her over money when she fell ill after giving birth."

Kokui could see Boris's attention glaze as he pulled out of the parking space.

"Do you want to gossip or direct me to the health center?"

"Ho. She was the one telling me her life story." Kokui held up the paper Frema had carefully written the directions on and motioned left. "Frema is stretched very thin."

"Then maybe you should support her."

"Ah!" She paused to soften the edge in her voice. "Boris, I just don't want to take on work for the sake of work."

He hissed, softly, also trying to be delicate. They were still feeling their way around their young marriage, getting to know the landscape, trying to figure out where the boundaries lay. "It's for the sake of money, Kokui. Just until we get to Erie. You don't have to complicate things for yourself. She is handing you an opportunity."

She turned to the window.

"I know you're thinking about the money your dad gave us," Boris said. "It's good that we have it, but living off it—or him—is not the plan."

It hadn't been the plan to sleep on a wiry couch bed for five months either. "Did I say I was changing the plan? I'm just thinking how we can make it work for the both of us."

"He's covering your tuition, but the rest, we are doing for ourselves," Boris decreed. "No allowance. The money he gave us is savings. Period."

Kokui sat in the silence of revelation, the particles between them shaken, falling and settling into a new understanding: Boris *wanted* them to struggle. And perhaps, more so, he wanted *her* to struggle. Kokui knew he resented the ladder that separated their classes. Though she had not created it, or done anything to elongate it, she would, too, if she were him. But she had never stopped to consider that a small part of him might want to push her to the bottom and make her climb so she would know how he felt. What she had thought was unimpeachable integrity was just another expression of his pride. She swallowed nervously, not sure what to do with this expanding view of her husband.

"You're willing to accept help from your cousin. Why aren't you willing to accept help from me?"

"It's not from you, Madame K. It's from your dad. We are not babies. We don't need your father to feed us. Sammy and Frema are simply easing our transition."

"So is my father," she said, exhausted by his ego.

"We can do it ourselves, Madame K." He forced a smile, like a salesman after a dubious pitch.

"We can do anything we want." One thing she had learned from Mawuli Nuga was it was possible to find, or make, a different way than everyone expected.

Boris nodded vigorously before she finished her sentence. "In this country, anything is possible. Look at how orderly everything is. If the trɔtrɔs had a meter like the taxis over here, you think the drivers could be changing the fares from moment to moment?"

Kokui smirked at his passion. "Look at you driving without a license, *like half of these drivers, no valid paperwork.*"

Boris snorted at her delivery in Sammy's voice. "I'll have to sort that out."

She resumed studying the directions Frema had given her, her eyes flicking from the paper to the buildings that stood behind the morning rush of people.

"I think it's here."

Boris slowed the car to a crawl. "I can't park here. Yesterday, Sammy didn't notice and got a ticket." He pointed to the sign that loomed above them.

"That's why he didn't have as much money as you last night," she said.

She watched Boris's jaw retract with the regret of a slip.

"No. Sammy will have to send the money in."

"Why were you parked? I thought you were driving all night." She made her eyes razors, waiting for his answer. "If I were Frema, I'd also be fuming by the kettle. Out all night working, you're supposed to be making money, not losing it."

"I didn't know my wife liked gossiping so much."

"You haven't answered me, Boris."

He exhaled. Like he had when she probed him about the eight-thousand cedi girl.

"I'm not gossiping." She tried to keep her voice steady, her mind rewinding to Boris's return. It was only Sammy who had gone straight to the shower. "I'm observing so we can know what to look out for."

"As long as we look out for ourselves, we will be okay."

"I am looking out for us," she said. "We have to be careful that their unhappiness doesn't infect us."

He scoffed.

"Maybe you should talk to Sammy."

"I'm not talking to him about anything except what we need to do to earn some money." He raised the hand brake. "Madame K, are you sure you don't want me to join you inside?"

"No, no, no." She wanted to mull over her conversation with Boris alone. She had come to America to find a way for herself free of her father's pressure to follow him into his business, and to build a life with Boris free from the shadows of her parents' marriage. She was starting to realize she would also need to take care not to get shackled by Boris's pressures to follow his agenda for them or for her—and that she would have to be careful to prevent new shadows from casting their length on her marriage. "Go make your hundred dollars," she told him.

"Where will you pass to look for work?"

"The same place you and Sammy parked."

He pursed his lips. "We went to Harlem, Madame K—he likes to go to a drinking spot called Shorty's after his shift. Me, I don't see the point of spending money we just made. I was just there watching him spend."

"Drinking spot?" She tensed. "Were there women there?"

She watched his chest fall and rise with his breath. "Not for me, Madame K."

Kokui felt the familiar lance of vicarious betrayal. "Poor Frema."

"Madame K, don't say anything to her about this."

"There's already enough tension between Sammy and Frema. I won't add to it," she said. "Thank you for letting me know."

She leaned to kiss her husband and got out of the car, glad to close the door on the argument they had tiptoed around, and grateful because she believed him. She knew if there was money involved, he was not spending it on any woman.

"You know your way back?" he asked.

She waved Frema's directions at him.

"I'll see you tonight."

She walked toward the brick building a bit depleted, thinking about Sammy and Frema's marriage.

"Madame K."

She turned at Boris's call.

"It's their business," he shouted through the window she hadn't rolled up. "Put it out of your mind."

Boris didn't understand. He had not grown up amid different fiefdoms of broken women turning their anger, bitterness, and shame on their children and themselves. He thought earning his own money was security. He didn't know fidelity was life's only true anchor.

20

The Women's Care Coalition shared a building with a chiropractor, a dentist, a media company, and a wholesale fabric manufacturer. Finding the office number on the directory fixed on the lobby wall, Kokui made her way up the stairs and pushed into a sitting room full of women. They all looked up at her, some holding clinging children on their laps. She touched her stomach. It had been five weeks since she had aborted.

She thought of Frema running out to pick up Jane, not trusting Sammy to remain awake behind the wheel. She thought, too, of Micheline's confusing devotion to her and Nami—her abandonment of them to their father's house, yet her decision to stay married to Mawuli to keep their inheritance secure. She wondered about her stepmothers. If they hadn't had children with her dad, would they have stayed as long as they did? Would Micheline have completely cut her ties with Mawuli if she and Nami didn't exist? What was keeping Auntie Hemaa around?

"I'm here for birth control," she told the receptionist behind the counter.

The bespectacled woman gave her a brochure and led her to wait with the others who had walked in without an appointment. Kokui pored over the pamphlet. She could choose to insert a device into her womb, have tubal ligation surgery, make it her job to either push a cup inside herself or ensure Boris wore a condom every time they planned to have sex, or she could swallow a pill every day with her breakfast. A menu with few appetizing options. The tea Auntie Hemaa had taught her to brew, and the one Mr. Koranteng had packed for her to take home, was no better. Why were so many things about womanhood so distasteful?

For more than an hour she waited before the doctor called her in to explain the selection of choices she had read. Like Frema, she opted for the pill, and left with the prescription.

The wind had stilled and the sun was beaming now. Kokui took her time moving down the block, inhaling courage as she surveyed the stacks of buildings around her. The area seemed mostly residential. She saw women pushing strollers, teenagers meandering, and dogs tugging their owners forward. But there were plenty of businesses—one of them had to have a decent job for her.

She slowed past a boutique, a beauty salon, a café, and a grocery store, peering into their windows before stopping into each one.

"I'm wondering if you have any openings. I'm—"

"Not at the moment," the woman at the boutique told her.

Kokui finished her sentence anyway. "—looking for work." She tilted her head up and walked out.

The man at the grocery store turned his face sideways at her. "You got papers to work?"

She nodded slowly. Technically, she did—she just wasn't allowed to use them outside of Erie.

"Oh." He seemed disappointed. "What I have is off the books."

"I can do that." She wasn't sure what she was agreeing to, but what harm could be found in Angelico's Community Kitchen and Grocer?

"It's a night position. We pay a dollar fifty an hour."

She narrowed her gaze. "Isn't the minimum wage two dollars?"

"It's off the books, so you don't pay taxes."

She hesitated. She supposed she was already on illegal ground working outside the terms of her visa, but not paying taxes sounded more dangerous.

"You got papers to work on the books or not?"

"Well—my student visa—"

"So, you can't work unless it's a campus job," he said. "Look, you want to make a little extra money outside school, I understand. We've had other people like you. Respectable. Professional. That's what we need.

"We're looking for someone to man the office at night, when we get our meat deliveries in. You check and make sure everything that's listed on the invoice is in the boxes and goes on the shelves. We provide free and discounted groceries for poor and homeless people so we can't have anything going missing. Can you make sure that doesn't happen?"

She nodded her reservations away and followed him inside. She would be helping people.

The interior was designed to look like one big kitchen. A series of center islands displayed respective bowls of fruits and vegetables while the shelves were designed to look like kitchen cabinets. She imagined it the kitchen of a faultless, benevolent family, as the owner intended, she was sure.

"We operate as a soup kitchen and grocer," he said. "Everyone in here comes through the homeless shelter and gets a voucher to eat and shop."

Koku tried to hide her surprise at some of the men and women she saw in the store. Some looked disheveled, but many looked neat and cared for.

The manager followed her eyes. "It's hard times in New York."

He led her into an office stacked with boxes, and she drew her coat closed.

"Why is it so cold here?" She could see the vapor of her breath.

"The meat freezer is next door."

"Is there a way to turn on the heat? It's very cold."

"We can't heat this room or it'll affect the meat, and it's against the law to have a space heater in here."

Kokui tried to imagine herself sitting in this office for more than five minutes, let alone until she went to Erie.

"You know what? I'll bump up the pay to a dollar sixty-five. Best I can offer."

She wanted to walk away, but she could hear herself telling Boris she had managed to find a job on her own and on her first try. Besides, it could be good training for the winter in Buffalo Sammy had warned them about, she told herself. "Okay, I'll take it."

"I didn't get your name."

"Kokui Nuga."

"Where's that from?"

"'That' is from me. I am from Ghana."

He nodded. "Okay, Ghana, you're gonna need that feistiness working here. I'm Paul from Staten Island. Can you start tonight?"

"Why not?"

Back in the sunshine, she giggled at her performed nonchalance.

She lit up a cigarette, savoring the return of the rush of excitement and pride she had felt her first moments in America.

Kokui pulled out the paper Frema had written the directions on. ASK SOMEONE TO SHOW YOU WHERE THE A TRAIN IS, Sammy's wife had scrawled, and so Kokui did, following the directions into New York's filthy, fascinating bowels. The urine stench thickened in the back of her throat as she navigated around a patchwork of New Yorkers, some in jeans, some in crisp suits, others in soiled rags. Some muttered, others raved, a few conversed, all were silenced when the train came roaring through, streaking the dimly lit station with bubble-letter paintings and cartoon drawings. With one hand, Kokui gripped her handbag as Frema had told her to, the bag's strap a diagonal slash across her torso. With her other hand, she held on as the train lurched forward like a theme park ride, the overhead lights flickering on and off the whole trip back to Bed-Stuy.

"How did it go?" Frema asked above Willie's whining welcome. Kokui had yet to put her keys down. "I just got a call from Jane's school. Again, her stomach is bothering her—she's been vomiting all morning. I don't know what's wrong with that girl."

She loosened the baby from her back and handed him to Kokui.

Kokui ducked the baby's grabbing arm, covering her left earring. "I got a job."

"You did?"

Kokui saw disappointment in Frema's wilted countenance. "At a grocery store. They want me to manage the deliveries that come at night."

"Oh. It's a night position."

"It's a respectable place. Angelico's Community Kitchen and Grocer. They support people who are struggling. They can go in and eat or shop for free," she parroted Paul.

"So, you can still help me with the children during the day."

Kokui blinked at Sammy's wife. Was the woman all right? "Frema, I'll have to preserve my energy if I'm to be working at night."

"I've told the parents in the building we can take on a few more children." She sounded as desperate as she looked. "We can all make some more money to help defray the extra costs. Potato powder isn't free."

Kokui arched an eyebrow. She couldn't blame Frema. It was clear she was stressed trying to hold her and Sammy's life together. She went to her hand luggage and pulled out the envelope her father had given her. "Will this defray your extra costs?"

Frema gaped at the two hundred-dollar bills Kokui handed her, and the envelope they came from. "Thank you, Madame K."

"Thank you and Sammy for allowing us to stay with you."

Frema yanked her handbag from the center table. "I'll be back, eh."

Kokui watched her scurry out, clicking the door shut behind her. She walked the baby in her arms past Whining Willie and the other toddler he was throwing plastic rings around the play-pen with, back to her and Boris's pile of suitcases in the corner of the living room. She returned the envelope to her carry-on with relief. She felt good giving Frema something that could lighten the load.

21

ammy and Frema's bathroom was Kokui's least favorite part of the apartment. Along with a naked bulb, a sprawling water stain glared down from the peeling ceiling in gradients of rust brown. To Kokui, the soil looked like an empty hourglass. She avoided glancing up at it as she showered, quickly and methodically scrubbing the lathered net sponge over her body.

She stiffened at the sound of the door opening, her anxiety about the broken lock realized. "I'll be finished just now!"

"It's me."

Kokui poked her head past the shower curtain, her apprehension giving way to tingling surprise at Boris putting the rubbish bin against the door. She giggled. "Aren't Sammy and Frema just outside?" The setting was far from aphrodisiacal, but she and Boris had not made love in the three days since they had landed in New York.

He folded his arms. "Madame K, Sammy is not happy that you gave Frema money."

Her smile sagged. Her husband hadn't burst in to congratulate her on finding a job on her first day of looking. Nor was he interrupting her bath to take advantage of the third time they had been alone since they had landed in New York.

"I know in your family you are used to receiving payments from your dad, but family doesn't have to pay to stay with family."

Kokui's eyes curled upward. Was her father's money, and Boris's lack thereof, going to be the running argument of their marriage? "If we were paying, I would have given considerably less. Two hundred dollars is double their rent."

She watched Boris's fingers gather into a loose fist. "Why are you so angry, Boris? Your family has opened their home to us, and even given you work. They've gone above and beyond. We can't be here five months eating and drinking, and not give them anything while we are working."

"It's not generosity if you receive payment for it."

She gasped her frustration. Her husband could be so simplistic. "It would be wrong for us to take, knowing they don't have much, while we save one thousand dollars that we were given."

"Who says they don't have much?" Boris huffed.

Kokui looked up to see if the stain had also heard the question. "Frema did. She told me she wanted me to help her with the kids during the day, then go and work my new job at night so she could take on more children and 'defray costs.'"

"Then help her with the children. That's what you should do."

She groaned. "Boris, yes, we are here to make money, but we don't have to go without sleep, working 'round the clock. I know you don't want to hear it, but my father gifted us some money. I don't see anything wrong in using it to make things easier for ourselves and for your cousin's family."

His arms, taut with frustration, fell slack. "You don't understand."

"What don't I understand?"

"Giving them money, when they didn't ask for it, is insulting to them."

"Maybe it's insulting to you and Sammy, but Frema and I understood each other."

"I just want us to be careful to respect them, Madame K. What they have, they are giving. It's not for us to say it's not enough."

"Did I say that?" She had already spent more time than she desired in this bathroom. "I just want to get ready for my new job in peace. You haven't even congratulated me." She tore the shower curtain across the bar and resumed her furious lathering.

He peeled the corner of the curtain back to watch her. "Sammy and Frema told me you found something, but they didn't tell me what it is. Tell me about it."

"Sammy told you I gave Frema money. Let him also tell you about the job I got on my own."

He stepped out of his trousers and briefs. "I want you to tell me."

She watched him grow larger as he unbuttoned his shirt.

He stepped into the tub. "I said tell me."

"I'm going to be managing deliveries at a soup kitchen and grocery store."

He began to graze her breasts, kneading her nipples into pebbles. "I'm listening."

"It's a night shift." She tried to keep her voice steady as he lowered his fingers, plucking moans from her throat.

"Keep going." He separated her thighs.

What she said next was incoherent as he slid inside of her. He clamped her mouth with his palm so only he could hear her pleasure. They clung to each other, jerking back and forth until the hot spray turned tepid.

"We should get out," he said. "We both have to go to work."

She thought he should stay home and sleep. He had been out driving all day, and hadn't slept more than three hours since they had arrived. But she didn't want to argue about it.

Boris left her in the tub and returned the small rubbish bin back to its corner behind the toilet. "I'll see you in the morning."

Kokui mopped the small tributary they had made on the floor with their opening and closing the shower curtain, before pulling on the blouse and trousers she had folded on the closed toilet seat.

She was still tingling when she exited the bathroom. Frema and Sammy sat on the couch, their arms locked under their chests, the veins at their temples bulging. "I'm here by myself," Frema was saying.

"Ah! What do you want me to do? Boss, I can't stay at home with you and also work and pay the bills."

"You don't pay the bills by yourself, Sammy."

Their daughter, Jane, sat on the floor at the center table, fidgeting over her homework.

"Hello, everyone." Kokui announced her entrance loudly to make them stop.

Jane dropped her pencil to run toward the bathroom.

"She's been waiting for you to come out," Frema said. "Will you make sure she wipes herself properly, Madame K?"

She had just come out of the shower and Frema wanted her to oversee her daughter's toilet use? "Of course."

She turned back to the bathroom and knocked at the slightly ajar door. "You finished, Jane? You wiped yourself?" She pushed in, the rotten stench of diarrhea smothering her. "Hmmph! The way you were shaking, I thought you were coming to urinate."

The girl laughed.

"Come on, wash your hands."

Kokui watched her roll the orange bar of soap over and under her hands and past her wrists. "Jane, stop playing with the soap and rinse off."

"I'm giving Mommy and Daddy time to finish fighting."

"And what about me? Eh? Eh?" Kokui performed the question, over-enunciating to make Jane, and the little girl she had once been, smile. "Maybe your booboo smells like flowers to you, but for me it's *fiu, fiu, fiu.*" She pinched her nose.

The bathroom door shook with the sound of the apartment door slamming. Jane turned off the water and shook her hands dry. "Daddy's gone."

Frema turned from the stove where she now stood ladling out a bowl of light soup. Next to the pot, steam began to burble from the kettle's diamond-shaped spout. "I didn't put any pepper in, so you shouldn't feel upset again. Drink all, okay?"

Jane walked the bowl slowly to the center table.

"I don't know what's wrong with her stomach," Frema said. "She says she's not eating anything she's not supposed to at school, but I can't tell what else. The doctor says she is fine. I haven't introduced anything new to her diet. Since you've been here you've seen. We eat the same things. Fufu and soup. Rice and stew. If they call me tomorrow to pick her because she's been throwing up . . ." She let her voice trail off and shook her head as she tipped the kettle over the tea bag waiting in her cup.

"It's because of you and Sammy fighting," Kokui said.

Frema raised her teacup to her face, exhaling a sad sigh before she drank. "Every couple fights."

Kokui gave Frema a consoling pat. "I know."

"I haven't seen you fight with Boris yet."

"Join us in the bathroom next time and you'll see," Kokui said.

Frema's beautiful face softened. "I thought you were doing something else in there."

"We did. After we fought."

The women chuckled.

"Newlywed. Enjoy it o."

"We are trying." Kokui met Frema's weary eyes. "I hope you didn't feel insulted by me giving you that two hundred dollars."

She waved the thought away. "Not at all."

"I don't want to cause problems between you and Sammy."

"It's not you causing the problem, Madame K. After a while you get tired of fighting over the same things."

Kokui smiled sadly. Was that the secret to a good marriage? Not getting tired? "Let me go and start this job."

She turned the key in the top, bottom, and dead-bolt locks of Frema's door before forcing the building's front door open into the icy evening. Instantly, her eyes became hot glass, atmospheric tears striping her face with tight, salty streaks. She looked like one of her mother's drip-dried fabrics by the time she moved down the subway stairs, blending into the madness. She became one with the others carefully looking away from one another on the garbage-strewn train car after nine p.m., each on their separate missions.

At the Spring Street station, she climbed out of the subway and tried to find her bearings back to the store in the frigid night. It was the veranda-style facade of Angelico's that had beckoned her to go in and try her luck, but she walked past it before realizing the veranda was now gated by a grated door. She could see people inside, past the plants, walking the aisles. She waved to get the security guard's attention.

"We close that entrance after nine," he told her.

"I work here," she told the tall, dark man. "Paul—"

"Oli nyuie ɖe?"

The guard's greeting in Ewe startled her, transporting her to her father's house for a moment as he slid the gate open.

"I'm Amos Ablor," he said. "When Paul said he hired another Ghanaian, and mentioned your name, I told him you are my Ewe sister."

He led her through the store, past the meat locker to her office. She blew on her cupped hands. It had not gotten any warmer since the morning.

"It's cold, eh? You can leave your things in the office, but you don't have to stay inside. The deliveries start after one a.m."

He held the door open as she set her bag on the chair and ran out.

"Is Paul here to show me what to do?"

"He says he has explained everything. You are just checking to ensure whatever is listed on the invoice is what is in the boxes, isn't it?"

She swallowed the globule of insecurity that formed in her throat. She didn't want to make a mistake.

"I'm going back to my post, but I'll be with you to assist when the delivery comes."

"Thank you, Amos."

"Akpe mehiã o. We have to help each other."

"So, what do I do?" she asked him as he locked her office door.

"You are new to New York, eh? Go out and explore—just as long as you are back to take the first delivery."

He nodded at her disbelief.

"It's just us here," he said. "I won't tell anyone."

If it was her dad's office, Kokui would already be gone, but she had come to America to do things differently. "It's okay, I'll stay around."

His eyes fluttered his surprise. "Okay, whatever you like."

She watched him walk away before she wandered the aisles. Again, it shocked her how many well-dressed people were in the shop, peering into the cabinets and fridges, plucking fruits from the bowls to squeeze and smell. She knew people were suffering everywhere in the world, but this was America, the headquarters of the World Bank.

She ended her stroll at Amos's stand.

"You sure you won't go out and see the neighborhood, my sister? You'll be tired walking up and down the store all night."

"I'm still on Ghana time," she admitted, covering a yawn. "Maybe sitting in that cold office will keep me from falling asleep."

He shrugged and walked her back. The clock ticked at just after ten-thirty as she sat in the chair behind the desk, curled into a heat-saving ball. Every minute seemed colder than the next. She shivered with the sweat building under her clothes.

Her door opened just as she was standing up to escape.

"Checking on you, my sister." Amos gave her a smile of pity. "You don't want to get sick. If you can't come in because you aren't well, they won't pay you."

"Is there anything I can help you with?" she asked through quivering lips.

"The boss's office is there. I'll open it for you. That one is heated, of course."

"Thank you, Amos." She gathered her bag quickly and followed him to the opposite side of the shop.

"Don't mention it."

She sat in the warmth blowing on her stiff knuckles, watching each second on the clock tick by. She sucked her teeth. She could not do this for the next five months. She paced the office to stay awake, the heat adding to her boredom, making her drowsy, even as she couldn't shake the chill that had settled in a film on her skin. At 12:50, she started back to her office to ready for the delivery. Amos wasn't at his post. The store was completely, eerily empty now.

Kokui wandered the store again, wondering if Amos had moved

to the other entrance he had mentioned but hadn't shown her yet. She returned to her office door, both relieved by the rustling she heard by the freezer, and scared.

"Amos?" She inhaled, bracing herself for whatever stood on the other side, including the lower temperatures, as she pushed past the heavy plastic slats into the walk-in meat locker.

Cases of meat surrounded her and two beef sides swung from hooks in the corner. She moved tentatively toward the open door blowing the wind outside in.

"Amos?"

Amos and two men were loading boxes onto the back of a truck parked in an alleyway.

"I thought you said the deliveries start at one."

Amos looked up at her, his arms full. "Sometimes they come early."

The men with Amos didn't acknowledge her presence.

"But are you delivering or packing away?"

Amos came over with the box in his hands. "You want some meat, my sister? They bring it from a farm. It's fresh, like back home. They are giving it free, anyway."

"Then why are you packing so many boxes onto the truck, Amos?"

"My sister, take some meat home to your family. You can even sell some. The money they pay us, we are working, but we are like the homeless who come here."

"Amos, what do you expect me to tell Paul?"

The men looked from her to Amos now, but they continued loading.

"He hired me to—"

"What did Paul expect you to do?" Amos said. "You think he doesn't know? He knows when the deliveries come. Instead of being here himself, he's left us alone. My sister, there are some deliveries that come and there are some that go. You will see for yourself."

Kokui left the freezer, back to the warmth of the store. She couldn't continue working here. She was a lot of things, but she wasn't a thief. Her shoulders slumped at the thought of telling Boris and Frema that Angelico's hadn't worked out—and at the thought of going back out to face the rejection of looking for another job.

Amos emerged through the heavy plastic flaps of the meat locker.

"I'm going home."

"That's what I've been telling you to do," he said. "It's late. New York is dangerous at this hour. I'll see you tomorrow, then."

"No, you won't."

"My sister, this is a job you can do in your sleep, and get some help while you are at it."

"Good night, Amos."

He pulled two hundred-dollar bills from his pocket. "Take something for your time then."

"No. It's okay."

"My sister, Paul gives me this money for situations like this. Take it."

Kokui started to protest, but the irony of the amount silenced her. That was the two hundred dollars she had given Frema and fought about with Boris. She walked back out into the night, thinking of Jane, oddly. How far would Sammy and Frema's daughter run to escape the shadow of her parents' marriage, she wondered, as she retraced her steps to the subway.

That night, she wrote her family.

She told her father she had found work on her first day, and

165

about Amos's, and potentially Paul's, scheme to steal and sell the free meat to suppliers, making sure to end with the note that she was undaunted. She would go back out and find a new job.

She told her mother how well she and Boris were adjusting to their new country and new routine. "It's been easier than I expected," she lied.

To Nami, she told everything.

22

When Boris's three weeks with the taxi had come and gone, Sammy got him a filing clerk position at his hospital.

"I see you don't want to be a cleaner either," Kokui couldn't resist saying to him.

Since the job was "on the books," he was using the Social Security number of Gyamfi, the friend who had loaned them the taxi.

"Can't we get our own Social Security number?" Kokui asked Sammy.

"You can, but it's better you wait and do it when you are at Erie so you are in the system the right way."

The right way. Boris was the moralist of the two of them, but Kokui seemed to be the only one uncomfortable with the underground nature of their life in New York so far. Boris had even chastised her for quitting Angelico's.

"I understand why you left, Madame K, but with the security

offering you free rein to leave, you could have even gotten another job and been making double money!" he said.

Boris had worked out a deal with Gyamfi to drive the taxi the hours the man couldn't work—yet still hadn't gone to get his driver's license. She worried that the police would stop him, arrest him, and everything would come to an end for them. But, of course, Boris hadn't gotten his license. When could he go and take classes and complete the necessary tests?

Every day, he left the house with Sammy before seven-thirty in the morning. He came home for supper at seven. He slept till midnight, before braving the subway after dark to make his way across the city to the Bronx, where he collected the car to drive, while Gyamfi slept from two to six a.m. It was dangerous—she hadn't needed Amos to tell her that. The papers reported two taxi drivers killed—one shot, one stabbed, both robbed.

The nights Sammy drove with Boris didn't give her relief. They always came back later than usual, Sammy heading straight to the shower when they arrived. She believed Boris when he said it was just Sammy entertaining other women, but she could see that skinny arm stabbing the night. *Mawuli Nuga, each and every one of your daughters will know the shame you've caused me.*

"Madame K, very soon we'll be at Erie," Boris said. "Let's just make as much as we can while we are here so we are set for our housing."

So far, life with Boris in America had required much deferral of pleasure.

She had spent the first days after her night at Angelico's trooping across Manhattan and Brooklyn, entering every establishment that would allow her in, asking if they had work. She filled out so many applications, she no longer needed to consult the paper Frema had written their address and telephone number on. "We'll call you," they all promised, but the calls had yet to come, and there was Frema suffering alone with the children. Kokui couldn't say no anymore—or give Frema more money. She was seeing that the thousand dollars her father had given her and Boris was not that much. It was enough to do what Mawuli had intended, set them up or bring them back to Ghana, but it would not cover life in New York for more than five or six months.

She and Frema minded six children between them—Whining Willie, Baby Joseph, who had just reached nine months, twin five-year-old girls, a six-year-old girl, and a three-month-old girl—not including Jane. Every day, between seven a.m. and seven p.m., the apartment seemed to be crawling, not only with the roaches that asserted their presence at mealtimes but with children. For just as long, Kokui held her breath, waiting for the last kid to be picked up each day. She longed for her and Boris's escape to Erie, though she knew now not to assume it would automatically be better. But, still, it wouldn't be this crushing cycle.

She hoped for inspiration in classes, an array of stimulating job options, and an apartment large enough for them to unpack the four suitcases and two pieces of hand luggage they currently had to take turns restacking in the corner of Sammy and Frema's living room whenever they wanted to wear something fresh. She looked forward to no Frema lurking as she and Boris whispered in bed, no children everywhere, and no hourglass stain on the bathroom ceiling. She would be able to scream aloud when they made love.

There was evidence the deprivation had some merit, though, Kokui had to admit.

Between the two of them, they had amassed $5,455—her contribution amounting to $1,890. An unfamiliar pride surged within her, counting money she had had to hustle for. The cash she and Boris gave Sammy to deposit into his bank account represented eighteen weeks of Whining Willie, sore arms and backaches balancing babies at her front and her back, changing diapers, holding children's running and crusted noses while instructing them to "blow," begging kids to eat, wiping faces and bottoms, scrubbing food, urine, and feces from the children's clothing and hers, sweeping, mopping, picking up toys, and an attendant soap opera addiction as the television blared, the characters on *All My Children*, *General Hospital*, and the commercials that played in between her and Frema's only adult witnesses.

"Erie is going to feel like a vacation," Boris said when she complained.

"Do you know the meaning of vacation?" She really wanted to know. He had elected to work at the hospital on America's Independence Day, eager for the time and a half he would be paid on the holiday.

"That's an extra ten dollars, Madame K."

* * *

The first two envelopes from Erie arrived the second week of July, with her and Boris's respective academic plans. The reason she had wanted to come to America in the first place was beginning to feel real. As she held her folder in her hands, Kokui swallowed nervously at the recommended courses listed out for her. Principles of accounting, business finance, macroeconomics . . . She could hear her father lecturing, see him waving at a shelf full of binders. *What do they all have in common, Kui?* She had been desperate when she checked the box for Business Administration, but she could not pursue this syllabus for two years, let alone four. She would have to explore the other available course tracks as soon as she set foot on the campus.

The third envelope came the week after with their orientation schedule, a copy of the classified ads listing local housing options, a brochure citing their employment opportunities, and the contact address and number of the family who was there to help them navigate life in Buffalo.

They were expected to report for orientation on August 27 to be ready for the start of classes on August 29, but their host family, the Bucketts, had included a letter inviting them up a week earlier.

"We spend that last week before school opens camping in the woods," Daphne Buckett wrote. "I know you're from the big city Accra, but I hope you'll join us on this 'country' family tradition. We'll bring the tents, food, and bug spray—just bring yourselves!"

"I don't mind telling them no so we can work one more week," Boris said.

"Boris, we are going. In fact, we should go even earlier, to look at the apartments before we decide."

Boris's brow puckered over the housing list. "Two hundred dollars a month! I thought Buffalo was a village. Sammy and Frema are paying half this for a one-bedroom apartment in Brooklyn."

But look at the type of apartment it is, she wanted to say.

"Maybe if we look farther away from campus, we can find something affordable."

"I don't want 'something,' Boris," Kokui said. "We're going to be living there for the next two years, at least. We have to be comfortable, else what are we working so hard for?"

Kokui pored over the employment brochure. There were office assistant jobs in a few of the department offices, and listings of openings in various businesses around Buffalo. Most interesting to her were the career coaching services. LET US HELP YOU FIND

WORK THAT MEANS SOMETHING TO YOU, the pamphlet read. She inhaled, her anticipation building, tempering some of her fear of the academics.

When the last parent came for their child that day, Kokui immediately got ready to gallop down the front stoop for a walk to Fulton Park. Now that the weather was warm, she made it a daily habit, her time to smoke her cigarettes and escape into a Janet Dailey romance. She savored the slow tease of misunderstanding and inconvenient attraction that ultimately unspooled to reveal love in the dramatic stories of rich, brutish men falling for beautiful, headstrong women—a holdover from her youth when she had prayed for her father's lie to be revealed as a misinterpretation, and an anesthetic when it wasn't.

She was readying for her stroll in front of Sammy and Frema's bedroom mirror, pinning her ponytail in, trying to smooth the flaring hairs on her aged wiglet, when Frema walked in.

"You have mail."

Kokui glanced past her reflection, expecting one of Erie's oversize envelopes, but the skinny white envelope bore the Nuga & Heirs logo. Nami had written. She started to rip the letter open, but Frema hovered. She would read it in the park.

"I'll be back," she told Frema when she was done fixing her hair.

"You promise?"

They giggled as Kokui made her exit, her ponytail, flaccid with too much pomade, hanging heavy behind her.

She greeted the neighbors enjoying frosty cans of Old English on the stoop. "What's up, Ponytail?" one of the men called after her as she continued around a group of kids drunk from the sun and the fun of running giddy circles in and out of the geyser of an opened fire hydrant. Normally, Kokui took her time strolling, drinking each solitary moment to the last drop before she had to return to help Frema cook, but she wanted to use the time she saved speed-walking to the park to linger over her first news from home since she and Boris had landed in New York. She had been so desperate to leave her father's house and the track he was trying to force her on, she hadn't expected to miss her and Mawuli's shared morning rides into the office. She missed Nami, too, and the slower rhythms of life back home, the comfort of sitting in the back seat while Nelson drove her wherever she needed to be.

At the park, teenage couples had taken over most of the benches, kissing or necking out in the open because they weren't allowed to do it at home, Kokui mused with a chuckle. She smelled marijuana wafting from some unknown location as she settled into a spot one pair had abruptly vacated. She filled her chest with air, preparing to enjoy Nami's letter like it was a meal someone other than she had had to cook, before opening the envelope.

"Sis," Nami began, "the house is not the same without you. I've been keeping to the hostel at school, but when I stop by, only Nelson, Evans, and Victor are home, standing around watching Sister Eyram chase Kofi down the veranda. They all ask of you. Nelson, especially."

That big house had always felt empty to Kokui, even when their siblings and stepmothers filled the rooms.

"I have to go to the office if I want to see Daddy. He's been pre-occupied with an inquiry. The Ministry of Lands has decided to investigate the land grants Nkrumah gave out and so they have sent Daddy a summons to produce all the original documentation. The paper king has what they need, but they've set a date for him to present in court. Auntie Hemaa has been especially supportive, going to the office with him and helping him prepare for the court date."

Kokui frowned at the letter, remembering Boris's former

colleague at the Ministry of Finance. She couldn't think of his name. *Solomon Something.* She shrugged at the memory of his vengeful face. If it was him leading this effort, he didn't know who Mawuli Nuga was. Her father would embarrass him to quash this inquiry. But still, the thought tugged at her, he had to feel a bit scared if Auntie Hemaa was getting involved.

"Daddy wants to know when you are coming back home so you don't have to steal meat to eat."

She snorted as she folded the letter over the letterhead and tucked it into its envelope, sitting for a few more minutes under the Brooklyn summer sun. She imagined telling her dad to his face that she had earned more than the one thousand dollars he had given them but thought better of the fantasy. She couldn't afford for him to rethink his promise to pay her tuition.

23

If August 17 was a song, Kokui would sing it. The morning was still dark, the house was still asleep, Boris's chest was still rising and falling with snores beside her, but soon the light would flood the sky, Frema would put the kettle on, Boris would wake up, Jane would putter in followed by Sammy, and they would go to pick up the rental car for the drive to Erie. She felt as if, after running for five months, the finish line was in view. Of course, they would not be completing the race when they crossed it—yet another new beginning lay ahead of them.

In some ways, she was glad she and Boris had come to America months before they started at Erie. Without leaving the awning of her father's money, she would not have understood that she had been naive to equate her husband's lower caste with a purer character. They had come to each other from very different places—they both had much to learn from one another, and about themselves. It had been humbling for her to beg for work without success, to take on Sister Eyram's role, to be a nobody whose name meant nothing, but she had done it—and she was still doing it, learning to build herself up.

She was proud that she and Boris had managed to maintain an overall tenderness with each other through this transition. He hissed, she huffed, but they had not sliced each other with their words or their actions. He did not have to tell her what Sammy had been up to, but he had trusted her with the truth, and she trusted that he had been true to their marriage. Yes, he was a man, fallible, but he was his own man. He was not her father.

She rolled over to lay her cheek on his chest, closing her eyes to the tears that signaled her gratitude. She had chosen rightly. As usual, the spring in the thin mattress squeaked with her movement, but she didn't hear it for the creak of Sammy and Frema's opening bedroom door.

"The man is still sleeping?"

Kokui raised her head, surprised to see Sammy.

"Ei, you are up. The two of you just got in." She didn't like it when Sammy drove with Boris. They both came back later than Boris did when he drove alone, and Boris had to split his earnings with him.

"Yes, I told Boris we should be early so we can get your money from the bank. You know it closes early on Saturday."

"Ah, yes." She shook Boris awake. In the last five weeks, they had added another $1,915 to their savings. They now had almost seventy-five hundred dollars in Sammy's account.

"Then we party. We haven't gone out together, all four of us, since you came. Mrs. Brown will watch Jane, and we'll enjoy a fare-well meal."

Frema strode in, balancing Jane in her arms. "Big baby wants to be carried."

"That's my baby!" Sammy gathered Jane from Frema and clasped her into a snuggle on his back. "You want to come with Daddy and Uncle to the bank?"

She nodded, rubbing the crust of sleep from her eyes.

"Daddy's girl," Frema said. "Of course she wants to go."

Boris sat up now.

"It's time to withdraw your millions from my account so you can treat us to your farewell dinner."

Frema went to get her daughter some shoes, and within minutes, the locks were clicking on the other side of the door.

Kokui rose to fold their bed back into the couch and put the cushions back in place. "You get your living room back," she told Frema.

"No more containing your 'fighting' to the shower, unless that's what you and Boris want."

The women chuckled.

"You will love Erie. Buffalo is smaller than here, quiet, but—"

The phone rang.

"—it's also a city." Frema walked toward the phone. "Hello?"

Kokui would not miss this utter lack of privacy. She could hear the person shouting as Frema pulled the phone from her ear. She started to move toward the living room, so at least Frema could converse in an empty kitchen, until she realized who was on the line.

"Gyamfi, what's happening?"

"Your fucking husband. He said he had paid the parking tickets. They towed the taxi yesterday morning."

Frema turned to Kokui. "But Boris and Sammy drove it last night."

Kokui felt her throat tightening, her stomach seizing. Where had Boris and Sammy been all night, then?

"When I went for it this morning, I thought it was stolen. I called the police before I found out Sammy reported it missing. The police have alerted the garage. If I lose my job because of this, hmmm. Right now your husband owes me one hundred and fifty dollars. I'm at the impound lot now."

"How do we know the tickets are Sammy's fault?"

"Don't play games with me, Frema," he shouted. "I just told you the police say Sammy reported the car missing before he realized it was towed, and he didn't even tell me! Besides, the tickets were all given in Harlem, near those bars he likes.

"We are all here helping each other," Gyamfi continued, "but you know the taxi is not for me. I, too, am leasing it from someone. Sammy should have been honest that he couldn't pay. Our arrangement is finished."

Kokui heard the line go dead. "What happened?"

"You heard everything," Frema said.

"Where do you think they were all night?"

Frema shook invisible water droplets from her hands, moving toward the kettle.

Kokui sat silent on the couch, burning, like oil left too long on low heat. She watched the door, waiting for the locks to turn. She could feel Uncle Joe grazing her shoulder with his thumb, could see her father making eyes at Afi and the receptionist, could hear Kofi's mother screeching her pain. She felt so stupid.

She popped to her feet at the sound of the key.

"Boris, where were you last night?"

He blinked blankly at her, the smile he had walked in with faltering. "What are you talking about?"

"Gyamfi phoned," Frema said, removing the kettle from the fire. "They towed the taxi for unpaid parking tickets, yesterday morning."

Jane squirmed in her father's hold. "Daddy, I have to go to the bathroom."

The women sighed as the little girl ran to the toilet.

"I need you to tell me where you were from two to six a.m., Boris."

She watched the apple in Boris's throat rise and drop as he quickly glanced at Sammy.

Sammy exhaled, raising scared eyes to Frema's face. "Boss, I went for a drink at Shorty's."

"Don't call me Boss. I'm not your boss, else you would support me instead of disrespecting me."

His nostrils bloomed.

Kokui bowed her head at the familiar feeling of disappointment in and violation by a man she loved.

"Madame K, Boris didn't join me. He hasn't been joining me for some time. One of our colleagues who works the night shift has been out on maternity leave, so he's been taking her shifts at the hospital."

She raised her gaze to her husband, not even sure what she was looking for. Her father never indicated a thing. Neither had Boris. "Why didn't you tell me?"

"I've told you I don't want to get involved in Sammy and Frema's business."

"You're very much involved," Frema said. "You've enabled him, Boris."

Boris glared at Kokui as she nodded.

"You enabled me, Frema," Sammy said. "Complain, complain, complain. *Sammy, you don't help enough with Jane. Sammy, don't you see I'm tired?* Meanwhile, all the months you couldn't work, wasn't it me hustling for us, working night and day? The pressure pounds, but you won't—"

Kokui leapt back as Frema hurled the kettle at her husband. The metal pot clattered to the linoleum floor, the cover shooting off, hot water splashing up. It just missed him. Just as fast, Sammy slammed Frema's face with his palm.

Kokui recoiled, shock mingling with fear and embarrassment. She wanted to fall to her knees and pick Frema up, but this public humiliation of a wife and mother too closely mirrored what she had run from and so she backed away. She felt so much sadness for this family even as the teapot's sharp oblong spout glinted a secret from the floor. The jagged diamond near Sammy's eye wasn't a birthmark.

"Boris, I want to set off to Buffalo. Now."

Frema growled, her palm covering her cheek. "Sammy, you know our situation," she croaked, "and yet you invited your cousin and his wife to stay with us for five months! Moving our daughter off her bed in the living room to come and sleep with us. When and where are we supposed to have sex with Jane kicking between us?"

From the moment Sammy had made them know Frema wasn't sleeping with him, Kokui thought, she should have put her foot down for Boris and her to find alternate living arrangements. They could have even gone up to Buffalo and settled there.

"He is my brother, Frema," Sammy said. "I've told you how his mother looked after me and my family."

"Boris, we can book a hotel room if the Bucketts can't accommodate us tonight."

"No," Sammy said. "We are going out tonight. I've made the reservation. Besides, you can't get the car without me."

Kokui gritted her teeth. She should have gotten her driver's license and not relied on Boris, but she, too, had been working. Now they had to sit in a car with Sammy for the six- or seven-hour drive to Buffalo.

Boris put his hand on his cousin's arm. "Sammy, we go do it another time, eh? Let's go now."

Sammy's face went tighter with anger and he left the apartment.

"Where is our money?" Kokui asked Boris as she flew to the door.

Her husband tapped his shirt pocket.

"Sammy! Wait. We are going with you to get the car and set off." She went to her handbag and removed the Quarteys' keys from her ring.

"Are you leaving, Auntie?" Jane stepped tentatively out of the bathroom.

"Yes, dear."

Jane moved to her mother and encircled her arms around Frema's hips.

Like a discharged inmate, Kokui's exhilaration mingled with pity. She felt so horrible for this family—and so relieved Boris had not been part of Sammy's overnight rendezvous, or had he? Her husband had lied to her, risking their marriage, to protect his cousin. Maybe Sammy, too, was lying to protect Boris. She pushed the thought away for the moment, returning her focus to getting out of this house. She pulled the trousers and blouse she had folded on top of her suitcase ready for their trip, and changed in the bathroom.

"Let's go." Boris had moved their suitcases to the door.

She turned to her friend. "Frema, thank you for everything."

The women hugged, and Jane joined the circle. "Enjoy school, Madame K."

Kokui nodded. "You, too. Finish and be free."

She grabbed the handles of her bag and followed Boris out, limping with the weight of the suitcase and the speed of her gait.

24

Behind the wheel of the water-blue Pontiac they had rented, Sammy met Kokui's eyes in the rearview mirror with the same look of bravado-cum-shame her father had given her when the officers at the Togo border finally released them.

"You all can't leave New York without a proper farewell."

"It was improper," Kokui said, "but we had our farewell."

Sammy swung the steering wheel. "At least we should stop for breakfast at Shorty's. Eh, Boris? Madame K, we haven't eaten."

She huffed, resigned to see this place he had been going to at the peril of his marriage and his money.

He led them to a bar with its name in red lights, the bulbs switched off for the morning. A sign in the window assured the establishment did indeed serve breakfast.

"Sammy Q!" the bartender shouted.

Their feet crunched on the sticky floors as the waitress, Tina, led them to one of two leather banquettes, gripping Sammy's hand on the way. When she returned with their order, Tina rested an arm on Sammy's shoulder, tracing the hairs on his arm with her fingers. Kokui sucked her teeth. This man was committed to humiliating his wife, she fumed, and putting her and Boris in the uncomfortable position of watching it.

"Tina, has Sammy ever brought his wife or their five-year-old daughter here to see you touching him like that?"

Sammy's eyes went wide with the confrontation, as Tina dropped her arm and returned to her post behind the bar.

"Kokui, it's not your place," Boris said.

"It's not your place to tell me my place, Boris." If no one could stop a man from doing what he wanted to do, no one would stop her from having her say about it, she decided. "Be good to your wife, Sammy. Think of Jane."

Sammy sipped his glass of Coke. "Maybe we should be calling you Prof K the way you are giving lectures."

"Well, I am ready for classes," she said.

She ignored Boris's twitching jaw, and left the cousins to talk among themselves over the casserole of baked eggs and bacon they shared.

When they returned to the car, she stretched sideways on the navy vinyl, drowsy with the meal, still trying to make sense of the morning's—and the prior night's—events.

She watched the city's dense pack of apartment towers give way to rivers and power plants. Through New Jersey and Pennsylvania, they cut their way to upstate New York. It was hard to believe Brooklyn and Manhattan were in the same state as the McDonald's they stopped at on a quiet street opposite a small steepled church. They drove through a series of similarly small towns of shingled houses, some with boats in their driveways, past general stores and roadside farmstands. She gaped as they passed a field of the heftiest bovines she had ever seen. She giggled to herself, imagining her dad and Nami guessing what kinds of meals these cows would end up in.

"Welcome to Buffalo." Sammy echoed the sign he maneuvered them past, into a city square that opened into its own mix of apartment buildings and shingled homes.

He pointed to a building under scaffolding. "This is Buffalo State, where Frema and I transferred after Erie. Boris, remember I was telling you my friend Linda Bonsu works in the admissions office there? She looks out for the Ghanaian students. She and her husband, Mike, were our big brother and sister when we were here. I should take you to her place and introduce you."

"Just take us to the Bucketts'." Kokui had reached her saturation point with Boris's cousin. She did not want to spend another few hours with him, nor did she want to be yoked to another Ghanaian couple. After five months with Sammy and Frema, she wanted the remove of foreigners. After Amos, she didn't want anyone calling her "sister" to pursue their own agenda. "The earlier we go, the better, so we'll know if we can stay with them or have to get a hotel."

"Linda and Mike will let you stay the night, no problem," Sammy said.

Kokui rolled her eyes. Sammy always had some convenience to offer. He had done them much good, but he had done them harm, too.

"By this time," Sammy was saying, "they will even be cooking. Linda is an excellent cook. Her palm nut soup is legend."

"Madame K, let's meet them," Boris said. "I could use some home food. We don't know the next time we'll get any with this camping we're going to do."

"Linda will show you where to shop for groceries," Sammy said.

She gritted her teeth and lay back on her seat, outvoted by the men.

"We've arrived at the Bonsus'."

Kokui sat up. "Already?"

Sammy parked the car in front of a blue, shingled two-story house. The pink tricycle on the wide front porch and the big green Chevy Impala in the driveway looked right out of a television commercial.

"Beautiful place," she said.

Kokui knew better than to assume this facade and its accessories meant the people living inside were happy, but she was weak for any suggestion of family perfection.

"The husband recently graduated from the medical school," Sammy said. "He's the one who got me the job at the hospital, and she works part-time in admissions supporting transfer students while finishing her math degree. They're only in their thirties—Frema's and my age—but they've done so well. Every Ghanaian in Buffalo looks up to them."

Kokui longed for a couple to look up to. The three of them unfurled from the car and climbed the porch.

"Ewuraba Linda!" Sammy pressed the doorbell and clapped the knocker.

"Sammy, paa." Kokui shook her head. "So loud on this quiet street."

"Linda is a woman of the people."

The door swung open to a man peering out, balancing a little girl on his hip. A woman in a long-sleeve T-shirt and trousers, her hair falling thick and full around her face, pushed in front of him. "Who's there?"

Kokui absently touched her ponytail, wondering if Linda's hair was real.

Linda's face relaxed into a smile. "Heh! Sammy Quartey!" The couple folded Boris's cousin into a hug.

"I came to introduce my brother Boris Van der Puye and his wife, Mad—"

"Kokui." She didn't want them thinking she thought herself better than them, when she already thought they were better than her, with their neat, warm house.

"They start Erie next week."

"Congratulations," Linda said. She waved them in. "We are heating up some food."

Sammy turned to wink at them as Linda led the way to the family room. "I told them about your weekly feasts."

"I was just telling Mike we should resurrect them."

Kokui took in the family portraits that lined the walls, interspersed with hopeful clichés. LET LOVE ABIDE WHERE WE RESIDE. HOME IS WHERE LIFE BEGINS AND LOVE NEVER ENDS. MORE BLESSING, LESS STRESSING. She admired the plants that grew green in the corners, the wooden bookshelves lined with schoolbooks and children's books, the leather couches, the peace.

"You have a lovely home," she said.

Linda smiled like she had heard the compliment before. "We weren't planning on settling in Buffalo when we came, but, well, now it's home," she said. "Mike, serve our guests something to drink. Nancy, come and greet your auntie and uncles. Samantha, go and lay the table."

Linda directed her husband and daughters from the embrace of the fat brown leather armchair she had settled in.

"The food should be out shortly."

"I hope we haven't imposed."

"Oh, come on. It's food," Linda said. "So, tell me. How are you finding America so far?"

"We haven't been doing anything but working," Kokui said.

"That's America."

"That was Ghana, too," Boris said. "For some of us."

Linda glanced from Kokui to Boris and back. "Ah, you come from money," she said. "Lucky you, Boris."

Kokui smirked at Boris's tightened jaw.

"Like my wife said, we were working 'round the clock to save money for our housing here," Boris said.

"Have you found a place yet? I know of several good places not too far from the campus, and also affordable. I'll show you," Linda said. "What course are you studying?"

"Accounting."

"That's great. And you, Kokui?"

"She is going for Business—"

"I'm not sure I want to go that way," Kokui said.

"—Administration."

Linda nodded. "No shame in not being sure. Finding your field is a bit like finding your spouse. You need to choose a course that develops your gifts and talents, else you'll be miserable."

Kokui exhaled her appreciation.

"We have to be practical," Boris said.

Mike brought the jollof and chicken out.

"To be continued," Linda said.

"Didn't I tell you Linda is an amazing cook?" Sammy broke the silence of heads bent over full plates.

Linda's husband, Mike, beamed proudly. Kokui did, too. She liked Linda. Very much. She was direct, generous, and seemed so in charge of her home and herself—the kind of woman Kokui wanted to be.

"I made Kokui and Boris detour to meet you all; they had planned to go to their host family," Sammy said. "The thing is, they have come a night early, so we were thinking of greeting their hosts and then looking for a hotel for the night."

"Sammy, you know you don't have to go 'round and 'round with me," Linda said. "You all are welcome to stay the night with us."

"We don't want to impos—"

"Stop with this 'we don't want to impose' talk, Kokui. In this America, we are all family. I'm your big sister."

They spent their first night in Buffalo in the quiet cool of the Bonsus' guest room, making love on a plush, firm mattress that didn't squeak.

The following morning, Linda dropped them at the Bucketts' with an invitation to come for dinner. "After your orientation, you'll be hungry."

"She's wonderful," they both said, arm in arm as they waved at her retreating Chevy.

* * *

"You're here!" Daphne Buckett did a little dance as she held the door open for them.

The sitting room was cluttered with people and overnight bags.

"I'm Missy."

"I'm Russ."

"I'm Craig."

"And this is Sunny, Carla, and Beau."

Kokui and Boris turned to each other and laughed. "We'll remember," she said, as another man came in from outside.

"Hi, I'm Tim." He went straight to Daphne's side.

Kokui blinked as Tim dug his palm in the back pocket of Daphne's jeans.

"Dad, would you please behave?" Missy said. "Boris and Coke-Wee haven't even been here five minutes."

"Well, it's been thirty-seven years for me, but who's counting?"

"Kokui," she corrected, but the family had already started grabbing their bags and trudging outside.

"Ready to sleep under the stars?"

Tim trailed Daphne like a hungry dog.

"I know, it's gross," Missy said, laughing. "They're grandparents, for God's sake."

"It's not gross," Craig said. "They weren't always this way."

Kokui followed them into the camper van, watching Tim stretch to kiss his wife before he started the car.

She should have been sleeping on her second hours-long ride in two days, but Kokui couldn't take her eyes off the Bucketts. They were almost four decades into their marriage, but Tim took every opportunity to brush against, rub, or otherwise touch Daphne, like Tina had with Sammy.

Daphne laughed as Kokui and Boris squinted at the rectangle of grass they ultimately parked on beside a charred square of bricks. "I promise you, you're going to love camping by the end of this week."

Missy and Craig showed them how to put up their tents, while the rest got to work unpacking the van and erecting their own tents. When Kokui and Boris's tent was set up, they went out to find Tim starting the fire. They helped him roast sausages and vegetables. The family ate and drank out of the tin bowls and thermoses Daphne had labeled with their names. Kokui and Boris lingered around the smoldering fire even as the others began to retreat for the night. It was the first time Tim had left Daphne's side since they had gotten to the campsite.

"And then there were three," Daphne said.

Kokui leaned into the fire to light a cigarette. "Wow, Tim is in love."

"In love, or in heat?" Daphne smiled in the direction of the tent. "We worked really hard to get here."

What kind of work, Kokui wanted to know, did it take to maintain a marriage to one person for almost forty years?

"What did you do for your marriage to be like this?" she asked.

"Madame K, that's so personal," Boris said.

"No, I brought it up," Daphne said. "But first, I'll take one of those." She raised a closed peace sign to her lips.

Kokui passed her a cigarette and the two of them puffed clouds of smoke into the air above the crackling fire.

"So, our marital work. Where do I begin?" Daphne laughed another cloud of smoke out. "Tim and I, we got married with all these expectations of what marriage and family were supposed to be, and we spent many, many, many years punishing each other for disappointing those expectations." Her eyes traveled to the memory, a wry smirk curving her lips.

"It was the kids who confronted us. Craig was thirteen, but he led his older sister and brother into our bedroom one night, and they just told us to figure it out or get a divorce. We decided on divorce, but we had just bought the house, and none of us wanted to give it up. We didn't have the money to buy each other out, and neither of us wanted to sell because we had put everything in the house. If we had split that up, we would have had half of not enough to buy something else. We were too broke to break up!" She shrugged, signaling for another cigarette.

"So, we went to counseling at church, and did the assignments our counselor gave us. No 'buts,' just 'ands.' *I love you, Tim,*' and *I would reaalllly appreciate it if you picked your shit up off the floor so I don't trip on it when I'm going to the bathroom at night.*' *Honey, I love you,*' and *I reaalllly need your eyes not to glaze over when I'm telling you about my day or sharing something that's important to me.*' *Darling, I love you,*' and *I'm not your fucking mother.*'"

Kokui could taste the bitterness that seasoned Daphne's snickering demonstration of their conversations.

"*And* what do you know?" Daphne said. "It started working. We stopped trying to destroy each other for not fulfilling our deepest hopes and dreams."

"But are you happy saying 'and' all the time, when you really mean 'but'?" Kokui asked her.

"No," she said, "bu—*and*—I'm happy with the outcome." Daphne squinted at her and Boris. "How many years do you two have?"

"Six months."

"Ouch. That's when the disappointment started to set in for me." She crushed her cigarette into the dirt. "But here we are thirty-seven years later."

Kokui sighed.

"Was that a sigh of disappointment?" Boris asked.

"I think that was a yawn, right, Coke-Wee?" Daphne pushed herself up off her folding chair as light cracked the black sky. "Well, if it had to rain, I'm glad it started now."

Boris muttered when Kokui zipped their tent closed. "If it had to rain, we could have stayed in the city to work one more week."

She chuckled. "My husband, we made good money. We are okay."

"For now," he said.

"That's a good thing," she told him. "To be okay right now."

"Spoken like a Nuga."

Kokui rolled her eyes in the darkness. "Actually, you sound more like my father."

"Just like you like it," he said, inching closer to her.

She pulled away.

"Boris, why didn't you just tell me you weren't driving the taxi those nights?"

She could hear his heart beating.

"You lied to me. For weeks."

"Sammy put me in a bad position."

"Yes, he did," she said. "If he wants to spoil his marriage, that's his choice, but we can't let anyone spoil ours, Boris. We have to be vigilant."

He was silent, his breath speaking for him.

"I'm serious."

"I've known how serious you were since before we married, Madame K. I'm here in these woods with you, aren't I?"

"We're here together," she said.

He clasped her hand. "Just the way I like it."

Kokui stared at the words in the black air. "Do you mean it?"

He released a fatigued breath. "You have to believe there's no one else I want to urinate in a thermos in front of."

"Heh?" She squeezed her face as Boris got up from the sleeping blanket, rooting around in the darkness, the thunder signaling Armageddon outside.

"You can't urinate in Daphne's thermos!" Kokui whispered sharply. "Go out and do it."

"I'm scared to go out there!"

"Ah! I'll go with you."

"We'll be wet."

Kokui pulled the zip down and dragged her husband out of the nylon shelter.

"Oh my God!" She caught herself and lowered her voice.

"What?"

She held out her hands. "Boris, it's dry! The trees are preventing the rain from hitting the ground!"

Tentatively, he stretched his arm through the tent opening. "Wow."

They giggled, darting to the dense woods that rimmed their site on the campground. He pointed, she squatted, and then they both shook, rinsing with the thermos that had almost been their toilet.

"It's amazing, isn't it?" She held out her arms again.

He clasped her hand. "I know it hasn't been easy for you at Sammy and Frema's, but you worked so hard."

She snorted. "You said 'so hard' with such force."

"I mean it," he said. "You've shown me we are in this thing together, that we can be like the Bonsus and the Bucketts one day."

She wondered what "this thing" meant to him. She swallowed, hopeful and unnerved as he pulled her closer. "Will you be satisfied when we get what we came here for?"

"I already am, Madame K." He led her a few feet from where they had marked their spots, deeper into the lushness, and bent down to show her.

She gave in to her body, and to love. Looking up at the leaves shivering in the thunder, but not letting the rain through, she willed herself to believe him.

"Will you be satisfied?" he asked her when they were back in their tent, curled into each other.

Kokui heard a faint plea in his voice that surprised her. "You think I won't be satisfied?"

"Sometimes I fear what you will do if the picture in your mind never matches our life."

She started to protest. Hadn't she shown him what she would do in their months in Bed-Stuy? But she stopped, allowing herself to consider his words. What *would* she do?

25

WELCOME CLASS OF 1976."

The banner hung high on the brick building that greeted them from the entrance, a promise of completion strung across the administration hall's facade. Kokui closed her eyes, a prayer that the next two years would find her on the other side of knowing what she was meant to do with her life. She and Boris alighted from the taxi and followed the flow of students, finding their way into the Student Center, scrawling their names on stickers they pasted on their chests. Tables draped in black cloth lined the atrium in rows, labeled for the different academic disciplines and student resources. She and Boris separated, him to Accounting, her to Academic Guidance.

The woman behind the table smiled at her tentative approach.

"What do I do if I want to change my concentration?" Kokui asked.

"Well, you change it! Perfect time to do it. Before you start down a road you know you don't want to go down."

"That's it?" Years of being told to discipline herself had instilled the idea that changing course should not be done, or be easy. She read the sticker on the woman's chest, swallowing her apprehension. "How do I do that, Kelly?"

"Do you know what you're interested in, Coco-Wee?"

She almost felt relieved by the mispronunciation. She would correct Kelly, and Kelly would guide her. "It's Kokui, and, honestly, I haven't a clue."

"Well, what are you interested in knowing?"

Kokui felt herself go pert with the query. She had never heard the question of purpose posed in that way. "I want to know about—" She felt puerile saying it, but if the truth could lead her to where she could freely be, she was willing to sound childish. "I want to know about men, fidelity, and marriage."

"Don't we all?" Kelly muttered. She plucked a booklet from the short stacks arranged on her table. "We have a Social Science curriculum, with a focus on Anthropology that explores coupling practices throughout history."

Kokui clutched the course catalog. "That sounds interesting."

"You don't have to decide right away," the man at the Social Science table told her. "Sit in on a few classes and see how it feels."

"I can do that?"

"You absolutely can, Coco. It might take you a little longer than two years to finish while you figure it out, but figuring it out's the most important part."

"Thank you, Jim. And my name is Kokui."

"Pleasure to meet you, Coke!"

Kokui found a bench to sit on to read the program description:

AN EXAMINATION OF NON-WESTERN SYSTEMS SUCH
AS THE NATIVE AMERICAN, AFRICAN, ASIAN, INDIAN,

AND OCEANIC PEOPLES, FOR THE PURPOSE OF GAIN-
ING AN UNDERSTANDING AND APPRECIATION OF HOW
OTHER CULTURAL GROUPS LIVE, COMMUNICATE,
MATE, CREATE FAMILY STRUCTURES, BUILD CUL-
TURAL VALUES, GOVERN, WORSHIP, AND EVOLVE.

She frowned at the words, curious about the focus on "non-Western systems." What did that even mean? In Ghana, the language of school and business was English, marriage increasingly involved a customary ceremony and a "white wedding," and the government was modeled on Britain's parliamentary system. Three and a half centuries under British rule, and historic contact with the Danes, the Dutch, the Germans, and the Swedes had mixed them all up. For better and for worse, what had started out as foreign to them they had absorbed and remade into their own. Their names said it all—Eleanor Kokui Nuga Van der Puye and Boris Nii Afutu Van der Puye—as did their lives. And yet, she was intrigued by this proposition to examine mating and family from a purely cultural perspective. She wanted to detangle what she knew and evaluate for herself the customs that had been in place before the British had come.

Kokui tingled with the flame of curiosity and the warm calm of a settled decision.

"There you are."

She looked up to find Boris holding his own paperwork.

"I'm going to shift my concentration to Social Science."

He squeezed his face. "Madame K, I thought we were going to focus on a practical course of study."

She handed him the course catalog opened to the Anthropology description. "Read it. This is what I need to be studying. You said it yourself. Remember when we were filling out my application at your uncle Joe's? You told me I should try Anthropology."

"Try it," he said. "Not make it your concentration."

"But this is what I want to study, Boris."

"Why do we have to keep rehashing the plan, Madame K? This is not a joke. We aren't here to explore our interests."

Kokui flinched. He made it sound so trivial when he knew that was exactly what she needed to do. Otherwise, why not just stay in Ghana working at Nuga & Heirs? Why not make him stay at the job her father had given him?

"We need to choose a course that will enable us to find good-paying jobs," he continued.

"Boris, I had a good-paying job in Ghana." She didn't add, "And so did you, once you married me," but he hissed anyway.

"Madame K, wasn't I right about you working with Frema? You wasted one whole week looking for work, but in the end, when you supported Frema, you were able to earn over twenty-five hundred dollars. Look what we were able to do together. Trust me," he said.

Kokui sighed.

"I'm not saying you shouldn't take the Anthropology course. I'm saying take it as an elective—or make it your concentration in addition to the Business Administration."

She looked back down at the booklet. She wanted to do the right thing for herself, and for her marriage—why did it increasingly seem that she had to choose one over the other?

"Okay," she said.

Boris smiled that salesman smile again.

* * *

In her letter to her mother, Kokui wrote of the camping trip, and the rain that didn't come through the canopy of trees. "I'm sure everyone in the village has experienced this, but it was so beautiful to me, Ma. Not every storm has to get us wet."

To her father, she wrote of the one-bedroom apartment on the first floor of a three-story house Linda Bonsu had helped them find just fifteen minutes' drive from campus, the used car they had bought, and the orientation that preceded the start of classes. "I've been renamed 'Coke,'" she wrote. "It's too tiring to correct each mispronunciation.

"In addition to Principles of Accounting, and all the other Business Administration requirements," she told him, "I've elected to take Cultural Anthropology. It's five classes instead of four, but I'm enjoying the Anthropology course."

To Nami, she told almost everything. The idyllic home the Bonsus had made for themselves in Buffalo, how warmly they had welcomed them, and how Linda Bonsu had encouraged her to take her time and find the right course.

I know you don't understand. You've always been so clear and so focused on what you wanted to do, Nami. I'm glad Daddy has an heir to carry on his business. Me? I'm still unsure. I have felt so ashamed of my uncertainty, but Linda has encouraged me to explore, even if Boris thinks it's frivolous for me to do so.

So far, I'm feeling led to pursue anthropology. I love that class so much I took a job as an assistant in the Anthropology department. We have started first by looking at the animals—how birds, snakes, frogs, and fish mate, and what they do after. Most, like the lions, either reproduce and go their own way or form arrangements with multiple partners, but some, like vultures and eagles, devote themselves to one partner for life. We humans are

*somewhere between the vultures and the lions, trying to figure out
how to balance our individual needs and wants with that of a
mate and children, if we have any.*

*Needs and wants. This has been my fight with Boris. I'm real-
izing a big part of marriage is determining what I'm willing to
give up or give in to to ensure our survival. Things have been better
since we left Brooklyn, but still, sometimes I feel he wants to grind
me into the ground—to make me pay for not having to struggle
as he did to get here. I keep trying to explain to him that struggle
is different for everyone, that every human being has their own
struggle.*

*Remember when I said that I liked that he didn't have money?
Now I wish he had some so he could stop obsessing over it. I miss not
having to consider the cost of every single thing, but it does feel good
to earn a living free of Daddy. Yes, he is still paying my tuition, but
if he stops, I know I can do it myself.*

*I miss you, too, Sis. As I try to balance five classes and work, I
think of you, my junior sister, beginning your third year at Legon,
working with Daddy. You are a marvel to me. Tell me how you do
it, and how you are.*

Kokui folded the letters in their envelopes and closed the flap of
her bag.

She bounced out of the library to make her way to the parking
lot to meet Boris. Wednesday evenings were the one night a week
neither of them worked, before the one day a week she didn't have
class. When it was warmer, they would drive to the park and lay
on the sheet she packed, shielding their eyes from the sun as they
talked about their classes and whatever else was on their minds.

Now that October was yielding to November, they spent the time at home, huddled in front of the fireplace enjoying leftovers with tall glasses of beer.

She smiled to find Boris waiting in their used Beetle, warming it up for her. It was another battle she had won after his initial complaint that running the heat ate into the gas. She slid into the front seat and rested her hand on his thigh as he pulled out of the parking space.

"How was your day?" She asked him first to save her news for when they got home.

"I just learned, after this semester, I'll have enough credits to transfer to Buffalo State. Linda says she can help me with the paperwork."

She felt jealousy prick her. Everyone, except her, seemed to have their path figured out. "That's great."

"The faster I get my full degree, the faster we'll be on our way to earning real money. Then you will see I'm not as cheap as you think. We, too, will have a couch bed to offer family to sleep on for five months."

"Very funny," she said.

"I got a letter from Sister Tsotsoo," he said, starting the car. "She says the house is in disrepair. My brother wants me to send money."

"How much do they need?"

"Five hundred cedis."

She bit her lip. That was over four hundred dollars.

"My brother who wouldn't even give me a key to my own mother's house. My brother who is still hoarding the rent for himself."

Between the car, their rent, schoolbooks, groceries, and proper coats, boots, and clothes for the weather, they had already spent close to half the money they had made their first months in New York, but Kokui didn't want to encourage Boris's miserliness. If it had been up to him, they would be walking an hour to and from campus every day.

"You know what, Boris, just send your brother the money," Kokui said. "We still have over three thousand dollars left, and we are working."

"I don't want it to become a habit."

"We don't have enough for him to keep coming back, but he is your brother. No matter what he did, he looked after you. Just give it to him. We are working."

"We aren't making what we were in New York, Madame K."

"Then don't give it. Ah!"

He looked startled by her frustration. "Okay, I'll give it to him. Maybe next month."

"Have you heard from Sammy?"

"Why?"

"I've been trying to reach Frema since we came to Erie, to see if she is okay."

"Kokui, you don't know how to mind your business."

"I've called a few times to check on her, left her messages, but she hasn't responded."

"Madame K, we can't afford to be calling long distance to Brooklyn!" he huffed.

She rolled her eyes, not in the mood to fight.

"It's you I'm concerned about," Boris said, his tone tender again. "How are you feeling? What did the nurse say?"

She had wanted to tell Boris when they were at home, out of the car, relaxed, but he had just turned onto their street.

"I'm pregnant."

She exhaled. This was the second child who had defied her birth control.

He turned from the road to look at her. "I thought—"

201

"You see me take the pill every day. I'm religious about it, but the nurse says it happens. She estimates I'm seven weeks along. Plenty of time to take care of it. She says I can have it done in Syracuse, or go to New York and do it. It will cost us two hundred dollars, plus some fees."

"Two hundred dollars!"

"It's not free, Boris."

He nodded. "Sammy can do it for you at the hospital."

Kokui frowned. "Do what?"

"He can assign your bill to a patient and then they can dispute the charge."

She searched her husband's profile for sense. "Boris, why would we do that?"

"You want me to give my brother four hundred dollars."

"Boris, we have the money to do both."

"But with Sammy's help, it will be free."

"I don't want to do anything underground. Not when we don't have to."

He hissed as he slowed the car in front of their house.

"Ho! Why are you angry? I didn't impregnate myself, Boris."

"I know," he said. He sucked in a deep breath. "We can ask Linda for the money. Or the Bucketts."

"What? Boris, why would we have to ask the Bonsus or the Bucketts to help us pay for an abortion, when we have the money to pay ourselves?"

He bowed his head.

"What is going on, Boris?"

He turned to face her. "I loaned Sammy the money."

"What money?"

"The garage fired Gyamfi for subleasing the taxi. He demanded Sammy give him four thousand dollars."

"Four thousand dollars! For what?"

"He's going to pay us back."

"How? Sammy doesn't have Gyamfi's taxi to drive anymore."

"Gyamfi used the money to buy a car he wants to use as his own taxi. They plan to split the earnings." Boris said it with his chest out. "I think we could all make some money."

She couldn't believe the words coming from her husband's mouth. "Boris, why would you give Sammy the money we both worked so hard for? Not to mention the money my father gave us!"

"Madame K, you said it yourself. Sammy did so much for us."

"You were mad at me when I gave his wife two hundred dollars to help them."

"Because you didn't ask me."

"What?" She almost laughed. "Did you ask me? Let's be clear, Boris, I don't need your permission to give money my father gave us."

"Here we go." He threw his hands up. "Your father."

"Yes, my father who paid for our flight to New York. He's the reason we were able to come when we did."

He punched the steering wheel.

"Get out of the car. I'm driving to Linda's."

"Why?" Boris demanded.

"I want to talk to Linda."

"You don't have to bring her into our business."

"You were just saying you were going to ask her for the money!"

"I wasn't going to tell her what it was for."

"Get out of the car, Boris."

He left the key in the ignition and slammed the driver's door.

Kokui crawled over the partition and turned the Beetle around. She heard herself wheezing, felt her hands shaking as she drove. She had gone too easy on Boris when she learned he had lied about driving the taxi with Sammy, she told herself. Maybe if she had thrown a kettle at him they would not, again, be at the bottom of another lie.

She stopped outside the blue-shingled house, trying to steady her breath, yearning for the calm she had felt inside, needing Linda's forthright, judgment-free wisdom.

Kokui climbed the porch and clapped the door knocker. She pulled at the streamer that plumed from the handlebars of Nancy's bike as she waited.

"Kokui," Linda said, surprise digging ridges into her brow. "Everything all right?"

"Can I come in?"

Linda closed the door behind her. "What is it?"

"I'm pregnant."

She inhaled. "Have you told Boris?"

Kokui nodded.

"What do you want to do?"

"This is not the time for us to have a child."

"You don't want the child, but Boris does?" Linda asked.

"Boris loaned Sammy all our money." She burst into tears. "Telling me Sammy can fraudulently apply my bill to another patient, if I abort at his hospital."

Linda filled her chest again. "How much time do you have?"

"The nurse says I'm seven weeks along."

"Good," Linda said. "You have time. I'll loan you the money."

"It's two hundred dollars. Plus hospital fees."

"Just pay me when you can," Linda said. "I've told you. We are family. My big sister did it for me, now I'm doing it for you."

Kokui drew back.

"What?" Linda asked.

She had forgotten all about it. "I'll be back."

Kokui ran to the car and drove home. She sat in the darkness for several minutes, only her cigarette lighting the car as she gathered the strength to enter their apartment and face her husband. This man was not her father, she told herself, he was worse! No, he wasn't cheating with women, but he was lying to her, the root of infidelity, putting their relationship and finances at risk to save his foolish, irresponsible cousin. It wasn't even a year into their marriage and look what he was doing. What would he do if she stayed? Her mother had warned her, and she hadn't listened, but she could hear clearly now. She had done her best, but this marriage wasn't working. She had forced it, rushed it—she had chosen wrongly. She would write and tell her mother so. Baby Kofi's mother had gotten her wish.

She walked out of the car and made the slow march up the stoop. Boris hovered on the other side of the door.

"I called you at Linda's," he said, "but you had left already."

"Boris, I can't—"

"Madame K, your father," he said.

Kokui wanted to scream. "What again about my father, Boris?"

"He's dead."

"He's . . . ?" Kokui studied Boris's face, waiting for him to finish his sentence: . . . *dead tired . . . dead-set against. Dead . . .*

"I've called Sammy. He is working on getting the money for your ticket home."

She heard all the air leaching out of her body as she sat down. She missed the sofa, falling in a clump on the floor.

Boris knelt beside her. "Madame K, did you hear me? Sammy is organizing the money for your t—"

"I have the money, Boris."

"You do? From where?"

"My mother."

He frowned, surprised. "Well, I—I'll come with you," he said.

"Don't, Boris."

She pulled herself up, passed the fire crackling in the hearth and moved into their bedroom. In the closet, she pulled her suitcase down. The hard plastic case clattered to the floor, empty, except for the envelope in its lining.

26

Micheline was the first person she saw in the crush of people waiting outside the airport baggage hall. Her mother, not in a shimmering silk boubou, but in the widow's duku, kaba, and slit. Nami and Sister Eyram stood on either side of her, the noon sun a burning outline around them, their hands clasped tightly.

"What do you mean Daddy is dead?"

Kokui had been wanting to ask since Boris had told her, and on the whole ride from Buffalo to Bed-Stuy, from JFK to the connection at Robertsfield, to the final leg to Kotoka. Now that she and her family were face-to-face, the Accra heat licking her pores open, the hope of misunderstanding died in her throat. She swallowed the dry lump of grief, the action a flame to her gullet, already swollen with tiredness and tears.

"Let's go to the car," Nami said.

Kokui marched alongside the women in their black cloth, wearing the pink suit she had worn to the airport the day she and Boris had left for New York, the last time she had seen her father. The porter who had noisily commandeered her luggage from the conveyor belt in the mayhem of the arrivals area silently trailed them to the car park, a sort of funeral procession. She blinked at the Togo license plate on the bottle-green Peugeot hatchback they stopped at. Afi was in the passenger seat, balancing Kofi on her lap. A driver Kokui didn't know started packing her suitcases into the boot.

"Nelson didn't drive you?"

She looked again at the motley mix they made as they clambered into the car. Sister Eyram, like the other Nuvis, had little tolerance for Micheline, and the feeling was mutual, but here she was now in this car from Togo. Why wasn't she at home with Kofi? Kokui searched Nami's face for the answer, even as she noted the others waiting with the bated breath of old gossip about to be shared with fresh ears.

Nami inhaled slowly, her lips setting in a straight line. Kokui gulped for air, dread setting in. Their father had died. What more could be making her sister speechless?

"What is it, Nami?"

"Auntie Hemaa," she said. "She has put us out of Daddy's house."

"Ah! What are you talking about?"

A dam of "hmmms" broke out in the car as the driver maneuvered them off the airport grounds.

"I'm at the hostel at school—at least until the term is up," Nami said.

"Kofi and I are with Efo Cletus and the rest," Sister Eyram added.

Kokui shook her head, trying to make room for what she was hearing. If her father's death was true, this, at least, had to be a mistake. She squeezed her face, then blinked, trying to picture it. She couldn't. The Auntie Hemaa she knew was too dispassionate to be vindictive.

"Ah!" she sputtered again. "How?"

"I told your father she was a witch," Sister Eyram said.

But Sister Eyram had also told Mawuli Micheline was a witch—as she had of Auntie Abui, Auntie Rebecca, and Auntie Hannah.

"From the day he brought that woman to the house," Sister Eyram continued, her voice and arm rising with her pointing finger, "she had him under a different kind of juju. Sister Abui had been holding on, but that woman's juju was too strong. No one could marry him after Sister Hemaa came."

Kokui looked to her mother. Micheline had also held on. Was it Auntie Hemaa's juju, her mother's, or her father's—or was it something else altogether?

"She's filed a claim seeking Letters of Administration over Daddy's estate," Nami said.

"A claim? On what grounds?"

"That she is the only legal Mrs. Nuga."

"Ah!" Kokui looked from her sister to her mother. "But?"

"He did Part Three with her," Micheline said.

Kokui closed her eyes. Her father had wed her mother, and each of his wives, in the customary way, first Knocking for them, then taking the second step of presenting their families the items listed on the dowry, along with the bottles of liquor to seal the nuptial agreement. Those who had divorced him had also done so according to tradition—the women's families returned the drinks. It was only with Auntie Abui and Auntie Hemaa, however, that he had taken a third step to celebrate in the Evangelical Presbyterian Church courtyard and submit a license to the Marriage Registrar. Auntie Abui had divorced him. His union with Auntie Hemaa was his only marriage, on paper.

"But we are his children. By law, we are his heirs, not her," Kokui said. Micheline had always made sure to emphasize this to her and Nami. "Have we contacted Daddy's lawyer?"

"Lawyer Denu is the one who told me. Under the Marriage Ordinance, as the 'Mrs.,' she's entitled to two-ninths of his estate," Nami said. "Ma can contest if she can prove she was his wife, too."

"I've filed." Micheline tilted her chin up. "You all are my proof."

"The rest of the estate is for the Nuvis and us to share," Nami went on. "But since Daddy had children with different women, our rights differ—which dilutes our individual positions, and makes hers stronger. For now."

Kokui bowed her head, her heart on fire for her mother. Her father had been dead less than seventy-two hours. She wanted to grieve him, not his libido. She had done the latter enough. But it remained unavoidable. Even from the grave he was humiliating Micheline.

"Doesn't she have to wait for his will to be read?"

"By doing it now, since all his other kids, except me, are in Abrokye, and the Nuvis don't have the funds to file, she assumes control of Daddy's estate until his will is read, or until we counter-file and get a judge to assign us power of attorney until the will is read," Nami said. "For now, the business, and any properties Daddy acquired before updating his will, are under her power, and any heirs he didn't mention before updating his will have to contest in court."

Sister Eyram collected Kofi from Afi.

"She can liquidate the estate or do anything else she wants until then. Not legally, but if she were to do so, it would be difficult to stop her. She won't give us access to the house so we don't even know what she is doing."

"But Auntie Hemaa has more properties and money than Daddy ever had," Kokui said.

"And no children to pass them on to." Micheline repeated what she had always banked on.

"Why would she do this?"

"I knew she would do this," Micheline said.

"I have told you why," Sister Eyram said, clutching Kofi tightly. "Just like I told your father: the woman is a witch."

Kokui's heart split for her stepmother. She had never understood why, or how, Auntie Hemaa stuck around, watching Mawuli leave her year after year to drive to Micheline, knowing full well he was also unfaithful with others. It couldn't have been for the "Mrs." title, Kokui mused. Auntie Hemaa's first cousin was the reigning Asantehene—royal blood ran through her veins.

Love had been the unsatisfactory answer Kokui came up with. Only love could make such humiliation seem worth it, she concluded, only love would need this validation beyond the grave. Or had it been masochism, she wondered. Had Auntie Hemaa been plotting to assume a control over Mawuli in death that had eluded her while he was alive?

"She is a businesswoman," Nami said. "We have to strategize, accordingly."

"I don't want to strategize!" Kokui heard herself. She knew she sounded like Whining Willie, but she didn't care. "Where is Daddy? Can I see him?"

Nami nodded. "We have control of the body."

"She wanted to do a One Week service." Sister Eyram twisted her head and tutted. "I told her he didn't become an Asante man when he put his penis inside her. We, we are Ewes," she said, slapping her chest.

Nami exhaled the ragged exhaustion of three more days than Kokui of hearing things like this. "We'll go to him after you settle."

"Settle where?"

"Ah!" Sister Eyram said, impatient. "I've told you we are at the house your father built us. We will never lose that house. He gifted it to us."

Kokui swallowed her protest. It had been one thing to stop in at the Nuvi house with her father for a quick visit on the way to her mother's, but to stay in Juapong, in that bungalow crowded with her cousins? She gulped her spit again, sobered by the abruptness of her new reality. Bed-Stuy had not been a test. It had been a preview.

She leaned her head against the window as the car rolled toward the Tema Motorway. They rode through the scarred road bordered by lush green land, past the small towns that led the way to the Adomi Bridge. The hawkers descended, as usual, as they waited to cross to the other side. Afi bought a small bag of adɔdi skewers. She held a kebab out to Micheline.

"Ma, you haven't eaten all day."

"You know I don't eat these roadside clams," Micheline said.

Afi was still smacking her lips on the dried seafood when they turned and stopped at the Nuvi compound.

Efo Cletus sat enthroned on a plastic chair in front of the uncles, aunties, and cousins, sitting thick and deep in their black mourning clothes, spilling off the veranda where they used to receive Kokui, Nami, and Mawuli. Instead of slipping his cousin a Christmas envelope, Mawuli leaned against the wall, his eyes blazing at them from a blown-up photograph. One of the boys was distributing bottles of Coke to the mourners.

"Ao, Nɔvinye, you were good to us." Sister Eyram spoke to Mawuli's spirit as they disembarked from the car. "If not for you, and this house you built us, where would we even cry your name?"

The driver began to unload Kokui's bags.

"How long are we staying here?" she asked Nami.

"We are here, for now. So far, Auntie Hemaa hasn't told us to vacate."

Sister Eyram dragged the lower lid of her left eye down. "Let her try and see."

Kokui felt her mind push against her skull. This was really happening. "We have to go and talk to her."

"You were closer with her. Maybe she will listen to you," Nami said. "In the meantime, you can stay here or go to Togo with Ma after Daddy's burial."

"You should stay in Accra," Micheline said. "You can go to Boris's people. Your sister can stay with you in your husband's room until we sort this all out, but I don't know how much time you have before you have to return to America."

Kokui felt her face go hot. She couldn't think about Boris right now—or the spirit slowly growing flesh and bone inside her body. "Where is Daddy?"

"At the mortuary."

"Take me."

"Go with your sister," Micheline said.

She clasped Nami's hand as they waited in the car for the driver to carry Kokui's suitcases inside. "What happened, Nami? How did Daddy die? How did things come to this?"

"I was in class when they called me out to tell me Daddy was gone."

"Who called you out of classes?"

"Auntie Hemaa."

That sounded more like their stepmother. Going to Nami so she would hear it from her and not anybody else. Auntie Hemaa never shrank from delivering difficult or uncomfortable news. "What did she say?"

"She told me she and Daddy went to bed, and the next morning, he didn't wake up."

"He died in his sleep?" Their father wasn't even fifty-four.

"The coroner at Korle Bu did the autopsy himself for Daddy. He says it was his heart. Apparently, Daddy's heart was so enlarged, it didn't have the strength to pump anymore."

Kokui wiped the tear that slid past her nose, the salt slipping between her lips at the irony. In the end, her father's heart had been too big for his body.

"Sister Eyram thinks Auntie Hemaa did it," Nami said.

"Maybe she did," Kokui said. Anything seemed possible now.

"After she told me, we drove to the house and she asked Nelson to pack my things."

"What?"

Nami nodded. "I think she filed her claim before she came to tell me Daddy was gone."

"Why did you leave, Nami?"

"What do you mean why did I leave?"

"That's our father's house. She has no right."

"But she does," Nami said. "We have rights, too. In fact, our rights are greater than hers if we can organize ourselves."

Kokui heard herself wheezing again. "How, Nami? Auntie Hemaa is a millionaire. She has the money to pay for a court case. Now, we have nothing, at least not until we know what's in Daddy's will."

"I've already contacted Bro Antony and Sister Esime and Sister Connie and Bro Yao and Sister Fafa and Sister Emefa and Sister Elikem and Sister Elinam."

Kokui lowered the corners of her mouth, impressed by the logistical and emotional effort she knew it had taken to obtain their siblings' contacts and reach out to them one by one. "What are they saying?"

"Sister Connie wants nothing to do with this, or us."

Kokui nodded. "Why would she?" Connie's mother had gone mad when she discovered Mawuli's infidelity, and died shortly thereafter.

"Sister Esime, Elinam, and Elikem say they will send whatever monies they can, but they are not coming to Ghana for the funeral," she continued. "Bro Antony is coming to represent himself, Bro Yao, Sister Fafa, and Sister Emefa, which is good, since he and Bro Yao are the eldest. We just have to be careful," Nami said. "As males, their rights to Daddy's estate may take precedence over ours."

Kokui rolled her eyes. "It's never 'woman's matter' when it comes to money." She sighed. "Where are we going to get the funds to fight this, Nami?"

"You wrote that you and Boris had saved some thousands."

She smiled sadly at the memory of herself writing that letter. If only she had known what the next few months would bring.

"Between you and Sister Esime, Elinam, Elikem, Fafa, and Emefa, and Bro Yao and Antony," Nami said, "we should be able to mount a strong defense. Ma is going to contribute, too."

This wasn't the time to tell her sister about Boris foolishly loaning their money to his cousin. "I know we'll get donations from Daddy's clients, the Colonel, the ministers."

"Hmmm," Nami said. "The Minister for Lands has been brought up on some corruption investigation, and there is one Solomon Kusi in the office who has made it his mission to scrutinize all existing land grants, including Daddy's. Remember, I wrote you about it."

Solomon Kusi. That was his name. Kokui could see the man's smirking face as he humiliated Boris.

"He found some exchanges between Daddy and the minister,"

Nami said. "Daddy temporarily transferred the deed to Auntie Hemaa's name to keep the land. She suggested it."

The sisters went silent with the driver's arrival, and held hands as he started the car.

* * *

A copy of the photograph that leaned on the Nuvi veranda hung in banner size on the white perimeter wall of the Eleanor Kekeli Nuga Hospital. WHAT A SHOCK, the poster read. WE REMEMBER OUR PATRON FESTUS MAWULAWOE NUGA, 1921–1974. *DADDY, MLƆ NYUIEDE!*

"They are preparing his body free of charge," Nami said. "We are very lucky."

Kokui nodded.

There was a time the small infirmary was a stop on their annual journey to Micheline's.

The year Micheline left Kokui and Nami with their father, Mawuli took over operations and financed a modest expansion to include more bed space, an operating theater, and a home for the doctor they brought in from Accra. But after the first coup, the visits stopped. It surprised Kokui to see the hospital still standing, and to know that her dad had remained committed to it all these years. Mawuli's ability to scatter his seeds didn't only apply to women and business, she could almost hear him saying to her.

Inside, she looked up at the framed photograph of her father's mother hanging above and behind the reception desk—the same one that hung in Mawuli's bedroom. In most of Kokui's childhood memories, her grandmother had been skin shrouding bones on a sickbed. This black-and-white photo of a twentysomething woman determinedly gazing at an unknown north was the only proof

Kokui had had that Eleanor Kekeli Nuga had once been everything Mawuli told them she was: a woman who had confronted insecurity to change her destiny. Kokui had never seen the resemblance the Nuvis gushed about, but she looked for it now, trying to discern a connection with the night-skinned woman in the printed head-tie as they waited to be taken to Mawuli.

One of the attendants at reception ushered them to the hospital morgue, through the main building and out to a small annex. The diamond shapes cut into the wall allowed light and air to pass through, but still the room felt dark and dank.

"Normally, the mortuary director would like to be here, but we will make an exception for your father."

The woman led them into a small room inside the annex where Mawuli's naked body lay on what looked like a wooden work table, still being prepared for presentation. Kokui gasped, grief brimming in her eyes again.

Death's brutality was its finality, and the mockery it made of a life once lived. Emptied of his spirit, Mawuli was almost unrecognizable.

His hair had been freshly dyed, his skin powdered, his eyes and lips sewn shut, his hands hidden under white gloves he never would have chosen to wear. Embalmer's thread made a chain of x's down his chest, disappearing under the cloth that covered his navel and hips. The cloth was one of Micheline's, the cock printed on the fabric staring at them.

"Oh, Daddy." Kokui sank onto the bench that protruded from the wall, twisting to turn her back to the cadaver. "He couldn't warn us of his death with sickness?"

Nami sat with her. "You know he would say, 'You have to prepare . . .'"

"'For every eventuality,'" they chorused.

The sisters shared a small smile even as Kokui shook her head. There were some things you could never prepare for, even when you did.

"Do you know if Auntie Hemaa intends to pay for the funeral?"

"Because of her claim, we think it will bolster our case if Ma pays—adding to whatever you and Bro Yao and Bro Antony and Sister Fafa and Sister Emefa and Sister Elikem and Sister Elinam and Sister Esime can contribute," Nami said.

Kokui snorted at the roll call. The third time her sister had done so in the last hour. "Don't forget Baby Kofi. He, too, has to bring his share."

"I'll leave it to you to tell Sister Eyram Kofi has to pay up."

"I hate that Ma is putting any money in this."

Nami sighed. "Well, he was her husband."

"And Sister Eyram says the women are the witches," Kokui said.

"I've always said his juju was the strongest."

Kokui stared at the cloth that dangled from the table. "He certainly was something."

Kokui and Nami's—and Yao's and Antony's and Fafa's and Elikem's and Elinam's and Esime's and Connie's and Emefa's and Baby Kofi's—father had been a magnetic man, to say the least, but how he had come upon this magnetism, perhaps only his mother knew.

Eleanor Kekeli Nuvi, then known as "Adzovi," was fifteen years old when she birthed Mawuli. There was talk he was the child of the cousin who assumed responsibility for her when her mother, Adzo, died, while others said Mawuli's father was the uncle who had taken her in after she ran from the cousin. But Mawuli gave sole credit for his appearance on Earth to his mother. Pregnant with him, and exiled to Juapong where her uncle Festus ran the small missionary printing and bookbinding shop he owned, she determined to change her, and his, life, and she did.

As Mawuli told it, his mother read the Bible and the other literature that arrived at Uncle Festus's shop like they were storybooks. She mooned over the Scripture's romances, in particular, Abram and Sarai's, and the triangle they had forced their young maid Hagar into, most capturing her imagination. In their story, God bestowed them each with new names pregnant with the promise of a future divorced from their past. Eleanor Kekeli wondered what might be possible for her if she had a new name.

Her first names designated her a bright light—but her whole life she had only been called "Adzovi," after her dead mother. *Little Adzo*. Compounded with her surname, she wondered if the reason she had felt not only small, but invisible, was because littleness was being spoken over her every time someone called her.

When the time came to name the baby boy she groaned, grunted, and growled out of her body, she changed both of their names. With hoarse conviction, she declared he would be called Mawulawoe Nu*ga*. "God will do a big thing for me and my child," she said.

Eager to confirm her conversion but focus it on who God was rather than what God would do for her, Uncle Festus nicknamed the boy "Mawuli." *There is a God*.

Mawuli grew into an uncommonly sharp child (his words). He was fast to parse the content of the pamphlets and books he helped Uncle Festus unwrap and repack for courier distribution to the different E.P. Church mission offices, and faster to intuit the unspoken yearnings of a soul. He knew what people needed to hear so they could receive what he had to say, a gift his uncle noticed as he watched the boy share the gospel tracts he gave him to disseminate in the market.

It wasn't that Mawuli was a charmer; it was that he sincerely desired a connection with everyone he encountered. Mawuli said he felt something go out of him each time he pressed the paper leaflets into the hands of a new soul—like Jesus must have felt when the woman who had hemorrhaged for twelve years was healed when she touched the hem of his garment. He saw the paper as a medium, transferring feelings, thoughts, hopes, and memories like a tradition, like a song, preserving them for eternity, and he sold it as such when he began peddling paper to different missionary societies for Weber und Söhne Papier, the manufacturers of the paper the tracts were printed on.

The success of his charismatic approach earned him the notice of Jan Weber and his sons, a ticket to their mill in Steinau an der Straße and an apprenticeship. To have Mawuli tell it, the Weber men were so utterly enthralled by his astral acumen, not even two years into his apprenticeship, that Jan Weber gave Mawuli the seed money to build his own mill in Ghana.

"Please, are you all okay?" The attendant poked her head into the embalmer's room, interrupting the sisters' reverie.

Kokui and Nami didn't answer. Nothing was okay right now. Instead, they rose and thanked her, and made their way back to the Nuvis' and to Micheline.

27

Her father's death-gray cadaver. Her stepmother's decision to humiliate her mother and her dead husband's children. Her failing marriage. The spirit growing quietly in her body. These were the things that had woken Kokui up, not the cock's crow, but she sat up at the rooster's piercing announcement of the new day. What had happened to this bird, she wondered, that compelled it, and its generations, to wail at the morning?

On the bed she had shared with her mother and sister, in the room her auntie had given up for them, she, too, bemoaned this day that promised more heaviness.

"We have to set off so we can pick up Bro Antony from the airport," Nami said.

"Now?" Kokui was up, but not yet ready to be up. "What time does his flight land?"

"Just after noon, but we have other things to do in Accra."

"I don't know why you got Antony and the rest involved. Their mothers divorced your father," Micheline said.

"Ma, they are still his children," Kokui said. "I'm sure Daddy has left all his kids something in his will."

"Your father promised me he would sort my daughters out differently," Micheline said.

Kokui closed her eyes. How, after all her father had done to her mother, could Micheline hold on to any promise Mawuli had made?

"Kokui, you have to ask your in-laws for a room to stay. After the burial, it will be easier for you all to navigate from Accra, and cheaper."

"But I'm not going to be here that long, Ma." She had to figure out how she would pay for her next semester of school. She had to deal with her marriage. "I have to go back."

"The room is not for you," Micheline said. "It's for your sister."

Kokui turned from her mother's penetrating gaze. To ask for a room at Boris's house, she would have to call her husband first. She knew she had to, for the practical reasons: confirm she had arrived safely, tell him all that was happening, ask him to send her paycheck. But she wasn't ready to speak with him, or to face the mess of their marriage on a phone call. She burned with remorse for her self-righteousness. She had been so smug with her mother. For so long she had judged Micheline's choice to stay. She had been so sure she could get right what her mother had gotten wrong, forgetting she was no better than either of her parents except in the ways they had enabled her to be.

Mawuli was many things as a husband, and his betrayal of her mother and their family was part of the reason Kokui fought a fundamental sense of feeling rudderless, but he was not her husband. He had been a good father to her, in spite of his weaknesses, heaping her with lessons and with luxuries his death had yanked away, while wrestling with the life he had been born into. The way Mawuli told his own story, he had been charmed from birth, and maybe he had been—but he had also been born to a girl on the run, a girl who had been violated first by a man and then by the whispers that cared more about who the man was than how she was, a girl so desperate to change her destiny she assumed a new identity. He was a powerful, intriguing, admirable man, but he was still a man, seeking the balance between his needs, wants, and responsibilities, like every other bird, snake, frog, fish, and lion.

Kokui crawled off the bed and carried the bucket of water her cousin had filled for her to the bathroom. She was grateful her dad had built the bungalow to specifications he would have wanted, and not gone cheap because his relatives were poor. He had invested in digging a borehole and installing plumbing inside the Nuvis' house. The neighbors had illegally tapped the aquifer, reducing the water pressure for everyone who used it until it was only the outdoor tap that flowed with full, reliable force, but when Efo Cletus cursed them, Mawuli chastised him.

"You can't be the only ones drinking and expect thirst to go away," he said.

Once bathed and powdered, Kokui and Nami sat for another hour-plus ride to Accra.

"You don't want to ask Boris's family about the room," Nami said as they bent to urinate behind the filling station. "Why?"

Kokui took the fold of toilet roll Nami handed her. She wanted to tell her sister that her marriage was not only struggling, as she had written, but not working—but she was not ready to talk through what she could or should do about it. Not now. "Let's go to Daddy's first. See if we can reason with Auntie Hemaa. I'm sure we can resolve this differently."

"We should wait and go with Bro Antony. She might be scared into giving up her claim if she sees us united."

"Are we united?" They hadn't seen their brother in over a decade.

"Well, he is coming to Ghana, and he stands to gain. We are on the same side."

They returned to the car, the driver and filling station attendant waiting for them with the bill.

Kokui gulped at the numbers scrawled on the limp carbon slip. "Ninety-five cedis!"

"Hmmm," the driver said. "Madame, the way fuel costs in this Ghana here, it's too much. Every day, another price."

She sighed. She needed Boris to send her money to her. "Let's make P&T our first stop. I have to call Boris."

At the post office, Kokui followed Nami behind the packed row that looked into the four glass booths of the communications hall, confused by the empathy that cautioned her to measure her words to her husband. She was inflamed by Boris's flagrant disregard for their marital and financial security, and the sacrifices they had both made to earn the money he had loaned his cousin without asking her first. He deserved the torrent of insults that lit up her mind, but when her turn came to go into the soundproof booth, at the sound of his voice, tears tore her throat.

"Tell me everything," he said, and she did, except that she hated him for making her pitiable to the little girl she had been who had watched her mother accept humiliation from her father. She wept the makeup off her face, her sobs rising over the clicking sounds warning that their time was running out.

"I'm sorry I put us in this position, Madame K. I thought Sammy would be able to pay me before we even missed the money. I was wrong. I just—I know what it is to be under pressure because of money issues. And Gyamfi helped us. I don't know how we would have earned what we did if he hadn't let us use his taxi."

He still didn't get what he had done. "Boris, you lied to me. Again."

"I'm sorry, Madame K."

They didn't have the time to go deeper.

"Go and tell my brother to give you my room. I sent him that money he asked for." He inhaled. "I'm sending you five hundred dollars today."

"How?"

Another warning clicked in his seconds-long hesitation.

"Linda."

Her pride flared uselessly.

"I'm still working on Sammy," he said before the phone clicked off.

"Everything okay?" Nami peered at her swollen face.

"No," she said. "But not now. Driver, please, we are going to Mamprobi."

She settled in the car and closed her eyes.

The last time she had been to Boris's family house, she was the Rich-imota Girl their Baby Last Number Six had had the good fortune to marry. After the wedding, she had declined the room Boris's brother Kwate offered them. Going from her father's villa, haunted as it was with the ghosts of wives and marriages past, to her husband's family compound house had felt like a step down to her. Now, she needed the room, and them.

"Number Six's wife." The old man across the road called from the plastic chair he kept watch of the neighborhood's goings and comings in. "You are welcome from Abrokye, but have you forgotten it's Sunday? They are all at church."

The last day she remembered was the Wednesday night she

learned her father was dead. She bowed her head and returned to
the car, preparing herself for the next stop on this march of confrontation when the gate creaked open.

Boris's sister-in-law poked her head out. "Madame K?"

A part of Kokui had been relieved to postpone submitting to the
humility of asking her in-laws for shelter, but now she would have
to kneel. She was realizing that, like Boris's, her pride was exhaust-
ing, too. She got out of the car, Nami at her heels.

"When did you get in from Yankee?" She looked past them to
the car. "Is Boris with you?"

"No, we didn't—it wasn't our plan to come," she said. "Sister
Tsotsoo, my father has passed on."

"Oh!" She bit her fist. "How? He was so young!"

"He passed in his sleep." Kokui paused, taking in the news again.
It still seemed like a dream. "It hasn't been one week yet but things
are moving fast. My stepmother has filed a claim as the Mrs. of my
father's estate, and we have to organize to get her out of the house."
She paused. She knew how to perform humility, but she had never
had to mean it. "Until then, we don't have a place to stay in Accra.
Can my sister and I stay in the room you offered Boris and me after
we married?"

Tsotsoo stepped aside and let them pass the gate. "You said you
didn't need the room, so we've rented it," she said.

Kokui wilted, following Tsotsoo up the stairs, past the bedroom
Boris used to share with his nephew, to Tsotsoo and Kwate's apartment. "Hmmm, Madame K, the place is full up, but there's no way
you won't get a place to sleep. This is your home." She gestured toward the sitting room's cane-backed, cushion-topped chairs and
love seat. "You can sleep here for now," she said. "We'll bring mat-
tresses for the floor."

Kokui swallowed her ego.

"Thank you, Sister Tsotsoo," Nami said for her.

"Don't mention it."

They sat down to drink the water Tsotsoo served them.

"My dear, I'm so sorry for you. Your father was such a strong man. What a shame."

She and Nami kept silent. There was too much going on to indulge condolence politesse.

"These inheritance issues are not a small matter," Tsotsoo said. "I've told you there were some skirmishes over Auntie Shika's properties when she died. Nkrumah's government seized everything except this house, and instead of helping her children, come and see Auntie Shika's brothers trying to take the place for themselves, saying she belonged to them, according to tradition. But where were they when Nkrumah jailed her? Ask them." Tsotsoo tutted at the memory. "Her husband's people were also plotting, trying to split the children, telling them Kwate believed he was the only rightful heir since he is a Quartey and they are Van der Puyes. Meanwhile, Kwate was doing everything to save this place for his junior brothers. I was there with him."

Kokui looked up at the picture Tsotsoo pointed to, her younger self in bridal white next to Kwate. Leaning beside it on the high hanging shelf was a portrait of Boris's parents on their white wedding day. There were other images of the couples, some in kente, some in cloth, some in skirt and blouse and suit and tie. Who was to say the photographs of Auntie Shika and her husband in their kente weren't taken at their Knocking or during the customary wedding, Kokui mused, but who was to say they were? You had to be told, or you had to be there, she thought ruefully of the impending litigation between her mother and Auntie Hemaa.

"Sister Tsotsoo, we have to be going. Our brother is arriving from London for the burial."

She nodded and rose to walk them out. "If I can open my mouth to advise you anything from our experience with Auntie Shika, I would say try not to let this nonsense cloud your father's burial. Focus on his life, not the show."

Kokui nodded politely. She didn't know how else to respond to her sister-in-law, except to say the show had taken over long before her father had died.

28

Mawuli Nuga's eldest son, Yao, had moved to London just before Kokui and Nami arrived at the Nuga house in Achimota. In his absence, Antony assumed the privileges of the firstborn, swaggering around the house ordering his junior siblings around with the full encouragement of his mother, Abui. Auntie Abui, Mawuli's first wife, had delivered two male heirs, and she made sure everyone in the house, from the wives to the children to Sister Eyram, understood their place in the pecking order for access to Mawuli. "I, and my children, are the First and the Last," she said.

Antony's arrogance notwithstanding, he was a jovial character. He admired how uncannily Kokui could parrot their father's lectures (he had never seen her impression of his mother), and often ordered her to perform Mawuli for his amusement. He loved laughing, and Kokui understood that making him laugh kept her and Nami safe. The stepmothers felt threatened by Kokui and

Nami because Mawuli had lied harder for longer to maintain his relationship with their mother. The siblings resented them because they had had the one mother–one father fantasy with Mawuli for twelve good years. Fafa, Elikem, and Connie—the Triplets, they called themselves, having been born the same year—bullied Kokui and Nami mercilessly the first weeks after their arrival, fanning Sister Eyram's accusation that they were the spawn of a witch. But Antony spoke up for them.

"If their mother were a witch, she would still have Daddy," he said. "Instead, her children are the most pitiable of us all. At least our mothers are here with us."

It was a defense that made Kokui feel worthless, but it slaked the Triplets' wrath. She and Nami lived in the relative peace of a truce until Mawuli went to knock for Auntie Hemaa's hand.

When Auntie Abui, or FirstandLast, as Sister Eyram and the kids called her behind her back, learned that Mawuli had married another woman, she gave up. In a wounded rage, she left Accra for her hometown. Antony, Kokui and Nami's only ally with power in the house, left for London soon after. He made it clear that his exit was in protest of Mawuli's disrespect of his mother, and he cursed their father—the only child who had dared do so to his face—in front of an audience of his children and the household staff.

Kokui would never forget the question Antony had lobbed at Mawuli.

"How can you, who loved your mother so much," her brother asked their father, "continually humiliate the mothers of your children? Isn't our love for our mothers as important as yours?"

The Nuga kids and the servants turned from Antony to Mawuli like they were watching table tennis.

"Today, I have only one son," Mawuli replied.

"Today," Antony retorted, "I have no father."

Everyone in the house was sure Mawuli would write Antony out of his will, but Mawuli paid for Antony's ticket to London and the fees for the technical school Antony attended before he dropped out.

It had been just over ten years since that day. Kokui had no idea what to expect of this reunion with their brother. However tenuous their bond, though, she took solace that they would be together for the burial. Only they as siblings could share the grief of losing their father.

"I've seen him."

Nami pushed to the front of the waiting crowd and stopped in front of a man carrying his navy gold-buttoned blazer in the crook of his extended arm.

Even under sunglasses and a full beard, Antony's face was Mawuli's, from his widow's peak to the pair of dimples that pressed into the corner of his mouth and the center of his chin. The resemblance was startling, transporting.

"Bro Antony." The siblings pushed into one another, tentative, lightly patting, keeping their distance even in the closeness they had initiated.

"So, the old goat is dead," he said.

Kokui could hear the ire threaded with wistfulness in Antony's voice. She reached out to squeeze his arm because she felt the same way. She, too, was aggrieved that Mawuli had died before she could resolve the hurt and resentment that sat curled like a cat between her love and admiration for him.

Her brother stepped back from the reach of her tenderness.

"What's the plan?" he asked as they led him to the car.

"We are doing the wake keeping and burial at the Nuvi compound," Nami said. "I know Daddy wanted to be buried by his mother. And then we'll do the thanksgiving service at the E.P. Church."

He slid into the front seat and closed his door. "When is the reading of the will?"

"I applied for a date at the Office of the Registrar the day after Auntie Hemaa sacked me," Nami replied. "We are waiting."

"So, we don't have a date yet?" He knocked his head against the seat back. "Why didn't you tell me?"

Kokui studied her elder brother's clenched fists. Their father often spoke of Antony in cautionary tones, telling Kokui, "The way you are going, you will end up like him. No steady job. Aimless." She swallowed, sobered by the thought now. She did not realize how desperate his situation was.

"Bro Antony, Daddy just died."

"Daddy's lawyer is seeing what he can do to expedite," Nami said.

"Which lawyer?" demanded Antony.

"Lawyer Denu."

"Daddy's drinking partner? Is that man competent?"

"Daddy trusted him," Nami said. "Lawyer Denu says we should have a date soon. In the meantime, we have to ready ourselves to pay the probate fee."

Antony raised a silencing hand. "I can tell you right now, I'm not paying a pesewa. I didn't come to give thanks at any celebration of life," he said. "I'm here for the money. That's all. It's the only thing of worth that man ever gave us."

Kokui heard the anguish in her brother's bravado. She could bet Antony's eyes were red under his shades.

"I say we strike a deal with Hemaa," he said. "Let's propose she buy us out of the estate with a lump sum we can split among ourselves. She can have the rest. The only Fourdrinier in all of West Africa . . . ," he muttered.

"No," Nami said. "It's not just about what Daddy's estate is worth today. We have to think about the future value. Bro Yao, Sister Emefa, Sister Esime, Sister Elikem, and Sister Elinam have childr—"

"Are they here?" Antony said.

"Didn't Bro Yao, Sister Fafa, and Sister Emefa send you to represent them?"

"I asked you if they are here?" He shook his head. "Let's go to Hemaa now and find out what she needs so we can get what we want."

"Bro Antony, I don't want any lump sum from her," Nami said. "I want us to keep what is ours. Daddy built the business for us to carry on his legacy."

"What legacy, Nami?" Antony said. "His legacy is a divided house. His widow is only making it official."

Nami looked to Kokui to back her up.

Kokui agreed with their brother somewhat. Her father's properties were probably worth close to six million cedis, not including the apartment in London. She couldn't begin to calculate the value of the business, even with the loss of the land in Bolga. If Auntie Hemaa would agree to give them a fair price to share among themselves, she wasn't opposed to settling this quickly and moving on. She didn't want to become ensnared in a court case that would only prolong their pain and drain finances. But what Kokui would not allow was a discounting of her mother's widowhood, too.

She had wanted her mother to divorce Mawuli for so long, but Micheline had chosen to stay in the marriage, and so had Mawuli. She was willing to go to court to assert that her mother's marriage to Mawuli was just as valid as Auntie Hemaa's, that her parents' marriage, complex as it was for Kokui to understand, was just as binding. The law could call the arrangement "bigamy" or "polygamy," but whatever it called it, the law had to acknowledge it.

"Auntie Hemaa is not his only widow," she said.

Antony's eyebrow arched toward his hairline. "Well, I'm not going to court to defend that," he said. "Driver, take me to my father's house in Achimota."

"Please, where is that place?"

"Ah! You don't know Achimota?"

Kokui rolled her eyes at her brother's nasalized enunciation of Achimota. "Bro Antony, my mother brought him from Togo. We have to direct him."

"Then tell him where we come from."

29

Achimota was one of Accra's oldest communities, carved out of the Achimota Forest that grew on the edge of the city. The dense woodland gave the neighborhood its name, but the area would go on to become synonymous with the Achimota School that cleared a large portion of it. Opened in 1927 as the Prince of Wales College and School at Achimota, the school's erection reflected a new generation of Gold Coasters who had only known colonial government.

They saw the British section off wide swaths of land to live four or five people in one family, in homes sized like compound houses traditionally fit for four or five families. They watched them send their children to mission schools that prepared them for a world of opportunity dominated by the sunset-defying British Empire. And they decided these minority tyrants could only be beaten by joining them. The resident colonial government stood to benefit, too. Linking arms with an amenable class of Gold Coasters eager to seize the spoils of their own country, and that of the crown that had colonized their tastes, would postpone the organizing push for independence a little bit longer.

Mawuli Nuga, a businessman, and his wife, Abui, a cloth trader, were members of this ascendant class. Shortly after Mawuli returned from Germany with the seed money to open Nuga & Heirs, he and Abui were part of the small wave who bought plots and built homes in Achimota. They sent their kids to the school started by an education activist from the Gold Coast, an Anglican vicar from Britain, and the then-governor seeking to "do something useful both for the Empire and for the natives of Africa."

Within a year of the Achimota move, Mawuli moved in a pregnant Rebecca Laryea, the caterer who held the contract to run the canteen that served all of the government ministries. A year later, he brought home Hannah Koomson, an assistant to the chief aide to the new acting Gold Coast governor, and their baby girl, Connie. More children began to fill the house, quickly outgrowing their mothers' suites to occupy the pair of dormitory-style rooms on the other side of the second floor from Mawuli's bedroom. Mawuli sent for his cousin Eyram to live with him as the children's caretaker. A compound family, in a house designed for an Ordinance union.

Before Kokui had known any of this, before she knew her father kept a second home in Achimota with his eight other children and three other wives, Kokui would sit in her mother's car on the drive to Achimota Primary, watching the whitewashed bungalows and two-story colonials of the predominantly British-settled enclave she lived in with her parents and sister give way to the cultural blur more pronounced in the wider city architecture.

There was the bougainvillea-pink apartment building with the leaf-green shutters. There was the sprawling three-story storehouse on a raised foundation buttressed by slim columns resembling masquerade stilts. And there was the sky-blue chalet with the thatch-reminiscent corrugated iron sheet roof advertising office space to let, among others. It all culminated with her mother slowing the car in front of the Achimota School's three-story administration building, a beacon of British colonial design with its shutter-trimmed windows, porticos, and clock-tower steeple—standing on ground that had once given the earliest-known Achimotans refuge from slavery.

When Kokui went to live in Achimota, Nelson and his dad told them the legends of the area's first settlers, people chased into hiding from Upper Volta and Cote d'Ivoire, escaping slave catchers. More than five generations later, Mawuli hid there, too, with three wives—for more than twelve years before Micheline discovered the truth—chased by what or who, Kokui never knew. In some ways, everyone in the Achimota house was hiding from something. Each wife, from the truth there was nothing they could do to make Mawuli love only them. The children, from the pain, shame, and rage their stepmothers unleashed on them instead of Mawuli.

At times, Kokui entertained the notion that her father had kept her mother separated from his other wives in another house on the other side of town from Achimota because she really was his Madame Nugaga, but she chased the thought with the truth that it ultimately did not matter. Loved most or least, Micheline experienced the same stinging betrayal as Mawuli's other wives, and Kokui and Nami had still ended up in the Achimota house with the rest of his kids. And, he had married Auntie Hemaa after her.

As the driver turned onto their road and stopped at the gate, she shivered at the sight of the two-story villa. Kokui had always felt a heaviness in the house, damp and clinging, like a towel soaked in cooking oil—but now that Mawuli was no longer physically there, the weight felt thicker, darker. Apprehension moistened her palms and dried her throat. In this day of confrontations, she had expected the one with Boris to be the hardest, but her body and her spirit were telling her different. This was the one she had feared most.

At the driver's beep of the horn, Evans stepped out of the pedestrian gate and immediately closed it behind him.

The gateman had seen the family expand, contract, and hemorrhage in his years manning the house's entrance, Kokui mused with sadness and embarrassment, as his eyes darted everywhere but her, Nami's, and Antony's faces.

"Hello, Evans," she said. "We've come to greet Auntie Hemaa."

"Madame has given us strict instructions not to allow"—he paused—"anyone to enter."

Antony got down from the car. "Do you see 'anyone' standing in front of you? I am Mawuli Nuga's son. Call Hemaa out."

Evans shifted his weight from one leg to another. The stance of a boxer—and the dance of delayed urination. Kokui empathized with his conundrum. Right now, Auntie Hemaa was his boss, but that could change once the will was read.

"She says she is not receiving visitors," he said.

"What kind of nonsense is this? If she likes, we can bring the police to compel her to allow us entry, or make her vacate immediately," Antony shouted. "Go in and tell her Mawuli Nuga's son is here! This is my father's house."

"Our father's house," Nami said.

"Kpɔ, let's leave her." Kokui was so tired of fighting in this house of hiding that she had lost herself in.

"Bring her out." Antony was still shouting. "Or, we will return with—"

They all turned to the opening car gate.

Kokui gulped, twelve years old again as Nelson held the iron barrier open.

"She says you can come," he said.

Even Antony became subdued as they entered the compound, the heaviness cloaking them all like a shroud.

Their father's Range Rover sat parked next to Auntie Hemaa's Benz under the car canopy, one of Auntie Hemaa's Prempeh Transport trucks on the side. They crossed the veranda, past the cushioned stool that had never made its way back into the house after Kokui's Knocking. Inside, Nelson led them to the dining table that had barely been used since the days when Auntie Rebecca conscripted Kokui, Nami, and their sisters to help her serve Mawuli multi-course meals Sister Eyram believed she put amati in.

The table was littered with Nuga & Heirs receiving slips and a stack of ledgers. Auntie Hemaa sat wigless, in the widow's black and red kaba and slit, and looked up from poring over the ledgers. Kokui felt her stomach turn to water at the sight. What was this woman doing with, or to, her father's accounts, she wondered. She heard Nami's breaths get short.

"Auntie Hemaa, what's going on?" Nami asked.

"I'm sorting out your father's books," she said.

"They're not your books to sort," Antony said.

Their stepmother's face twitched with impatience. "Who are you?"

Antony had left before Auntie Hemaa moved into the house, but she knew who he was. In the bedroom Mawuli had shared with Auntie Hemaa, opposite the wall where the picture of his beloved mother hung, beside his and Auntie Hemaa's white wedding portrait, were photographs of each of his children.

"I'm your ex-husband's second-born son, representing his firstborn son, and his firstborn and sixth-born daughters," Antony said. "Who are you?"

"I am your father's widow." Auntie Hemaa turned to Nami and Kokui. "The one who bailed him out again and again and again."

Kokui raised an eyebrow. She had no idea whether her step-mother had personally loaned her father money, but she did know her father paid Auntie Hemaa for use of her trucks to ship the wood from Bolga to Accra. Boris had made his predictions about how her father's spending threatened the company's health, but Nuga & Heirs was not in debt when she had helped her father with his books those months she had worked with him. It had been almost two years since then, but she doubted things could have changed that fast.

"You have the land in Bolga," Nami said. "It's worth millions."

"What! She has the land in Bolgatanga?" Antony put his hands on his head. "Lawyer Denu allowed that? Where will the press get the wood for the paper?"

"I had agreed to rent the land to your father for five hundred cedis a month." She plucked a sheaf of documents from the table, the red rubber stamp of the Notaries Public on the top page.

Kokui gulped the saliva that had collected in her mouth. Once upon a time, Micheline had tried to destroy her father with fire. Auntie Hemaa was using paper.

Mawuli loved to lecture about the importance and power of paper, yet knowing this, he had given Auntie Hemaa that power over everything he had worked for, and over his children. What-ever had chased her father into so many arms, between so many legs, Kokui would never know, but she felt such grief for him now. Mawuli Nuga had deceived his wives and, by default, his chil-dren, but everyone who knew him was clear about his desire to propagate his legacy. He wanted his children to take advantage of every spoil he had amassed. Now, his legacy was in limbo because of his libido.

"Auntie Hemaa, you understand that anything you do to tamper with Daddy's finances—"

Kokui stopped her sister from continuing.

"Let's go," she said. "We can continue this conversation after the reading of Daddy's will."

"We can continue this conversation in court," Antony said.

"Whichever comes first," Auntie Hemaa said.

She hadn't shouted or sneered, but Kokui heard the fury her stepmother had swallowed when Baby Kofi's mother came to leave her son at the house. Now she saw the rage her father's wife had suppressed when Mawuli spoke of driving to his other wife in Togo. Now she knew why Auntie Hemaa hadn't left Mawuli the moment she learned he was married to another woman; and that the polygamy she had grown up in and sought to escape for herself was her marital reality. Now Kokui understood what had held Mawuli Nuga's wives in place for so long, why none had immediately divorced him.

It wasn't love, or the children, that had kept her father's wives with him humiliation after humiliation—it was the pain. By staying tethered to Mawuli in whatever way they could handle, they believed they could find some way for his treachery to make sense, for it to have some purpose, to extract some value from the betrayal they had received in exchange for what had begun for them as tenderness and trust.

"Auntie Hemaa, I'm sorry for what he did to you," Kokui said. "I really am. He did it to our mothers also, and in so doing, he did it to us, too."

Auntie Hemaa did not react, not that Kokui had expected her to. What could she say? What could any of them say? It was Mawuli who should be apologizing to them all.

"Nelson, show my husband's children out of my house."

30

'm coming for the funeral," Boris said.

Kokui stood in the wooden booth of the Akosombo post office branch, the phone hot on her ear. The last thing she needed right now was the shadow of her failing marriage cast over the darkness surrounding her father's send-off. "No, Boris. It doesn't make sense for us to spend all that money for you to come for a few days. I just want to bury Daddy and return to classes, catch up on what I've missed."

"I've spoken with your professors," he said. "They've all agreed to let you make up the work you are missing over the winter break. They've given me your assignments to bring to you when I come."

She closed her eyes, both relieved he had taken care of that for her, and resentful of the pressure she felt now. "I don't want to do schoolwork while I'm dealing with my father's death, and Auntie Hemaa, Boris."

"Okay." He returned the growl in her voice before taking a breath. "You can do it when we come back in the new year."

"Are you hearing me, Boris? I don't intend to be here that long."

"Why not stay through the end of the year, until the will is read?"

"First of all, I'm not sleeping on your brother and sister-in-law's floor till the new year," she said.

Boris sighed. "When I come, I will demand a room. I know my brother and his wife are greedy, but this is too much, putting my wife on the floor! That is my mother's house, too."

Kokui shuddered to think that she and her siblings might be fighting over rooms in the Achimota house with Auntie Hemaa if her father made it so in his will.

"The way Auntie Hemaa was talking, I doubt this will be over in two months. We are still waiting for the registrar to give us a date for the will to be read. And depending on what the will says, this whole thing could take at least a year to settle. More, if Auntie Hemaa really wants to fight in court."

"I'm sorry you are going through all this, Madame K. I want to support you, and I want to honor your father. I can't miss celebrating his life. Not after all he did for me. If not for him, I couldn't have come here when I did."

Now he wanted to acknowledge her father's help. She pursed her lips. "We can't afford it."

"I've demanded the money from Sammy. He's given me two thousand. He says he can give me the rest when we get back from Ghana."

He paused. She knew he wanted her to applaud his work to get their money back, but Kokui refused to congratulate him for what she believed he should never have had to do.

"Boris, why don't you send me the money you would spend on the ticket? If you come here, you won't be able to work. We still have to pay our rent."

"Some things are more important than money."

She squinted at the phone. Had her husband really just said what she heard?

"Madame K, you and I need to talk face-to-face, and it can't wait."

Kokui swallowed now, new anxiety seizing her. Did Boris want to end their marriage, too, she wondered. "What do you want to talk about, Boris?"

The phone clicked a warning.

"We'll continue when I come on Thursday."

"Thursday!"

"You said the burial is on Friday."

The line dead, Kokui walked to the car, her emotions even more muddled. The thought of having Boris close in just three days lit her up with apprehension and with pride. He was coming for *her*. The salty shame of insecurity stung her eyes, even as she exhaled from the flush of relief. In the deepest parts of her, she needed to believe that she was someone's *nu ga ga*.

She blinked back the tears as she bent into her seat. She had told Nami she didn't need to come since she was going to the Akosombo post office branch closer to the Nuvis', but her sister had not left her side since she landed. Kokui's heart ached for Nami. Her little sister was the only one of Mawuli's kids who had intended to carry on the business; she had wanted so badly to build upon Nuga & Heirs with their dad. Now, her next term at Legon was not secure.

Kokui started calculating. She would have to help her sister pay her fees, and she would have to find extra work to pay for her own. She touched her stomach. She needed to see Mrs. Koranteng.

"He says he's coming," she told Nami as she closed the car door behind her.

"It's good you'll have that support."

"You know I'll do everything I can to help you with your school fees," Kokui said.

Nami nodded as Kokui took her hand. "Let's focus on burying Daddy. We can talk about the rest later."

At the Nuvis', Efo Cletus, Sister Eyram, and Antony sat enthroned among a panel of chairs in the sitting room, Micheline on the three-seater opposite them reviewing the funeral poster. Kokui couldn't tell if the pained look on her mother's face was from mourning or frustration.

"Come and sit." Micheline called her daughters in. "We are discussing the funeral arrangements."

She passed them a sample of the funeral program flyer. Next to "wife," only Micheline's name was listed.

"We've already left the body too long. I know you all are Accra people," Efo Cletus said as Kokui and Nami flanked their mother, "but our tradition calls for us to do the burial, then the funeral, then the kɔnuwɔwɔwo, then—"

Micheline inhaled. "Efo Cletus, what you are describing is all going to be money. Since I am fronting the costs, let's keep things simple as I had suggested. Burial on Friday. Funeral on Saturday. Thanksgiving service on Sunday. Finish."

Efo Cletus's nostrils doubled in diameter. "My brother was not a simple man," he said. "Aside that, you know we will get donations to cover all the costs and even leave us with profit."

"Let's focus on ensuring a profit," Antony said.

"You know your brother was an E.P. Church man," Micheline said. "He didn't agree with libations, except to drink them himself."

"Faaa!" Efo Cletus sprang from his chair, the legs scraping the floor with his movement. "You, the traditional wife, are fighting his Christian wife for your children's rights, but you want to go around the custom? Decide for yourself what it is you want to do and tell me, since you are the one 'fronting the costs.'"

Micheline sucked her teeth. "Which custom? Was I there when

you all were creating your customs and traditions so you could bed as many women as you like, whether in church or in the village? In fact, you wear your customs like costumes—when you don't like one, you switch to the other, mixing and matching to suit yourselves.

"Me, the custom I fell into when I married my husband was love," Micheline said. "I loved the man, not knowing he had pledged himself to many others, and when I learned the truth, I bound myself only for my children. I will get for them what I stayed for."

"We all have to get something out of this," Antony said.

Sister Eyram jabbed the air between her and Mawuli's second-born son. "Ewò Antony, you have gotten plenty." Sister Eyram turned to Micheline. "Sister, you have to play your part wisely, else that witch will take everything from us."

"One of my mother's cousins works in the Office of the Registrar," Antony said. "I'll see if I can get him to expedite and get us a date for the reading of the will."

Kokui saw Micheline tighten at the mention of their father's first wife. She and Nami did, too. Unlike Micheline, they did not want their father's estate for just them, but Kokui was loath to involve her stepmother. Of all of them, FirstandLast had made no secret of her wish that she and Nami had never been born.

"Thank you, Bro Antony." What else could she say, she wondered, given their delicate alliance?

"Maybe Boris can assist when he comes," Kokui said when they were alone in the sitting room. "He knows Solomon Kusi, the one who was investigating Daddy."

"I was wondering when your husband was coming," Micheline said.

Nami peered at Kokui. "Sis, what is going on with you and Boris? Every time we mention him you start twitching."

Micheline's eyes jumped to her eldest daughter. "Is everything okay?"

She did not want to admit to her mother that she had failed, but it would all come out anyway when Boris arrived. "It's not what I thought," she said.

"What do you mean, Sis? What's not what you thought?"

"Marriage."

"Hmmm," Micheline said. "I told you to take your time."

Kokui swallowed her rebuttal. She couldn't continue to hurt her mother with talk of how her marriage to Mawuli had driven her decision.

"Sometimes I feel happy with Boris," she said. "I love him. I admire him. But I also feel trapped by him. Like, if I push for something I need or tell him how I truly feel or show him who I truly am, I will spoil everything between us. And he lies, Ma." She told her mother and sister about Boris lying for Sammy to go and see Tina at Shorty's, and loaning Sammy their money without telling her.

Nami's face squeezed tighter and tighter, gasping as she went on, but Micheline kept silent.

"I have to end this marriage."

"My daughter," Micheline said, "you know Boris is not the one I would have chosen for you, but this is not something to end your marriage over."

"It's not?" Nami asked.

"Ma, I can't stay like you did."

"Stop comparing yourself to me, Kokui. You were foolish to give your husband charge of your money. You have to take control so he can never do that nonsense again."

"I didn't give him charge, Ma."

"You have a bank account and you are not checking the balance? He had to tell you before you knew he spent the money?" Micheline shook her head. "Kokui, you are not a small girl. You have to start taking responsibility for your own actions and stop blaming others for your poor decisions. Discipline yourself!"

Kokui couldn't count the number of times both her parents had commanded her to discipline herself. What did that even mean?

"You knew when you married that Boris didn't have money. How did you expect him to behave when he gets some and the cousin who helped him come to America needs some funds?"

"I don't expect him to go behind my back."

Micheline snorted. "You think harmony happens just because two things have come together? No. The two parties have to do what they can to prevent a collision! You have to be alert. You have to keep your hands on the wheel and steer," she said. "My daughter, you all are just beginning. You have to teach each other how things have to be. You have to correct him and give him a chance to make the correction."

"Did you do that with Daddy?"

"How could I correct what he did? Tell me," she said. "All I could do is correct what I did. That's my advice to you."

"You left, Ma."

"I had to, but you are not in the same situation, Kokui. You got your wish, and my wish combined," she said. "Your marriage is better than mine."

If her marriage was better than her parents', it was only because it had not lasted as long, Kokui thought. "Ma, I'm sorry for all the things I said to you."

"You can't be sorry for what you meant."

She had meant it, and still did. She did not want her parents' marriage. But she knew now that was never going to happen. "I didn't know what I was saying. I didn't know then that every marriage is its own thing."

31

Why had she wanted to marry Boris so badly? Kokui mulled the question as the driver slowed the car in front of the airport. The only marriages she had seen up close were laden with lies and undergirded with sadism. Why had she thought she, of all people, could crack the nut? She could never have a marriage like the Bonsus' or the Bucketts', she told herself—not that she even knew the terms or constitution of their unions. The truth was, her fear of failure in marriage was almost as great as her fear of what it would take to succeed. She had watched her mother and Auntie Hemaa accept deception and humiliation to stay married. She chose not to do the same.

As much as she admired Linda, what did she really know about her or her husband's arrangement beyond what they showed? Daphne Buckett had described the hard work she and her husband had put into their marriage. Could she similarly survive a lifetime of measuring her words and emotions before pouring them out?

She didn't want to be careful of everything she did and said to prevent a fight. She didn't want to have to tell an adult man it was wrong to lie, and that he had no right to loan out the money he and his wife had both worked around the clock to earn without discussing it with her first. But more than that, she didn't want to have to keep fighting against the wall of the different ways they saw life. If that was the only way to stay married, Kokui was ready to cut her losses.

She stepped out of the car and waited among the watchers craning their necks as the first passengers began to emerge from the evening flight Boris was on. For the third time that week, she spied families swamping their arriving loved ones, slapping their palms, snapping their thumbs, relieving their shoulders of thick luggage straps. It was a special gift to be received by someone, she thought, and to have someone to receive—until it wasn't.

Kokui lit a cigarette, her first since she had landed in Ghana. Exhaling deeply, she tried to exorcise her anxious thoughts, but the cloud that escaped had nothing to do with the one that grew thicker and darker in her mind. What did Boris have to say to her that he couldn't over the phone? Now that Mawuli was dead, and she would have to pay her own tuition, she imagined Boris lamenting the burden she would become to the plan they had so carefully crafted for their future. He just wanted to do the decent thing and tell her to her face, she told herself, and maybe even resume his relationship with the eight-thousand cedi girl he had supposedly left for her. Or maybe there was someone else. One of Tina's friends. Sammy could not have been spending all of those nights at Shorty's alone. She had been a fool to believe otherwise.

"Madame K."

Boris pulled her close. As he clung to her, and she to him, in the warm relief of their tight hold she agonized. Was she, as her mother had said, making more of Boris's lies than she should? She had married Boris for many reasons, primary among them to escape her father's house and her life in Ghana. Now that she had achieved that, was there enough between them to try to steer their marriage from a crash? Was Boris even willing? She swallowed, fear thickening in her throat at the thought of asking him.

"I've missed you," he said.

"I've been thinking about you, too," she said carefully. It felt safer to withhold the fullness and complexity of her emotion, and hide in the ambiguity.

He jerked his head, absorbing her aloof reply like a fist to his face, and her heart ached for hurting him.

"I've missed you, too," she said, surrendering the words like an offering.

In the car, they sat quietly looking out of their respective windows, but touching, their knees pointing toward each other. The driver propelled them through the early November streets, slowing for the soldiers standing around other officers enthroned on folding chairs in the middle of the road.

Boris barked as Kokui rummaged in her purse: "Don't give them a dime."

Kokui tapped the driver's shoulder with the one-cedi note, but Boris stretched to snatch the paper from her hand. The limp note, already tattered, ripped with his action. The soldier who rose to peer into their car had not seen the violence done to his tip, but Kokui recoiled, gathering her knees to herself. "What was that for, Boris?"

A motorcycle was flashing police lights behind them. The officer had no choice but to stand at attention as the cars behind them piled up to let the eight-vehicle convoy pass.

"Some big man," the driver said as the officer waved them on.

"The only way to get respect in this country," Boris said. He turned to the window, his jawbone twitching under his skin.

"The big man myth," she corrected him.

The anger Boris carried confused Kokui. He was mostly mild-mannered, obsequious in the face of most disrespect, but then, without warning, his rage leapt like a lion. Her asking questions about his family. Her giving Frema money toward their stay. Her father's money. So far, these had been the revealers of the wrath that lurked inside her husband, but she couldn't find the thread that stitched them together.

"Myths are still legends," he said.

She rolled her eyes. "Boris, if you came to my father's funeral to support me, support me. I can't manage your pride and my grief."

"You're not the only one grieving, Kokui."

"I know you liked him, Boris, but he was my father."

"I'm not talking about him," he said. "You're not the only one who didn't have a fantasy childhood."

She turned to him. "I know yours wasn't perfect either."

"No, it wasn't," he said, "but I don't punish you for it."

"I don't punish you, Boris."

"You want me to be me, and you want me to be your father," he said. "You have to choose one and commit."

"Is that what you couldn't tell me over the phone, Boris?" she hissed. "You are the one trying to stifle me!"

"I gave Sammy the money as an investment," he said. "You saw how much money I made driving the taxi. It being our own car, we stand to make so much more if we split it three ways."

"It wasn't your money to give him."

"But it was your money to give Frema."

Kokui sighed. "Boris, I'm tired."

"Madame K, I know I don't have enough to satisfy you now, but I promise you one day I will. Can you stick with me until then?"

Kokui gritted her teeth, the plea in his voice surprising, annoying, and rebuking her. So much for making Boris eat her adɔdi, she thought. He wanted his own envelope, and his own altar to make her kneel at.

She had married her father, after all.

"Boris, my whole life I thought my father was an exceptional man, and he was, but he was also unremarkable. He wanted more for himself, like everyone else. He was just willing to do more than most of us to get it. But when he got it, he never made the connection that what he had was what he had started with. He had to go after everything because he believed he was nothing. He didn't believe in himself."

"It's hard to believe in yourself in this country if you don't have anything."

"It's hard to believe in yourself if you have something, too," she said. "But I believe in you, and I know you believe in me."

That was why she had wanted to marry Boris, she realized. He was the only one who had believed.

"If we are going to survive, we have to keep believing in each other," she said. "We have to be truthful and faithful. Some legends are based on truth. Some aren't. I want the one that's true. Can you commit to that?"

He nodded.

"I don't want Cinyras," Kokui said. "I want you."

32

It dawned on Kokui, as she rose to ready for her father's burial, that the union between Mawuli Nuga the man and Mawuli Nuga the myth had been Mawuli's first marriage—the only one he had been faithful to. He had used the myth to hide his insecurity. In return, it had helped him attract wealth and power, and given him permission to continue hiding in women. Now that Mawuli the man was a spirit, his body about to be lowered into the earth, only four of his eleven children present to witness, Kokui wondered if he would have chosen differently if given another chance.

The morning still black, she stood with her mother, sister, and Boris, together with the Nuvis, and the reverend from E.P. Juapong, staring solemnly at the gaping chasm of soil that waited to hide the man forever as Sister Eyram led them in worship.

"Mawu li nam nu ga lo. Mawu li nam nu ga kpi. Mawu li nam nu ga lo. Mawu li nam nu ga vivi. Indeed, God has done great and mighty things for you and for me."

Headlights cut through the dark morning service and Antony emerged from the taxi with his mother. Kokui's hands stretched to find her mother's and her sister's hands as Antony began to distribute a flyer among the family gathering.

Kokui bent to pick up the circular Micheline had let fall to the ground. It bore an image of a much younger Mawuli—the one who had wooed Abui Dei from Juapong to Accra—and it omitted mention of a wife. Instead, it listed Mawuli's children and their mothers, from the firstborn on. Kokui huffed, frustrated by this bog that determined to sink them no matter how far, fast, or long they ran.

Sister Eyram fingered the paper. "You've forgotten Kofi."

"Let's continue," Micheline said.

In another life, Abui Dei and Micheline Miadogo might have been friends. Mawuli's first wife was a cloth trader and Micheline a fabric designer, but because of the man between them, they stood on opposite sides of the hole that had been dug.

Sister Eyram resumed singing as the man they had all shared was lowered into the ground.

"You return man to dust," the reverend recited from the Bible. "You sweep them away as with a flood; they are like a dream . . ."

Kokui closed her eyes as he spoke, watching her father take his place by his mother's side.

". . . let the favor of the Lord our God be upon us, and establish the work of our hands; yes, establish the work of our hands."

The gravediggers began to cover the coffin. A mason slathered cement over the top. The sun rising over them now, Antony led his mother to the waiting taxi.

The women were opening the pots on the stove, readying to fill their plates when Antony returned.

"You're back," Sister Eyram said, her tone thorny.

"I was able to secure a date for the reading of Daddy's will," he said.

The tightness in the air loosened, the tentative alliance they had formed still in place.

"It will be next Wednesday."

"Thank you, Bro Antony."

"Thank my mother," he said. "It's her friend who expedited for us."

They kept silent, the tension returning because it could never fully go away, could it?

* * *

All of Juapong, scores from Accra, and several internationals assembled under the black and red tents on the Juapong football field to honor Mawuli's spirit. Draped in black, red, and brown cloths, they spilled off or stood around the white plastic chairs, listening to testimonies of Mawuli's uncommon life.

Extended family, Nuga & Heirs staff past and present, E.P. Church congregants, and a small parade of townspeople from Juapong and the surrounding municipalities held the microphone at the lectern on the dais. They told of children whose school fees Mawuli had paid, hospital bills he had settled, homes he had built, kiosks he had bought for women to open shops, and investments he had made in farming businesses. In the seats, personal eulogies abounded. Men Mawuli had squired many a girlfriend with, including the Colonel, jokingly and jealously recounted his effortless charm, his winking audacity. Ministers and members of Parliament whose pockets he had lined recounted their memories, too, of Mawuli's brilliance as a negotiator and his big vision for Ghana. A contingent of E.P. Church moderators from across the Volta Region remembered his humility.

Common to all the reminiscences was a marveling at the story of the boy from Juapong who had risen from birth to a poor mother to funding a hospital in her name. Then, the invitation that followed: to find similar motivation to do the same. It really was an incredible and inspiring story, Kokui thought, even if it didn't take into account that not everyone had the gifts, calling, or desire to follow in her father's footsteps—or wanted what it had come with: the gossip about what would happen to Mawuli's holdings in his wake.

It shocked Kokui how many details people knew. Yes, Auntie Hemaa's absence at the wake-keeping, burial, and now the funeral was a glaring sign that all was not harmonious in the family, but how did one of the E.P. Church congregants know that Kokui had asked Boris's brother to allow Nami to stay with them in Accra?

"I was so sorry to hear."

Kokui looked up at the woman who had eulogized Mawuli at the top of the service, now hovering over her on the dais as the Juapong Kpekpe Troupe danced borborbor at the center of the field.

"Thank you, Auntie." Kokui gave the same bland reply to each mourner who approached her in tears, eager to end the interaction quickly so she could return to her own grief.

"That wicked woman trying to tear a family apart," the lady persisted. "Pushing you to beg your husband's brother for a room. The greed in this country is just too much. Can we take anything with us when we die?" She turned to descend from the dais and into the crowd.

Kokui looked around helplessly as another mourner sought to make eye contact with her. Boris, together with Tsotsoo and Kwate, had followed Micheline and Afi to the food stands set up on the edge of the field. Sister Eyram stood beside Efo Cletus at the head of the dais, surrounded by a circle of people paying their respects and jockeying for position in case the court case went their way. Behind her, Nami, Antony, and Lawyer Denu sat in a tilted-heads conversation. Nami had taken the lead on gathering the information to understand the fight they were in for their father's estate. Mawuli had always said Kokui had the flair, but Nami was maneuvering their stepbrother and her father's lawyer quite handily.

"Sis," Nami said as Kokui settled beside them.

"Lawyer Denu, hello," Kokui said.

"My daughter, how is it?"

Their father's lawyer had been among the men who used to sponsor her and Nami's drinks at the Ambassador, but since Mawuli's death, the lustful leer in his eyes had been replaced by the tender sharpness of paternal protection. The men of her father's generation seemed to be masters at sliding between the poles of prurience and benevolence.

"I was just telling your sister that I need the two of you to submit written statements attesting to your parents' marriage so we can add together with photographs and any other documentation between your parents."

"But why do they need to do that if we already have a date for the reading of the will?" Antony asked.

"Well, it's for the official record, in case there are any other beneficiaries we don't know of, or if Hemaa decides to contest the will's contents. It weakens her position if there are two legal Mrs. Nugas," he said. "I'll be honest with you. It's tricky because she didn't know your father was married to your mother when he married her, so she can say she entered a monogamous union in good faith. But in the same vein, Micheline was there before her—though in a customary arrangement, which presupposes she was open to a polygamous union. Are you understanding me?"

Kokui nodded. "My mother and Auntie Hemaa have to fight for my dad all over again."

33

The waiting room at the Office of the Registrar General started on the veranda. Rows of chairs stood under the shade of the building's raised foundation entrance, and people sat on the edges of their seats with the particular restlessness of waiting to record, or unseal, a life moment. The clerk manning the desk next to the soldier guarding the door looked equally impatient. A parade of registrants approached him with repetitive questions about the needed paperwork and how much longer they had before their turn would come, while an entitled stream sidled up to drop names of personnel so they could jump the queue. Kokui, Boris, Nami, Micheline, Afi, Efo Cletus, Sister Eyram, Kofi, Antony, and Auntie Abui made a river of the stream.

"Please, take your seats," the clerk huffed as the ten of them swamped his desk. "Whether you know Kojo Bigman or Jesus Christ himself, your matter is no more important than that of your fellow Ghanaians."

"We are here to see the Registrar General," Antony said.

"Tell him Mrs. Abui Nuga is here."

The clerk's jaw tightened as he pushed the notebook to them. "Please, each of you enter your names in the book and indicate your purpose."

"She's here," Nami said, passing the notebook to Kokui.

Hemaa Prempeh-Nuga (Mrs.), their stepmother had written.

"We knew she would be."

They moved inside the government building, bypassing the pews of people waiting inside. Kokui noted a woman in a white lace kaba and kente slit gripping a bouquet of flowers. She wondered if the woman's intended was the white-suited, tea-colored man seated to her left, or the black-suited, biscuit-colored man on her right. All three wore the queasy, confused expression of an imminent moment of reckoning.

"Charlotte, are they all here?"

Afi collected Baby Kofi from Sister Eyram and sat to wait as the registrar's secretary ushered them toward the voice beyond the half-open door behind her. Ibrahim Bashiru, the name imprinted on the doorplate read. "Sir, it's left with one more."

"Sister Abui." Mr. Bashiru rose to greet his friend. "Long time. How are you?"

"Hmmm," she said. "I'm managing."

A sympathy that seemed, to Kokui, deeper than politesse indented the space between his brows. He turned to the rest of them. The chairs were arranged in a half circle, and Auntie Hemaa had taken the center, her pocketbook perched on her lap like a handgun. With her arm crooked through Antony's, Auntie Abui strode to the cushioned seat beside Auntie Hemaa.

Micheline took the room's roll call with her eyes as she stood beside Lawyer Denu. "You said there is one more, but we are less three seats."

Mr. Bashiru grimaced now, his face ridged with mortification. "I'm sorry to say, Madame, but Mr. Nuga has asked that you, and Madame Hemaa, and"—he paused to swallow—"and Sister Abui not be present for the reading of the will."

Lawyer Denu's face froze with surprise.

"What are you talking about?" Auntie Hemaa's grip tightened around the handle of her bag.

"He—he was explicit. He made mention of one Madame Rebecca Laryea, as well—that you all should be notified of the reading, but removed from the hearing."

"The man was my husband," Auntie Hemaa said. "I demand to hear his last words!"

Antony bowed his head. "Those were his last words to you."

Auntie Abui shook her head as Micheline tilted hers upward. Kokui trembled with anger. This would be her mother's last humiliation.

Charlotte poked her head in the door as the mothers, stooped, began to file out. "Sir, he is here."

Kokui jerked at the sight of the biscuit-colored man from the waiting room sinking onto the last seat of the arc.

Auntie Hemaa stopped. "Who are you?"

Lawyer Denu and Ibrahim Bashiru exchanged the wide eyes and pursed lips of a shared secret.

"I'm Festus Weber," the man said.

The silence that followed was thicker than his accent—and deeper than the dimples that puckered the corner of his mouth and the center of his chin.

Given who her father was, it was surprising there weren't any other dimpled heirs in the room, Kokui thought. But still. The familiar flame of shame rose within her, complicating her anger, compounding her grief. Her father had kept yet another secret from them all these years. Boris's palm rose behind her neck, massaging her gently, keeping her head up, and causing her to shiver. Could she trust that her husband would choose truth instead of lies, as he had promised?

"Yes, have a seat." Mr. Bashiru turned to the mothers. "Please. Let us finish the proceedings and we can answer any questions you all have after that."

After her father's wives left the room, Mr. Bashiru cleared his throat. "Now that we are all here, we can begin."

Charlotte walked a brown A4 envelope on a scratched metal tray to her boss.

"This envelope contains the last will and testament of Mr., uh, Mr. Festus Mawulawoe Nuga, colloquially known as Mawuli Nuga," he said. "But before I unseal it, Charlotte will pass it 'round for you all to attest that the seal is unbroken. Is that okay with you?"

They nodded.

"Please, I need audible avowals to avoid any possibility of misunderstanding," he said.

They mumbled over each other. "Yes." "It is."

Charlotte walked the will around their crescent of chairs.

"Are you all satisfied? Do you all confirm that the seal containing Mawuli Nuga's will has not been broken?"

"It does not appear to have been broken," Antony said.

"You can feel free to touch it if you want to be sure."

Antony shook his head.

"So, you agree?"

"From what I can see, it has not been broken."

"Good." Mr. Bashiru pulled the letter opener from his desk and sliced through the wax with the precision of his position. Gingerly, he removed the thin sheaf of papers and flipped through it before looking up.

"Before I begin to read, I want to caution you all to listen without any kind of vocalized reaction so everyone in the room can hear without disturbance. There is an officer outside my office who stands ready to forcibly remove any mal actor," he said.

"In my twenty-three years in the Office of the Registrar, I can count on one hand the number of times everyone at a reading was happy with the will's contents. There will be disappointments, but as in life, everyone has free will to express their wishes, and this represents the wishes of the testator, Mawuli Nuga.

"Additionally, everyone in this room is here because they were notified and invited to be here, at the request of Mawuli Nuga himself. I will now read the names of those who declined to be here."

The names of Mawuli's other children elicited an assortment of reactions in the room. Nods. Bowed heads. "Hmmms." Memories of tortuous bullying, whispered curses, foisted nicknames, bedtime laughs, the overlapping marriages that had swung like Damocles's sword above them all. What a childhood each of them had survived, Kokui mused.

"Without further ado, I hereby read:

The Last Will and Testament of
Festus Mawulawoe Nuga

This Will is made on this 7th day of December 1972 by me, FESTUS MAWULAWOE NUGA, of house No. 10 Achimota

Forest Road, Achimota, Accra, in the Greater Accra Region of the Republic of Ghana as my last Will and Codicil.

I hereby revoke all previous Wills and Testamentary Dispositions made by me before this day.

1. I appoint Albert Denu (my lawyer and friend of twenty-seven years) and Sophia Eyram Nuvi (the daughter of my mother's first cousin, who became a sister to me, and would not let any man, woman, or child put a foot against me) to be the Executors and Trustees of this Will.

2. I direct my Executors and Trustees to use the monies in my underlisted bank accounts to pay any testamentary expenses only.

3. My Executors and Trustees should note that I am not in debt to any man, woman, or child, dead or alive, and any such claim should be vigorously refuted at the expense of any claimant who alleges the opposite.

4. I direct my Executors and Trustees to pay my son Festus Mawulawoe Mensa Nuga Weber a sum equivalent to the 5,000 Reichsmarks his grandfather Jan Weber gave me, including any interest, adjusted for inflation. I give it to him not because Jan Weber expected back his investment in me and my talent, but because I reject outright the secondary reason he made the investment. He did not want to acknowledge my consensual relationship with his daughter Julia Weber or my paternity of our son. I was "the smart man" until I became the "monkey" who impregnated his daughter. I supplied Julia a monthly allowance of 100 Marks until our son's eighteenth birthday, and covered every expense to do with his education. Through several sources, I confirmed that my son was

being treated equal to his mother's other sons, and I am pleased to know that Jan Weber recognized the sharp intellect my son inherited from me and listed him among the beneficiaries of Weber und Söhne Papier. God knows I did much to enrich that man and his family, and in fairness, he seeded the riches of mine.

5. I direct my Executors and Trustees to transfer equal ownership stake of my business Nuga & Heirs, and all its subsidiaries, to my children. They are permitted to gift or sell their stake to one another, but under no circumstances may they gift, sell, or license their stake to any other individual or entity. They are to tithe ten percent of all profit to the operation of the Eleanor Kekeli Nuga Hospital in Juapong. This should be done in perpetuity, a provision made in their own Wills for their children current and yet to be born.

6. I devise my under-listed properties in Accra to all my children equally. They are permitted to gift or sell their share in the properties to one another, but under no circumstances may they gift, sell, or license their share in the properties to any other individual or entity.

7. I devise my under-listed property in Juapong to Sophia Eyram Nuvi. She is permitted to gift or sell the property to Cletus Nuvi or my children, but under no circumstances may she gift or sell the property to any other individual or entity.

8. I make no direct provision for the mothers of my children. Any promises alleged by them to have been made by me in the haze of love are not legally binding and to be vigorously refuted if purported to be so. Just as my mother's loving devotion to me elicited the loving response of my total care for her till the end of her life,

I expect my children's respective relationships with their mothers to dictate.

9. I have had many loves in my life—among them Abui Dei, Julia Weber, Rebecca Laryea, Hannah Koomson, Micheline Miadogo, and Hemaa Prempeh, to name a few—but in the end, I have discovered, I have no wives. Any legal claim to the contrary should be disproven at the expense of the claimant.

10. Any Will presented in my name after this date should be considered fictitious.

34

Kokui pushed out of the Women's Care Coalition office and skipped down the stairs. She paused at the security guard's desk to shake on her coat, squinting through the window as she dug in her pocket for her gloves. She hadn't realized how long her appointment had kept her inside. The darkening afternoon had begun to make a mirror of the glass, the lobby's menorah and the miniature Christmas tree glowing in front of and behind her.

"That's a big umbrella you got for those bitty flakes," the guard said.

She shrugged, pulling her hat on. "I won't get wet, though."

"Certainly won't." He buzzed her out into the frigid swirl.

Kokui bent into the weather, as four New York winters—two in Buffalo—had taught her to do, aiming her umbrella at the sky. She wove impatiently through the meandering holiday foot traffic, scanning the corners on both sides of the street.

"Madame K!"

She twisted around, her body relaxing at the sight of Frema trotting across the street. The women shivered into each other, their cheeks practically rubber.

"There's a Burger King just there," Frema said.

They locked arms and strode toward the restaurant.

"Ei, Frema, should I call you MRS or MSW?" Kokui asked as her friend loosened the buttons of her black coat for the navy skirt suit underneath.

She snorted. "MSW, please."

"Congratulations. You did it."

"We did it," she said. "And we are doing it."

Kokui nodded, hesitant to ask. "How are things with Sammy?"

"You, let's order and we'll talk."

They made their way to the counter, looking up at the options. "We should have met in Brooklyn," they said in unison.

"The same burger and bread . . ."

"Three dollars more," Kokui finished for her.

The women tutted and ordered, pulling the bills and coins from their handbags.

"Anyway, it's nice not to rush home straight from work for a change," Frema said. "Jane will be happy, too. No one to worry her to do her homework."

"Ei, Jane. How is she?"

"Daddy's girl is fine. As for her daddy, he is the same," she said. "Now that he and Gyamfi are doing that taxi service, Sammy has every excuse to stay out till morning."

Kokui frowned at her friend. "How are you managing, Frema?"

"As I've done since Jane was born," she said. "I split the bills with my roommate."

Kokui knew from experience not to say more. No woman stayed with a man for any other reason than that she wanted to.

"How about you and Boris?" Frema asked.

Kokui inhaled. "Much better."

"You don't sound convinced."

"Frema, with the way things have been going, I'm not convinced of anything, or anyone, anymore."

"The court case."

"Court *cases*," she said. "Nuga vs. Nuga. Nugas vs. Nuga. The amount of money we've wasted, I can't even tell you. Then there's my brother's own: Nuga vs. Weber." She shook her head. "Meanwhile, my father's estate is frozen until each suit is resolved. I think my stepmother is prepared to fight until she dies."

"How long are you prepared to fight?"

Kokui took another bite of her burger. "It's really my mother I'm doing it for. I mean, the woman locked herself to my father for twenty-five years because she was resting on the law, and then for him to use the law against her—against them all—the way he did . . . Our marriage laws just humiliate women," she said. "I mean, if you do customary wedding, the law says the man can add as many wives as he likes. If you do white wedding, they tell you the marriage is invalid if the man has entered, or enters, another customary marriage, even if you don't know. Protect the man's prerogative at all costs! I don't know why we even bother marrying."

Kokui paused to swallow. "But Boris has been behaving. I also don't give him room like I used to. I have my own account. We sit down and pay the bills together. And we—I do love him."

"He loves you, too," Frema said, a resolved smile tightening her face. "Shall we go?"

The women resealed themselves in their wool and down coats and rewound themselves in their scarves. They separated at the subway, Frema on the Brooklyn-bound platform, Kokui heading to the Bronx.

The pungent scent of a homeless man greeted Kokui as she stepped onto the car. As always, when she was pregnant, her gag reflex was heightened. She spent the whole ride heating up from the inside, doing everything she could to keep her Whopper down, trying to figure out why, for a third time, a being had attached itself to her at an inopportune time despite her every precaution.

She pressed her way off the train at Grand Concourse and made her way home, through the streetlamp-lit night, past the security, up to their seventeenth-floor apartment.

The apartment smelled of groundnut soup, and Boris stood at the stove stirring, the television keeping him company.

"Hello," she said, hanging her coat in the closet.

"How's Frema?"

"She called Sammy her roommate."

"Hmmm," he said. His answer of choice now when he felt she was gossiping. He joined her on the couch. "How are you?"

"Eight weeks," she said, leaning into his arms.

"What do you want to do?"

She sighed. "I still haven't found work." She braced herself for his recurring complaint about her choice to drop Business Administration, but it didn't come.

"You will," he said.

"And these court cases."

"If all else fails, you can go back to Angelico's."

"You can go to Angelico's."

"They only hire Ewes," he said.

"Very funny."

They lay curled into each other, the *Jeopardy!* game show casting a blue glow over their living room.

"I think we should keep this one," he said.

She swallowed, fear joining her nausea.

"Just like our marriage isn't your parents', our childhoods won't be our child's."

Her eyes turned to glass, brimming tears blurring the television screen. "How can you know?"

"I can't," he said, "but I know we can do better."

"How do you know, Boris?"

He folded his arms around her. "Because we want to, Madame K."

ACKNOWLEDGMENTS

Thank you:

LORD for the gift of writing, which has continually helped me make sense of myself and my world. In 2008, when I wrote the first words of what I thought would be my second novel, I had no idea it would morph into this story, or that trying to get it published would take me on a journey worthy of its own book. You kept me going, and writing, through it all, raising encouragement and Encouragers from unexpected corners.

Judith Curr for believing in me and rooting for me.

Tracy Sherrod for all you did.

Abby West for your immediate warmth and support.

Rakesh Satyal for your patience as I took the time I needed to revise and rewrite.

Acknowledgments

Ryan Amato for keeping me on task and deadline.

Jennifer Baker for asking the question that helped me get to the heart of the story I wanted to write.

Vince Bielski for dotting my i's and crossing my t's.

Essie Brew-Hammond McCabe for reading draft after draft after draft for the past decade-plus.

Norma Jaeger Hopcraft for taking time out of writing your own book to read one of my deadline drafts and for offering such thoughtful feedback.

Redeemed Writers Group for listening to early drafts of this novel and sharing constructive critique.

Stephanie Nikolopoulos, Jane Park, and Nimma Bhusri for letting me vent and praying me through the hardest parts of writing this book.

Grace Powers for your very specific words about the refinement process, and the entire 10@10 fam. Tosh Ernest, I'm eternally grateful you shared your two fish and five loaves with us!

Fleur Lee for your morning prayers.

Charlotte and Ally Sheedy for your tenacious, early support.

Malaika Adero for keeping it one hundred, always.

Martin Egblewogbe for all you do to uplift and advocate for Ghanaian and African writers, and for always extending the warmth of community. I'm so grateful to you, and the entire Writers Project of Ghana team, including Mamle Kabu and Lizz Johnson, for cheering me on season after season.

Nana Awere Damoah for easing the way for me to get my books in Ghanaian readers' hands via Book Nook, and for all you invest in writers and readers.

Breena Clarke, Cheryl Clarke, Barbara Balliet, and the Hobart Festival of Women Writers family for giving me the space to be and express myself.

Acknowledgments

The Hedgebrook 7—I still get the shivers when I think about our sessions around the table and in front of the fire.

Bisi Adjapon, Kwame Alexander, Keisha Bush, Chris Colderley, Kim Coleman Foote, Nana-Ama Danquah, Jennifer Franklin, Ayesha Harruna Attah, Abeer Hoque, Abi Ishola-Ayodeji, Marjorie Light, Kinna Likimani, Deanna Nikaido, Maya Nussbaum, Nii Ayikwei Parkes, Randy Preston, Maritza Rivera, Shawn Stewart Ruff, KC Trommer, Vanessa Walters, Frankie Edozien, Zukiswa Wanner, George McCalman, the S.W.A.N.'s, and the others, too many to name here, that I am blessed to be in literary community with.

Francisca Valerie Afun and Elizabeth Esi Mainoo Brew-Hammond for your towering examples.

Nii Allotey Brew-Hammond for the gift of reading, and your passion for developing my intellect. I will never forget how patiently you listened as three-year-old me sounded out *The Princess and the Pea* to you.

Delphine Brew-Hammond—you are an inspiration, and you are my inspiration.

Dustin Haffner for keeping me loved and laughing.

Kwam Brew-Hammond—I love you.

VWK Agbodza and LE Kojo Brew-Hammond, you are dearly missed!

Auntie Wolanyo Amoa.

Auntie Della Sowah.

Abrahams, Afuns, Agbodzas, Amoas, Amoonoo-Monneys, Binkas, Brew-Hammonds, Dankwa-Smiths, Ghansahs, Haffners, Kpatakpas, Ofori-Attas, Segbedzis, Sowahs—it's a blessing to call you family.

Readers for the gift of your time and attention.

ABOUT THE AUTHOR

Nana Ekua Brew-Hammond is the author of the children's picture book *Blue: A History of the Color as Deep as the Sea and as Wide as the Sky*, illustrated by Caldecott Honor artist Daniel Minter, and the young adult novel *Powder Necklace*. Her short fiction for adults has been included in the anthologies *Accra Noir*, *Africa39*, *New Daughters of Africa*, and *Everyday People*, among others. Most recently, she edited *Relations: An Anthology of African and Diaspora Voices*. Visit nanabrewhammond.com to learn more.